DEATH WATCH

The new Charlie Woodend mystery

Angela Jackson has been missing for over twenty-four hours and, in the opinion of Dr Stevenson, the psychiatrist who Woodend turns to for advice, her kidnapper will first torture and then kill her. With damaging strains operating within his own team, the more the investigation proceeds the less hope Woodend can see. And he knows – deep within himself – that he will fail in bringing Angela back alive...

DEATH WATCH

A Chief Inspector Woodend novel

Sally Spencer

Severn House Large Print
London & New York

This first large print edition published 2010
in Great Britain and the USA by
SEVERN HOUSE PUBLISHERS LTD of
9-15 High Street, Sutton, Surrey, SM1 1DF.
First world regular print edition published 2007 by
Severn House Publishers Ltd., London and New York.

British Library Cataloguing in Publication Data

Spencer, Sally.
    Death watch.
    1. Woodend, Charlie (Fictitious character)--Fiction.
    2. Missing children--Fiction. 3. Police--England--
    Fiction. 4. Detective and mystery stories. 5. Large type
    books.
    I. Title
    823.9'14-dc22

ISBN-13: 978-0-7278-7896-0

Severn House Publishers support The Forest Stewardship Council
[FSC], the leading international forest certification organisation. All
our titles that are printed on Greenpeace-approved FSC-certified paper
carry the FSC logo.

MIX
Paper from
responsible sources
FSC® C018575
www.fsc.org

Printed and bound in Great Britain by the
MPG Books Group, Bodmin, Cornwall.

PART ONE:

The Invisible Man

One

The horse-chestnut trees in the corporation park were tall and strong and, having lived through so many of nature's annual cycles, they should have been prepared for the autumn. They should have known that their aggressive lushness in the spring was only a passing phase, that the complacently deep green of their summer foliage could not last, and that when their leaves started to turn a gentle russet brown it was the beginning of their yearly death. Yet still they looked surprised, as they stood starkly against the darkening sky – like blackened skeletons ashamed of their own nakedness – while, beneath them, their former glory had formed a thick and crinkly carpet.

This carpet of leaves, while it might have embarrassed the trees, had not gone unappreciated by a small army of Munchkins. All afternoon, children enveloped in several layers of clothes had been ploughing happily through it, giggling constantly and attempting to push each other over.

But not any more!

Now, the whole area was effectively sealed off by the bulk of half a dozen large uniformed

7

police constables, while several other bobbies were busily shepherding the children and their parents into the park cafe.

Set slightly apart from this scene – closer to the swings and seesaw than to the carpet of leaves – were a woman, a man, and a little boy.

The woman had long blonde hair which, though she sometimes tied it in a bun, now cascaded over her high cheekbones. Her eyes were blue, her nose a little larger than was common in Whitebridge, and her mouth full and promising. She was wearing a stylish check suit, and while she was crouched down so that she was on the same level as the small boy, she was actually giving her full attention to the man who was standing beside him.

'Freddie was in a real state when I found him,' the man was explaining. 'It took ages to calm him down enough for him to tell me what had happened.'

'But when he *had* calmed down, the first thing he told you was that his sister had disappeared?' DS Monika Paniatowski asked. 'Is that right, Mr Lewis?'

'Yes, that's right,' Lewis agreed. 'Angela had gone missin', he said. Just vanished into thin air. An' I remember thinkin' at the time that that was just not like her.'

'So you know the family, do you?'

'Should do. They live next door but one to us, an' I've known Angela since the day she was born.'

'How old is she?'

8

'Well, let me think. She was born around the same time as our Elaine, so that must make her thirteen.'

And the boy looked to be about five, Paniatowski guessed – not old enough to be let out on his own, but perfectly safe when accompanied by his big sister.

Except that it was now looking as if it had been the sister who hadn't been safe.

Paniatowski reached across, and gently stroked the boy's cheek. It was cold to the touch – much colder than it should have been, even on a chilly autumn day.

The lad was terrified, she thought. And why wouldn't he be?

'Don't worry, Freddie, everything's going to be all right,' she cooed reassuringly.

'But Angela's gone!' the boy said tearfully, as if to imply that things could *never* be all right again.

And maybe, as far as his family was concerned, that was not too far from the truth, Paniatowski told herself.

She looked up at the man again. 'What did you do once you'd found out what had happened, Mr Lewis?' she asked.

The man looked uncomfortable. 'Well, I suppose the first thing I *should have* done was to call her dad,' he said awkwardly. 'But I didn't. Instead, we went lookin' for Angela. I know that it sounds like a stupid thing to have done now, but I didn't want to cause any unnecessary panic, you see.'

'You were quite right to make sure you had all the facts first,' Paniatowski assured him. 'It was the natural thing to do.'

But she couldn't help wishing that he *hadn't* done the natural thing.

'Anyway, when we still hadn't found her after about ten minutes, I *did* call her dad,' Lewis continued. 'An' he said he'd ring the police, an' I should keep searchin' for Angie – which I've been doin'. But there's still no sign of her.'

This didn't have to end in tragedy, Paniatowski told herself. There was still a chance that the girl would simply turn up again and wonder what all the fuss had been about.

She switched her attention back to the boy, and as she did so she forced her lips in a warm smile. 'Does your Angela have a boyfriend, Freddie?'

Freddie shook his head. 'No, she doesn't.'

Paniatowski chuckled. 'Are you sure about that?' she asked quizzically. 'You have secrets, don't you? Maybe Angela's got a few of her own.'

'She tells me everythin'.'

'Really?'

'Yes! Honest she does! Because she knows I wouldn't tell our mum an' dad, even if it meant a smackin',' the boy said firmly. Then, as if he thought the nice blonde lady required further convincing, he added, 'Our Angela thinks big lads are horrid, an' she says she'd rather be out with her mates.'

Paniatowski nodded. 'I think big lads can

10

sometimes be horrid, too,' she said. 'Tell me, Freddie, did you notice anybody hanging around, just before Angela went away?'

'Hangin' around?'

'Just standing there, doing nothing.'

'There were lots of people doin' nothin',' the boy said, puzzled. 'This is the park.'

'But did you notice anybody acting strangely?' Paniatowski persisted.

The boy leant closer to her, so only she could hear him. 'There was a girl who did her poo in the bushes,' he whispered.

Children only really noticed what impacted on their own narrow world, Paniatowski thought – so it had always been a long shot that he'd have seen anything important.

She tousled the boy's hair, and stood up. 'Take him to the cafe,' she said to the neighbour. 'There'll be a couple of constables on duty there. Tell them that I say Freddie can have the biggest glass of lemonade they've got on offer.'

'An' an ice cream?' the boy asked, showing a sudden interest in something other than his sister's disappearance.

'And an ice cream,' Paniatowski agreed, though she found herself shuddering at even the thought of eating an ice cream on a nippy day like this one.

As the neighbour led the boy away, Paniatowski lit up a cigarette, and looked around her. The area under the horse-chestnut trees had been cleared of civilians. The uniformed officers had retreated to the pathways which

11

surrounded it. And beyond the pathways, close to the rhododendron bushes, stood a young, fresh-faced man who was dressed in what looked like his Sunday best suit, and who was gesturing that she should come and join him.

Paniatowski took a quick drag on her cigarette, waited a second for the smoke to curl its way comfortingly around her lungs, then walked towards DC Colin Beresford.

It was the sound of a soft moan – her *own* soft moan – that made Angela Jackson realize she was awake. But even with this knowledge, she did not open her eyes.

It was far too soon for that!

She had been in the corporation park, she remembered, watching little kids crunching the leaves under their Wellington boots. She hadn't wanted to be there. At the age of thirteen, she'd argued to herself, she had the right to choose how she spent her time and it seemed so unfair that, instead of hanging around the boulevard with her friends and having a good laugh, she should have been ordered by her tyrannical parents to babysit a little brother who, though she loved him to pieces, could still be a considerable pain.

She'd glanced down at the watch on her wrist, and seen that it was nearly three o'clock.

They'd been in the park for nearly an hour. Surely that was plenty long enough, and nobody could call her unreasonable if she took Freddie home now?

She'd looked at the watch again, and felt a pang of guilt. Her mum and dad had given her that watch for her thirteenth birthday, and she'd known – though they'd never have told her themselves – that it had cost more than they could actually afford. So what kind of daughter was she, then, to resent doing a little for them in return?

'Was it you who abandoned that poor little kitten in the bushes?' an angry voice behind her had asked. 'It was, wasn't it?'

She'd turned to face her accuser. 'What kitten?'

'Don't come the innocent with me,' the man had said harshly. 'You're all alike, you young girls. You treat animals as if they were no more than playthings, and when you've finished with them, you just cast them aside.'

Angela had not been frightened of the man. Why should she have been? Unlike many of the men who hung around the park, he was smartly dressed, and even his rage was understandable, given the crime he obviously considered her to be guilty of. In fact, rather than unsettling her, his anger did quite the reverse.

It showed he cared.

It showed he was a decent person.

The man's annoyance had drained away and had been replaced by, what seemed to Angela, to be an expression which was a mixture of shame and embarrassment.

'Sorry, love, I shouldn't have flown off the handle like that,' he'd said. 'I should have seen

13

right away that you're far too sensitive and grown up to have done anything so wicked.'

'Yes, it is wicked, isn't it?' Angela said, and though her face had still registered a real concern for the kitten, her insides were glowing at the compliments the man had just paid her.

Grown up! she'd thought. He says I look grown up.

They'd both fallen silent for a while, then Angela had said, 'So what happens now?'

'Now?' the man had repeated, as if he'd had no idea what she was talking about.

'To the kitten?' Angela said.

The man had shrugged his shoulders. 'I suppose the kindest thing would be for me to go back into the bushes and wring its neck.'

Angela had felt a shudder run through her.

'Kill it?' she'd said, half-hoping that the man had meant something else entirely.

The man's face had mirrored her concern. 'I know that sounds horrible, but it'll all be over in a second. And in the long run, it'll be a kindness.'

'But ... but I thought there were shelters where they took care of homeless animals.'

'So there are. But the last I heard, they were all full to bursting, so even if I take her in, all they'll do is put her to sleep.'

'She's a little girl, is she?' Angela had asked.

The man had nodded. 'But it's best not to think about that. As I see it, there are only two alternatives: either she's put out of her misery now, or she's left where she is until the rats find her –

14

and I certainly wouldn't wish that on the poor little thing.'

He was wrong about there only being two alternatives, Angela had thought. There was a third, and though it would involve an awkward scene with her parents, she was fairly confident she could pull it off.

'I could take the kitten home with me,' she'd suggested.

The man had looked doubtful. 'You're sure about that?'

'Yes,' she'd said.

And suddenly, she had been. She'd known that her friends would laugh at her – say she'd gone soft – but she didn't care. Though she had yet to even see the kitten, she had already fallen in love with it.

'Well, I suppose that would be one solution,' the man had admitted, almost grudgingly. 'But I don't see it working myself.'

Then he'd turned, and walked quickly away from her.

For a few moments, Angela had stood rooted to the spot, not quite understanding what had happened. A minute earlier, the man had been so friendly and sympathetic. Now he seemed to have no interest in what they'd been talking about at all.

It was almost as if he didn't want to be seen with her!

By the time she'd recovered herself enough to follow him, he'd already disappeared into the rhododendron bushes, and she'd had to run to

*make sure that she didn't lose him completely.
But there was no danger of that. As she'd reached the bushes, she'd seen that the man was
standing in a small clearing with his hands
behind his back, waiting for her.*

*'Where's the kitten?' she'd asked, in a panic.
'You haven't...you couldn't have...?'*

*'No, she's fine,' the man had assured her. He'd
nodded his head towards one of the bushes. 'The
poor little thing's over there.'*

*She'd wondered briefly why he'd made the
imprecise head gesture, instead of pointing with
his finger, but then she'd caught sight of a blaze
of colour under the bush, and she was lost.*

*She'd rushed over to the bush, and squatted
down. 'Here, Kitty-kitty,' she'd crooned softly.
'Come to Angela. I'll look after you.'*

*But the kitten had made no attempt to either
come to her nor run away. It hadn't flinched –
hadn't seemed to move even a muscle.*

*What's wrong with it? she'd wondered. Had
the man lied to her when he'd said the kitten was
fine? Had he already wrung its neck, even as he
was speaking those reassuring words?*

'And what happened after that?' she asked
herself now, her eyes still tightly closed, her
body as still as the kitten's.

What had happened after the little creature had
refused to respond to her?

She didn't know, she realized with true horror!
She couldn't *remember*!

DC Beresford led DS Paniatowski into a small

clearing in the middle of the rhododendron bushes.

'This must be where he grabbed her,' Beresford said.

'You're sure there's a "he" involved?' Paniatowski asked.

Beresford nodded gravely. 'Look down there.'

The ground just beyond them was already close to being winter-hard – two or three degrees away from frozen – but even so, the struggle which had occurred had left its impression on the earth. Paniatowski examined the heel marks – some small enough to have been made by a child, others the definite imprint of a larger and heavier adult.

The sergeant glanced over her shoulder. This clearing was almost completely hidden from the rest of the park, she noted, which was why – of course – it had been chosen.

'What's that?' Beresford asked, pointing to something lying at the base of one of the rhododendrons.

'A handkerchief?' Paniatowski guessed.

But when she bent down to pick it up, she discovered that it was much thicker than a hankie – that it was, in fact, a pad of surgical gauze.

She lifted it to her nose, and sniffed at it gingerly. It reminded her of her rare and reluctant visits to hospital – and dealt the final death blow to the possibility that the mystery of Angela Jackson's disappearance would have a happy ending.

'Look what else I've found,' said Beresford,

who had been searching under a second bush.

And when Paniatowski turned towards him, she saw that what he was holding in his hand was a fluffy toy which vaguely resembled a real cat.

'Do you think this has anything to do with the abduction – or is it just something a kid dropped here?' the detective constable asked.

'It could be either,' Paniatowski said.

But the odds were heavily in favour of it being what the kidnapper had used to distract the girl, just before he drugged her.

'Hang on,' Beresford said. 'I think there's something else down there, as well.'

He bent down again, and what he retrieved this time was a lady's wristwatch.

It was a fairly expensive timepiece, Paniatowski decided, which argued for it belonging to an adult rather than a child. On the other hand, it had a rather modern look about it, and it was hard to imagine it on the wrist of a matronly woman.

She took a closer look. The leather strap, from which Beresford was suspending it, was broken, and the glass which covered the face had been smashed. The hands of the watch showed it had stopped at two minutes past three.

'Do you think it's the girl's?' Beresford wondered.

'It has to be,' Paniatowski replied.

She stepped through the gap between the two rhododendrons – brushing away the overhanging branches with her hands – and found herself standing at the edge of the car park.

The kidnapper had planned it well, she thought. Once he had lured the girl into the bushes, it would have been simplicity itself to dope her and then carry her to a waiting vehicle.

She was still standing there when the old Wolseley arrived on the car park. The driver – a big man wearing a hairy sports coat – had his foot pressed down hard on the accelerator, and for a moment it looked as if he was intent on smashing his vehicle into the line of parked cars. Then he slammed on the brakes, the engine screamed in protest, and the Wolseley came to a shuddering halt.

'The boss is here,' Paniatowski called back through the bushes to Colin Beresford.

There was no physical reason for Angela not to have opened her eyes, yet she still had not chosen to do so.

There was something rather comforting about the darkness, she told herself.

Or rather, if she was being honest, there was something frightening about what might lie beyond it.

And so, instead of taking the big step of finding out where she was, she began with smaller ones – first moving her fingers and then twitching her toes. But even before she had started to make these simple movements, her body had already started telling her things.

It had informed her, for example, that she was lying down.

But not on a bed.

On something very hard and very cold.

She became more experimental, stretching her legs and feeling the surface below her with the tips of her fingers. There was nothing to stop her doing this – no restraints, no obstacles. Perhaps, she decided, now was the time to start looking around.

The first thing she saw when she allowed her eyes to open was the light. It was a long neon tube, fixed to the ceiling, and it crackled occasionally. For a while, it mesmerized her, but then she grew bored with it, and decided to expand her vision of the world.

She raised herself up on one elbow, and looked around her. She was in a room with no windows – a room in which the floor and walls were made up of dusty grey concrete. There was a metal door in the far wall, and the second she noticed it, her heart leapt and she was on her feet and rushing towards it.

The surge of hope did not last long. There was no handle on the door, only a keyhole.

And she did not have the key!

She made her hands into fists and banged on the door. Then, when that seemed to have no effect, she kicked and kicked until her toes were bruised and aching. And all the time she was screaming at the top of her voice.

'Let me out of here. Please let me out of here. I want to go home.'

But nobody answered.

Two

The cafe in the corporation park had been designed to cater for thirty customers, with space for another sixty on the outside terrace, but the season when it would be comfortable to sit on the terrace had long since passed, and all the potential witnesses to the Angela Jackson abduction had therefore been asked to go inside.

No one was happy with this arrangement. There were not enough chairs for all the adults to sit down on, and no room at all for the children to play. The kids were growing increasingly bored and restless, the grown-ups puzzled, concerned, and frustrated – and as the windows began to steam up, tempers were becoming frayed.

The arrival of the big man in the hairy sports coat did not seem to offer an immediate solution to the problem, but at least it promised the possibility of a little variety, and when Woodend finally spoke, he had everyone's full attention.

'I must apologize for keepin' you here for so long, an' I can assure you that as soon as you've made your statements to the officers, you can leave,' the chief inspector said.

'What's this all about?' demanded a young

woman whose headscarf did not quite conceal the row of plastic curlers around which her mousy brown hair had been wrapped.

'There's been an "incident",' Woodend said heavily.

'Meaning what?'

'Meanin' just what I've said.'

The woman put her hands aggressively on her hips, which was no mean feat, given the limited amount of space available to her in the crowded cafe.

'My husband will be home in half an hour, and he'll be expecting his tea on the table when he walks through the door,' she said.

'Then you'd better get yourself off now, then, hadn't you?' Woodend countered.

The response had clearly not been what the woman had expected, and it knocked her a little off balance. '*Can* I go?' she asked, somewhat subdued. 'Just like that?'

'Of course,' Woodend replied. 'Why not?'

'Well, I thought...'

'Let me tell you somethin', love,' Woodend said in a voice which anyone who knew him would have read as a danger signal. 'There's a family in this town right now that's experiencin' a heartache that I hope an' pray you never have to go through yourself.'

'You never said anythin' about—' the woman began.

'In fact, their whole world's collapsin' around them,' Woodend interrupted her. He paused for a second. 'But whatever else is happenin' – however much anybody else is sufferin' – you'll have to make sure your husband gets his tea on time, won't you?'

Woodend was angry, Paniatowski thought, observing the exchange from the cafe doorway. And that was not like him at all.

True, there were a number of detective chief inspectors in Central Lancs who used anger as a tool – a way of keeping both their subordinates and the general public permanently on their toes – but Charlie Woodend wasn't one of them. He didn't lose his temper often, and when he did it was usually because he considered that the object of his wrath had been stupid, inefficient, or insensitive.

What she was seeing now was something quite different. This was a display of rage she'd only observed once before – during the Helen Dunn kidnapping.

The curlered woman who'd complained was looking distinctly uncomfortable. 'Well, I suppose it wouldn't do my Harry any harm to wait for his tea just this once,' she said grudgingly. 'As long as it's important.'

'It's important,' Woodend confirmed. 'That's why I'd like to thank you in advance for your cooperation, madam.'

There might possibly have been more questions put to him, but he did not wait to hear them. Instead, he turned, brushed past his sergeant, and walked out onto the terrace. Once there, he stopped, lit up a cigarette, and waited for Paniatowski to join him.

'A few years ago, it could have been my Annie that had gone missin',' the chief inspector said.

Paniatowski nodded. Annie Woodend, she remembered, was just completing a course in Manchester, and would soon be a fully qualified nurse.

Woodend took a deep drag on his cigarette. 'I want everybody in that cafe questioned, but I want special attention paid to the men,' he said.

'You think the kidnapper may have returned to the scene of the crime?' Paniatowski wondered aloud.

'I don't know,' Woodend admitted, with a disturbed edge creeping into his voice. 'An' that's the whole problem, Monika.'

'Sorry, sir?'

'I simply can't get into the heads of bastards who do things like this, so I just don't bloody *know*.' Woodend looked around him, as if half hoping that a sudden and obvious clue would present itself. 'I want every inch of this park goin' over with a fine-toothed comb,' he continued.

'Naturally,' Paniatowski agreed.

'Inspector Rutter had better supervise that,' Woodend said. 'I wouldn't trust anybody but Bob to be in charge of the job.'

There was an awkward pause from Paniatowski, then she said, 'But Bob's not here, sir.'

'Not here?' Woodend repeated, as if he couldn't quite comprehend what she was telling him.

'No.'

24

'Then where the bloody hell *is* he?'

'He's gone down to London.'

'London!'

'To pick up his daughter. He *did* tell you about it.'

'Jesus Christ!' Woodend exploded. 'Is he a bobby, or isn't he? Because if he *is*, he should be here when I need him.'

He was being unfair, Paniatowski thought, but that was only because he was so distressed.

'They're arriving back sometime this afternoon,' she said.

'Then the moment he *is* back, I want him right here, leadin' this investigation. Is that clear?'

Paniatowski nodded. 'Perfectly,' she said.

The lecture slot immediately after lunch was not popular with most of the teachers at the University of Central Lancashire. They complained – with some justification – that at that time of day many of their students were far more interested in going to the bar than in pursuing their studies, and so those lecturers with some influence in campus and departmental politics did their damnedest to ensure that *they* weren't the ones addressing half-empty halls.

Dr Martin Stevenson was not one of these academic rats who sought to flee a barely floating ship. Experience had shown him that his lectures were well attended at whatever time of day he was scheduled to give them, and the one he had delivered that afternoon had been particularly successful. The subject had been the psychology of Gilles de Rais, a fifteenth-century French nobleman who had abducted, raped, and killed at least a hundred young boys who he had taken into his castle as pageboys, and when the bell had rung to indicate the end of a session, there were quite a number of students who had remained firmly in their seats.

Seeing them still sitting there, Stevenson sighed inwardly. On the one hand, he told himself, there was a research paper back in his office that he was under some pressure to finish, and had been hoping to work on for the rest of the afternoon. On the other, he supposed he should be grateful that he could arouse such interest from his students, and it seemed almost a crime to nip their enthusiasm in the bud, especially since he knew for a fact that the seminar room next door was free for most of the afternoon.

He would give them fifteen more minutes, he decided in the spirit of compromise. Fifteen minutes would surely be more than enough. But the discussion was still going on an hour and a half later, when his secretary – who had finally managed to track him down – informed him that his wife had rung and said she needed to speak to him.

'Ring her back, and say I'll call her as soon as I can,' said Stevenson, who was rather enjoying the heated debate with his students.

The secretary gave him one of those disapproving looks of hers, which always managed to somewhat disconcert him.

'I can't ring her *back*, because she's still on the

line,' the woman said. 'And she did tell me it was *urgent.*'

Stevenson shrugged apologetically. 'The joys of married life,' he said to the students, who giggled.

When he reached his office, two minutes later, he was half expecting that his wife would have grown bored with waiting and hung up. But she hadn't.

'Where've you been?' Rosemary Stevenson demanded.

'Working,' her husband told her. 'And aren't you supposed to be on duty yourself, darling?'

'I *am* on duty,' Rosemary told him. 'That's why I'm angry it's taken you so long to answer the phone.'

'If I'd known you were going to ring—'

'Listen,' his wife interrupted, 'a girl's gone missing from Whitebridge corporation park – and there's a tremendous flap on down here.'

'Oh dear. How awful,' Stevenson said with feeling. 'I suppose we must all hope that she turns up again soon.'

'Is that all you've got to say?' his wife demanded.

'I don't think there's much more I *can* say, except I'm surprised that, given the circumstances, you've found the time to ring me at all.'

'You don't get it, do you?' his wife asked, with just a hint of hardness to her voice.

'Don't get what, Rosemary?'

'The girl's *thirteen*. Chances are, she's been abducted by some kind of pervert.'

'Oh, I don't think that necessarily follows,' Stevenson said. 'There are lots of other reasons she could have gone missing. She might be the subject of a parental custody battle and—'

'She isn't.'

'Or perhaps her mother and father don't approve of her boyfriend, and she's run off with him. But if that is the case, they won't get far before they start to see how unrealistic they're being.'

'Everybody down at the station thinks this is a sex crime,' Rosemary interrupted him impatiently.

'Unless they have considerably more data than you've provided me with, I think they must be on very shaky ground to make such a broad assumption,' Stevenson countered.

'This is your big chance,' his wife told him.

'My big chance?' Stevenson repeated.

'DCI Charlie Woodend's in charge of the case,' Rosemary said. 'Cloggin'-it Charlie, they call him.'

'Interesting. Why do they...?'

'Because instead of keeping his fat arse parked on a seat behind his desk, like most of the other buggers in his position do, he likes to clog it around the scene of the crime.'

Stevenson grimaced, and wished his wife would not resort to such crude language quite so often.

'Well, from what you've told me, Mr Woodend seems to be the right man for the job,' he said.

'No,' Rosemary said firmly. 'You're the *right* man for the job.'

'I'm a theoretician – an academic!' Stevenson protested.

'So you don't have any patients, or conduct any interviews?' his wife asked sarcastically.

'Well, of course I do. You *know* I do.'

'Then you're basically involved in the same kind of work as Cloggin'-it Charlie – except that you've got brains, and he hasn't.'

'Really, darling...'

'It's time you started making a name for yourself.'

'I'm already doing that. In case you've forgotten, the paper I presented at the symposium in Toronto was *very* well received.'

'Are you deliberately being thick?' his wife demanded.

'No, I don't think so,' Stevenson replied – and he was only *half* lying.

'It's time you started to make a name for yourself *with the public at large.*'

Stevenson glanced out of his office window at the shiny glass and concrete structures which made up the UCL campus. It was an ultra-modern university and made no pretence at being anything else, he thought. And yet, in many ways, it was just as peaceful and contemplative as any of the colleges in Oxford and Cambridge – just as much a place to think and dream.

'Did you hear what I said?' his wife asked. 'It's time that you started to make a name for yourself with the public at large.'

'Do you know, I'm not sure I really want to do that,' Stevenson told her.

'Then what about me?' Rosemary replied. 'Don't I count? Don't you see how it might help to advance my career?'

Stevenson laughed lightly. 'I'm sure that a woman of your obvious ability doesn't need any help from me,' he said.

'Then what about your sense of duty?' his wife persisted. 'If there's a nutter running amok and you can help to catch him, don't you think you're pretty much obliged to?'

Stevenson sighed. 'Perhaps you're right,' he agreed.

'So you'll do it?'

'So I'll *think* about it.'

'If it wasn't for me, you wouldn't be where you are today,' Rosemary said.

'I quite agree with you there,' Stevenson agreed. 'You've been a wonderful guide.'

'So why won't you let me guide you now? Why won't you see that what I'm suggesting would be good for both of us?'

'I really *will* think about it,' Stevenson promised. He paused for a second. 'Shouldn't you be getting back to the investigation, darling?'

'Damn right,' his wife agreed. 'If I'm not careful, that bitch Monika Paniatowski will go ahead and grab all the glory, because not only has she got a protector in Cloggin'-it Charlie, but she's free to sleep with anyone she wants to – which is well known to be a good way to get on.'

'I'm sure your own virtue will be rewarded in good time, darling,' Stevenson said.

'I don't want to wait for "good time", Martin,' his wife said. 'I want my reward *now*.'

'I'll talk to you later,' Stevenson said, replacing the phone on the hook, and renewing his contemplation of the university campus.

Three

The man alighting from the train which had just pulled into Whitebridge's late-Victorian railway station was in his early thirties. He had alert brown eyes and a determined jaw. His dark hair was neat without being austere, and he was wearing a smart blue suit. An uninformed observer might well have taken him for a tough London business executive on a whistle-stop inspection tour which was intended to put the fear of God into the quaintly provincial managers of his company's old-fashioned northern branches. Closer examination, however, would have revealed an air of uncertainty about him which would not sit well on the shoulders of a company hatchet man. And a moment later, when he reached up into the carriage and gently lifted down a small child, the initial impression would not have had a leg left to stand on.

'Well, here we are. We're finally home,

darling,' Bob Rutter said to his daughter.

Louisa, who was not quite four, looked up at him questioningly. 'Home?' she repeated.

'You remember, don't you?' Rutter asked, with some concern. 'This is where we used to live before you went to stay with the *abuelos*.'

The *abuelos*. Louisa's Spanish grandparents, who had taken her in when Maria, Rutter's wife, had been murdered, and Rutter had found himself incapable not only of fulfilling his duties as a detective inspector but even of taking care of his own daughter.

But that was all in the past. He was back on Charlie Woodend's team, pulling his full weight again, and now he was ready to take responsibility for his little daughter, too.

'You *do* remember, don't you?' he asked, almost pleadingly.

The little girl looked at him with a serious expression in her eyes. 'Yes, Daddy,' she said.

She was lying, he thought. She'd only agreed with him because she could tell that he was worried about her answer, and wanted to please him.

But at least she *did* still want to please him – which, after he had abandoned her for so long, was more than he had any right to expect.

'I told you about Janet, didn't I?' Rutter asked.

'Janet?'

'The lady I've asked to look after you when I'm not there. I'm sure you're going to like her.'

'Why can't *abuelita* look after me?' Louisa wondered.

'Because she's in London, and we're here,' Rutter explained patiently. 'Besides, *abuela*'s quite old now, and she finds looking after an energetic little girl like you more than she can handle.'

'Is *abuela* olderer than you, Daddy?' Louisa asked.

'Not olderer, just older,' Rutter replied.

He corrected her automatically, but the moment the words were out of his mouth he found himself wondering, as an anxious parent determined to get things right, if that had been the proper thing to do.

'Is she *older* than you?' Louisa asked, enunciating the word with extreme care.

'Much older,' Rutter told her, and he was thinking: There are so many things that are obvious to an adult that don't seem obvious to my baby at all.

There was the sound of a whistle blowing, and the train started to pull out of the station. Louisa watched its departure with growing panic, as if she had only just now realized that this wasn't merely a day's jolly excursion with Daddy – this was to be her *life*.

'It's all right,' Rutter said soothingly. With his right hand, he took hold of his daughter's hand. With his left, he picked up her suitcase. *'Everything*'s going to be all right.'

He started to lead her gently towards the ticket barrier. She did not resist, though it would have been stretching the truth a little to say that she went completely willingly.

It was then that Rutter saw the blonde woman standing by the barrier. Monika Paniatowski was doing her best to display a welcoming smile, but for some reasons already obvious to Rutter – and some that were yet to be revealed – she was not making a particularly good job of it.

'Hello, Bob! Hello, Louisa!' she said.

'Who are you?' the little girl asked.

'This is Monika,' Rutter said. 'I work with her.' And silently, he added, She's the woman who I betrayed your mother with. The woman your mother was going to divorce me over, even though I'd already forced myself to break off the affair.

'Are you my auntie?' Louisa said.

Paniatowski laughed gently. 'Now whatever made you ask that?' she wondered.

'Because Daddy used your first name,' Louisa said seriously.

'I don't understand.'

'He didn't call you Mrs Something-or-other, like he does with most ladies. He called you Monika, instead.'

Paniatowski's eyes watered slightly. 'I'm not your auntie,' she admitted. 'At least, not your *real* auntie. But you can call me Auntie Monika if you want to. Would you like that?'

'Yes,' Louisa said. 'You're nice.'

And so she was, Rutter thought. In many ways, she was bloody wonderful. But what was she doing there at the station – edging her way into his new life before that life had even really started?

34

'The boss sent me,' Paniatowski said, by way of explanation to the unspoken question.

'That was kind of him,' Rutter replied, surprised to hear how sour his own voice sounded to him. 'But I'm a big boy now. I can probably find my own way home.'

'I'm sure you can,' Paniatowski countered. 'But he doesn't want you to go home – he wants you to report to him immediately. That's the main reason I'm here – to look after Louisa so you'll be free to see the boss.'

'This is outrageous!' Rutter protested. 'I've only just arrived back, for God's sake!'

'I know,' Paniatowski said sympathetically. 'But a thirteen-year-old girl's been kidnapped from the corporation park, and the boss thinks it could turn very nasty – very soon.'

'But why does he need me?' Rutter asked, almost petulantly. 'Why can't you handle things for a while?'

'Because I'm not the one he's asked for. You are. You should be flattered.'

'So I'm suddenly bloody indispensable, but he doesn't mind *you* nicking off?' Rutter said angrily. 'Well, screw him!'

'He's watching you, you know,' Paniatowski said ominously.

'I've absolutely no idea what you're talking about,' Rutter countered.

Paniatowski shook her head, slowly and sceptically. 'You don't really expect me to believe that, do you?' she asked.

'Believe what you like,' Rutter said.

Paniatowski sighed. 'All right, if it's necessary to spell it out for you, I suppose I'll have to do just that,' she said. 'The boss is worried that you can't both do your job *and* bring up Louisa single-handed. So he's watching you to see if you really can cut it. And it wouldn't do you any good to fall at the first fence.'

She was right, Rutter thought. He might not like it – but she was undoubtedly right.

'So you'll take Louisa home?' he said defeatedly.

'That's right,' Paniatowski agreed. She crouched down, so that her eyes were at the same level as the child's, just as she had done with Freddie earlier. 'We'll have a little party,' she said. 'Just you, me, and Janet, who's going to be your nanny. There'll be loads of fizzy drinks and lots of cake. And even though it isn't Christmas yet, we'll have crackers. Won't that be nice?'

'Will there be paper hats?' Louisa asked.

'*Of course* there'll be paper hats!' Paniatowski agreed. 'That's why we've got the crackers.'

She stood up and held out her hand, which, Rutter noticed to his own chagrin, Louisa took willingly.

'See you later, Daddy,' the little girl said, and though she had not framed it as a question exactly, the questioning was undoubtedly there.

'Of course you will,' Rutter agreed. 'I'll be home before you know it, sweetheart.'

But he avoided looking into Monika Paniatowski's eyes for any sign of confirmation.

* * *

The Jackson family home was a solid, respectable, mid-terrace house which had probably been built some time in the mid-twenties. As Woodend drove up to it, he saw that a small crowd had already gathered in the street outside the front door. He was a little dismayed at the sight, but not entirely surprised – because however hard the police tried to keep a lid on secrets in a town like Whitebridge, the news would still spread like wildfire.

He parked the Wolseley, and climbed out. Several of the spectators noticed him for the first time, and he heard one man say, 'See that big bugger? That's Chief Inspector Woodend.'

As he drew level with the gate, he turned to face the crowd. 'Why don't you all take yourselves off home?' he asked. 'There's nothin' at all for you to see here – nor is there likely to be.'

Several of the watchers looked down at the ground – perhaps with shame, perhaps with embarrassment – but none of them moved a single step.

Well, it was a public street, and there was nothing he could do about it if they wanted to stay there, he told himself. Besides, there were much more important matters to deal with.

A uniformed constable was standing on duty at the door. 'Are the parents inside?' Woodend asked.

'They are, sir.'

'Anybody with them?'

'Yes, sir. Sergeant Stevenson.'

Woodend nodded. It was a good choice,

because though he didn't like Rosie Stevenson personally, he acknowledged that she was a solid bobby who knew how to keep her head when all around her were losing theirs.

He knocked on the door, then, without waiting for an answer, lifted the latch and stepped into the hallway.

Sergeant Stevenson appeared in the living-room doorway almost immediately. She was around the same age as Monika Paniatowski, Woodend remembered, but there the resemblance ended. Stevenson was slightly shorter and slightly chunkier than his bagman, and wore her dark brown hair in a tight, controlled perm. She managed somehow to be simultaneously both more aggressive and more deferential than Monika, and while Paniatowski's obvious ambition seemed to gently back-light her every action, Stevenson's glowed like a blazing warning beacon.

'How are the parents?' Woodend asked softly.

Stevenson shrugged. 'About like you'd expect, sir.'

'You take a ten-minute break, Sergeant,' Woodend said.

'Sorry, sir?'

'Take a break. I'll talk to them alone.'

'I don't need a break, sir,' Rosemary Stevenson said firmly. 'I think I'd be of more use assisting you.'

'I'll be the judge of that,' Woodend told her. 'You need to get away from this house of sorrow for a few minutes, Rosie. Walk up an' down the street a couple of times. Fill your lungs with fresh air. But whatever you do, don't say a word to the gatherin' ghouls outside.'

For a moment, Stevenson looked as if she was about to argue, then she shrugged again, squeezed past him, and stepped out through the front door. Woodend took a deep breath himself, then entered the lounge.

Mr and Mrs Jackson were sitting on the sofa. Mr Jackson had his arm over his wife's shoulder, and they both looked as if they'd been crying.

They were both in their late thirties, Woodend guessed. That was rather old to be bringing up such a young family, but he suspected that Mrs Jackson was probably one of those women who refused to be led to the altar until she and her future husband had scraped together enough money to put down the deposit on a house, a dining-room set, and a good three-piece suite.

'Have you found her?' Mrs Jackson asked frantically.

Woodend shook his head. 'No, I'm afraid we haven't.'

'Oh, my God!' the woman moaned.

'But it's early days, an' you shouldn't necessarily take the fact that there's no news yet as a bad sign,' Woodend told her.

He regretted using the word 'necessarily' the moment it was out of his mouth, but it was said now. Besides, it would have been cruel to give Angela's parents any false hope.

'She's such a good girl,' Mrs Jackson said.

'Such a *reliable* girl – and so fond of her little brother.'

'I'm sure she is,' Woodend said.

'She's doing very well at school, as well,' Mrs Jackson continued in a rush. 'Her teachers are always telling me that she's destined for great things.'

She was putting her daughter's case, Woodend realized – arguing that bad things should only ever happen to bad people.

But it didn't work like that!

'I'm sorry, but I'm goin' to have to ask you a few questions,' he said.

Mr Jackson nodded. 'Of course.'

Woodend reached into his pocket, and pulled out the watch that Beresford had found under the bush. 'Is this Angela's?' he asked.

Mrs Jackson moaned softly.

Mr Jackson said, 'Yes, it's hers. It's the one we bought for her when she turned thirteen.'

'My daughter always keeps her watch runnin' ten minutes fast,' Woodend told him. 'She says it's her way of makin' sure she gets to places on time. Is your Angela like that?'

Mr Jackson shook his head. 'No. Our Angela takes real pride in the fact that her watch is always accurate.'

So if the watch said two minutes past three when it stopped working, then that was the time it had actually been, Woodend thought.

He cleared his throat. 'The next question I have to ask you is if you've seen any strangers hangin' around in the street?' he said.

40

'Strange *men*, you mean, don't you?' Mr Jackson asked.

'Yes,' Woodend admitted. 'That's what I mean.'

Mr and Mrs Jackson exchanged helpless glances.

'I wouldn't have noticed if there was. I'm out at work for most of the day,' Mrs Jackson said. 'You need two wages coming in when you've got a growing family to support,' she added, as if she felt the need to justify herself.

'An' at night?'

'At night – with winter drawing in – I close the curtains as soon as I get home, and never step out of the house again.'

'What about you, Mr Jackson?' Woodend asked.

'I'm out most of the day *and* most of the evening,' Angela's father said. 'I'm a taxi driver, you see, an' in my job, you have to take the work when an' where it's available.'

'But we should have taken more care,' Mrs Jackson sobbed. 'We needed to have taken *more care*.'

Her feelings of concern were being drowned in a tidal wave of guilt, Woodend recognized. It did not surprise him. He'd seen it a thousand times before – and he was far from immune to it himself.

'You mustn't blame yourself,' he said gently. 'Even if he has been watchin' the house – and that's far from certain – he'll probably have taken care not to be spotted.'

'Do you think it was all carefully planned in advance?' Mr Jackson asked, the thickness in his voice showing that he was close to tears again.

'I don't know about that – one way or the other,' Woodend admitted.

'But you *do* think she's already dead, don't you?' the anguished father demanded.

'I don't know whether you remember this or not, but a couple of years ago another girl of about your daughter's age disappeared from the corporation park,' Woodend said, sidestepping the question.

'Helen Dunn,' Mr Jackson said dully.

'That's right, Helen Dunn,' Woodend agreed. 'She was missin' for several days, but when we did eventually find her, she was alive and well.'

That was all true enough, but even as he was speaking the words he was well aware that that had been an entirely different case – that young Helen Dunn had been of no interest to kidnappers in herself but had merely been a pawn in a much bigger game.

If he wanted to compare cases – and he didn't! – then the one that came to mind concerned the little girl in London whose disappearance he'd investigated early in his career. He'd never forget the day he found her – never forget the sight of her poor mutilated body, as they pulled her out of the river.

Never *forget* it?

Twenty years on from the case, and he could not even stop himself from *dreaming* about it!

'We're doin' all we can,' he said. 'If it's humanly possible to return your daughter safely to you, then you can rest assured we'll do it.'

It wasn't enough for them. He knew it wasn't enough. But what else could he say?

Four

The basement of Whitebridge Police Head-quarters had a dual role. For most of the time it was a dumping place for unwanted or redundant equipment – traffic signs, police barriers, and the like – but when there was a serious crime it came into its own as the only room in the entire building which was big enough to accommodate a large team of investigators. A couple of hours earlier, it had still been in its dumping-ground phase, but by the time Woodend reached it to address his new team, its transformation had been completed.

The chief inspector looked around him – at the desks laid out in a horseshoe, at the eager faces of the detective constables, pulled in from all over Central Lancs to work on the case.

By Christ, they all looked so young, Woodend thought. In fact, each new team seemed to be younger than the last. Give it a couple of years, and he'd find himself addressing babies.

He cleared his throat. 'We don't *know*, for

certain, that this poor kid's been grabbed by a pervert,' he said, 'but given that she seems a steady, responsible lass, an' that her parents are nowhere near rich enough to pay a sizeable ransom, it seems more than likely that that's exactly what happened. Which means that speed is of the essence. Or to put it another way, we have to collar this bastard before he's had time to do his victim too much damage.'

The detective constables all nodded sombrely – but also hopefully.

They didn't question for a moment the idea that the abductor *could* be caught before he'd done too much damage, Woodend thought. They were still labouring under the illusion that right and justice always triumph. Well, there was nothing wrong with hope – when that was all you had. And in many ways, it was a pity that after a couple of years at the sharp end – after they'd seen for themselves just what one human being can do to another – they'd discover that hope was being elbowed out of the way by dis-illusionment and cynicism.

'We haven't yet got any leads as such,' the chief inspector continued, 'but there are areas of possible investigation which might *give* us leads. For a start, there's the park itself. Every-one who was there has already been interviewed by the uniformed branch, but they're not trained detectives like you are, and they may have missed something.' He paused, noticing the new arrival in the doorway, then continued, 'Isn't that right, Inspector Rutter?'

Bob Rutter nodded. 'In this job, you soon learn that you never cover the ground just once,' he said. 'You go over it again and again, until you're absolutely certain there's nothing more to be extracted from it.'

'Which means that all those people will be re-interviewed by you lads,' Woodend said. 'Next there's the car park to look at. It's more than likely that the kidnapper left his vehicle there – which is why he chose to attack the girl where he did – so we need to find out which cars *were* parked there at the time, an' follow them up. Detective Constable Beresford will be super-visin' both those operations. We'll also have a team, led by Inspector Rutter, goin' over every inch of the area around the bushes, to make sure the kidnapper didn't leave any clues behind.' He lit up a Capstan Full Strength, and took a deep drag. 'Any questions so far?'

The detective constables looked at each other, and then back at the chief inspector. None of them said a word.

'That's the *chasin'* part of the investigation,' Woodend continued, 'but we're also goin' to be doin' what in Western films they call "headin' the bloody bastard off at the pass". A team led by Sergeant Paniatowski an' me will be pullin' in any known deviants in the area.' He paused again, and looked across at Rutter. 'Any idea where Monika is at this moment, Bob?'

Rutter look distinctly uncomfortable. 'I be-lieve she's sifting through all the information we've collected so far, sir,' he said.

'Siftin', is she?' Woodend asked dubiously. 'Anyway, as I was sayin', me an' Sergeant Paniatowski will be talkin' to all these perverts, an' the grillin' we intend to give them will make any other police interview they've ever had seem like a Sunday School outin'. Because believe me, lads, the gloves are off this time, an' if you have to step over the line to help get a result, step over it without a second's thought, an' we'll worry about the consequences later. Any questions *now*?'

One of the bolder detective constables raised his hand. 'What exactly did you mean by the last remark, sir?' he wondered.

'I meant that if you don't exactly stick to what's laid down in the Police Handbook, I'll protect you in any way I can,' Woodend said. 'An' if you take a fall for what you've done, you won't be doin' it alone – because I'll be fallin' with you.'

There'd been a time when, on entering a pub with his boss, Rutter would have ordered a pint of best bitter for Woodend and only a half for himself. But that had been in the south. Now they were up north, where a half pint was a ladies' drink, served in a straight glass, and men – who took their drinking seriously – supped their ale from a heavy mug. And so it was that as the two men approached the bar counter of the Drum and Monkey, Rutter held up two fingers to the barman, and the barman reached up to the shelf for two pint pots.

'I think you might have been a little unwise in what you said back in the briefing, sir,' Rutter told the chief inspector, while they were waiting for their pints to be pulled.

'Oh aye?' Woodend replied. 'Are you referrin' to anythin' in particular that I might have said?'

'The comments you made about supporting anyone who stepped over the line.'

The barman placed their pints in front of them, and Woodend took a large swig of his. 'That was a mistake, was it?'

'I think so,' Rutter told him seriously. 'There are plenty of bobbies serving on this force who'd be more than ready to go right over the top, in a behavioural sense, if there were no restraints on them. That's why the Police Handbook's there – to put that restraint in place – and what you've just done, if you'll forgive me for saying so, sir, is give the rogue element virtual licence to act in any way it wants to.'

'What I've just done is increase the chances of gettin' that little girl back alive,' Woodend told him. 'An' however slim that chance may be, I still think it's one worth takin'.' He looked around the bar, to see if they could be overheard, then continued, 'Movin' on. What was all that bollocks you gave me in the briefin' about Monika siftin' through the information we've got so far. There's bugger all information *to* sift through.'

'I imagine there isn't,' Rutter agreed. 'But I thought the team might take it the wrong way if they learned what she was *actually* doing.'

'An' what *was* she actually doin'?'

'You know, because you were the one who told her to do it. So when you asked me in the briefing what she was doing, I just assumed that because of the pressures of the moment, your instruction to her had slipped your mind.'

'An' they still seem to be slippin' it,' Woodend said. 'Just remind me of what them instructions were.'

'You told her to take Louisa home.'

Woodend was silent for some time, then he said, 'I told her to see to it that you got to headquarters as soon as possible. I never mentioned anythin' about her becomin' your personal babysitter.'

'I hardly think that's fair,' Rutter said hotly.

'I'm sure you don't,' Woodend agreed. 'But it's right enough, whether or not. She wants to protect you, Bob. An' I can understand that, because I want to protect you, too. But there are limits to what we can do – an' I won't see Monika dragged under just so that you can stay afloat. So while she's lookin' after your interests, it's your job to see that you're lookin' after hers.'

'I still thing you're being unfair,' Rutter said.

'*Life*'s unfair,' Woodend said flatly. Then he softened a little and put a sympathetic hand on Rutter's shoulder. 'Life's *very* unfair. An' after all that you've been through yourself, I would have thought you'd have understood that long ago.'

* * *

48

The windows of the house were all boarded up, as was the front door. In what had once been the small front garden lay any amount of rubbish which had simply been dumped there – broken-down refrigerators and superannuated prams, glass bottles and rusting tin cans. To anyone who happened to be passing by, therefore, the house looked derelict and totally uninhabited.

The Invisible Man knew better. He knew, because he owned the house, that while most of the rooms had fallen into irredeemable decay, there was one on the ground floor which had been fitted up for his special purpose. In this room, which was illuminated by a paraffin lamp, there was a camp bed, an easy chair, and a small gas stove. But, more importantly – *much* more importantly – there was a spyhole in the wall, which was virtually undetectable from the other side.

He had begun thinking of himself as the Invisible Man while he was still at school. No one else knew then – or knew now – that he called himself by the name. It was a secret he had never revealed – and would never reveal.

Back in his school days, the name had had an almost literal meaning for him – he was the boy who other people appeared not to see, the boy whose opinions mattered for nothing, the one who was the last to be picked for the football team and was looked straight through by the girls he admired.

It didn't have that meaning now. Now he was invisible only in the sense that other people couldn't see what he was doing, couldn't even guess at his plans, and had no idea how he meant to order their lives until it was too late to stop it.

Invisibility was no longer a sign of weakness as it had once been, he told himself. It was a cloak that he used to hide his true power.

He sat down in the easy chair, pulled back the cover of the spyhole, and pressed his eye against the glass.

He could see the girl! She was huddling in the corner of the room, hugging herself tightly and sobbing. Illuminated as she was, by the flickering neon light over her head, it seemed almost as if she was on a stage, performing. And in a way, she was. Performing for her director. Performing for *him*!

He had been imagining this moment for weeks.

No, not for weeks!

For months!

For years!

For almost as long as he could remember.

Yet never had he thought it would be like this – never come anywhere close to grasping how wonderful it would actually be.

The tears were still running down the girl's cheeks. Yes, she was desperately unhappy, the Invisible Man told himself. Who wouldn't be in her situation? But if she knew – if she had even the slightest inkling – what was in store for her, she wouldn't be just unhappy. She would go quite mad.

He looked down, and was surprised to see that his right hand was steadily massaging his crotch. What an explorer that demon hand of his was, he thought. What a mind of its own it had.

He was tempted to let it continue with its busy work, yet he forced himself to resist the temptation. Half the pleasure of all this was in the anticipation, he reminded himself. Perhaps it was even *most* of the pleasure, for though he prayed and prayed that it would not be the case, he suspected that the climax would come as something of a disappointment.

He heard a car pull up in the road outside, and felt the hairs on the back of his neck tingle. He pushed himself out of the chair and crossed the room, noting, as he did so, that his heart had started to pound furiously.

He was anxious, he told himself. He was perhaps even a little bit frightened. But so what? Wasn't fear also a part of the process – a part of the excitement of the game?

He reached the window. Like all the others in the house, it was boarded up, but that did not bother him because he had thought about this problem in advance, and – clever, clever man! – had installed a second spyhole in the wall which gave out onto the road.

The vehicle which had pulled up was a police car, and two uniformed officers were just getting out of it. He had anticipated this might happen, too, but he was not worried.

Honestly, he promised himself, he was not worried at all.

As the two constables stepped onto the pavement, he quickly read the language of their bodies, and decided that whilst they might be alert and ready for trouble, they were certainly not expecting any. They had no idea they were so close to the girl, which meant that they would not find her – would not *save* her.

Nobody could save her now!

Five

The man sitting across the interview-room table from Woodend and Paniatowski was called Cedric Thornton. He was in his early thirties, and had greasy dark hair and very bad teeth. Patches of sweat had begun to form under the armpits of his cheap white shirt.

'I haven't done nothin',' he whined.

Woodend took a deeply pensive drag on his cigarette. 'I believe you,' he said finally.

Thornton looked surprised. 'You do?'

'Yes,' Woodend confirmed. 'I've had a little chat with Mr Bowden, your probation officer, an' he tells me that since you've come out of prison, you've been keepin' your nose very clean.'

'I should never have been banged up in the first place,' Thornton said.

'Now that's not quite true, is it, Cedric?'

Woodend asked mildly. 'You did *rape* the girl, after all.'

'She wanted it as much as I did,' Thornton said. 'It was only later that she changed her mind and started to claim that I'd raped her.'

Woodend tut-tutted softly. 'She didn't go out on the moors lookin' for sex, now did she, Cedric? She went to look for a missing dog – a collie called Prince, if I remember rightly. And even if she had agreed to let you do what you did to her – and there's not that many women around who will agree to have their backsides penetrated – she was still underage.' He paused. 'But that's by the by. Your probation officer says you're clean, an' I for one am prepared to believe—'

'Probation officers!' Paniatowski snorted.

'Is there some point you'd care to make at this juncture, Sergeant?' Woodend asked.

'Only that probation officers know bugger all, and if you want the living proof of that, you've only got to look at the pathetic specimen we're talking to now. He's a natural rapist if I ever saw one, forever trying to compensate for the fact that he's got a very tiny prick, and always having to *force* girls into having sex with him because they'd certainly never go with him voluntarily.'

'Here, you can't go saying things like that,' Thornton protested.

'I just did,' Paniatowski told him.

'A lady shouldn't be using them sorts of words,' Thornton muttered, almost to himself.

53

Woodend shook his head regretfully. 'Ah, but that's the problem, you see – Sergeant Paniatowski's a lady only in the biological sense.'

'We're wasting our time,' Paniatowski told Woodend. 'Let's charge the bastard with Angela Jackson's kidnapping and have done with it.'

'Is that what this is about?' Thornton asked. 'The girl who went missing from the park?'

'Look at how he's trying to come over all innocent now,' Paniatowski sneered.

'I am innocent!' Thornton said. 'I've got an alibi for the whole of the afternoon.'

'I doubt even *I've* got an alibi for the *whole* of the afternoon,' Paniatowski said sceptically.

'It's true,' Thornton told her. 'I was up at the VD clinic.'

'All afternoon?'

'They know all about me up there, and they don't like me – so they make me wait for my treatment.'

'And this alibi will check out, will it?' Woodend asked. 'Because I swear to you that if I find out you've been wastin' my time...'

'It'll check out,' Thornton promised.

'I think we should charge the bastard anyway,' Paniatowski said. 'It'll get the newspapers off our backs, and we can always trump up some other charge to hold him on once we arrest the real kidnapper.'

'You can't do that,' Thornton said, almost sobbing now.

'Can't we?' Paniatowski wondered. 'Do you really think the people at the VD clinic will

54

confirm your alibi...'

'Yes, they're forced to.'

'...if we ask them not to?'

'I can see the appeal of what you're proposin', Sergeant,' Woodend admitted, 'but in the interests of fairness, I really do think we should give Cedric another chance.' He turned his gaze full on to Thornton. 'Don't *you* think we should give you another chance, Cedric?'

'I'd appreciate it, sir,' the sweating man moaned. 'I really would.'

'But if we're goin' to be nice to you, you'll have to do somethin' for us in return,' Woodend pointed out.

'What?' Thornton asked.

'See what you can find out for us, you scumbag,' Paniatowski said. 'Have a quiet word with your slimy little mates, and see if they know what's happened to the girl. If you can bring us something useful, it might – and I'll say no more than "might" – get you off the hook.'

'I ... I don't have any mates,' Thornton stuttered, 'but I'll...I'll see what I can find out.'

'You do that,' Woodend said.

'So ... so can I go?'

'You can go,' Woodend agreed. 'But remember, if your alibi doesn't hold up, we'll have you back in here quicker than you can *say* "venereal disease". And once we've got our hands on you again, havin' the clap will be the least of your worries.' He turned to the uniformed constable standing in the doorway. 'Show Mr Thornton off the premises, will you, officer?'

The constable opened the door, and Thornton rose to his feet warily – as if he believed this to be some kind of elaborate trap which was just about to be sprung on him.

'Don't act like you've got all the time in the world!' Paniatowski said harshly. 'Piss off as quick as you can – before we change our minds.'

Thornton crossed the room in a scuttle, which, by the time he reached the corridor, had almost turned into a run.

'He didn't do it,' Woodend said to Paniatowski, once the door was closed. 'Even if his alibi doesn't check out at all, he's simply not organized enough to have arranged the abduction.'

Paniatowski sighed. 'You're right, of course, sir,' she said. 'Do you think my playing the complete bitch will give him the incentive to try and find out who the kidnapper really is?'

'Yes, it probably will,' Woodend said. 'You certainly scared him enough to make him do anythin' he possibly can to avoid havin' to go through the experience again. Still an' all, however hard he tries, I don't hold out much hope of him getting us a result.'

'No?'

'No! You heard what he said to us. He can't get us a lead through one of his friends, because he doesn't *have* any friends. An' none of the other perverts I've ever met have had any friends either. They're solitary, lonely creatures, though whether being lonely turns them into perverts or whether it's the other way round,

I've absolutely no idea. But whatever the case, I doubt that our kidnapper's goin' to go out drinkin' with a few of his like-minded mates an' brag to them about what he's done, as a burglar or a car thief might do in his place. No, Monika, he's goin' to keep it entirely to himself.'

Paniatowski sighed again, and lit up another cigarette. 'Shall we see the next one, then?' she suggested.

'Aye,' Woodend said heavily. 'We might as well.'

Rutter stood on the terrace of the cafe in the corporation park. The potential witnesses who'd been rounded up earlier had all had their statements taken and been sent home more than an hour earlier. Now the only people in evidence were the uniformed constables who were searching the ground in front of them, inch by careful inch, under the harsh glare of portable floodlights.

'I should be at home,' Rutter told himself. 'I should be with my little baby, reassuring her that she'll soon stop missing her *abuela* and that she's really going to like it here.'

But Monika Paniatowski was right – Woodend would be watching him carefully, and he could not be seen to fall at the very first fence.

He supposed he didn't have to put up with any of this if he didn't choose to. He could always resign from the force and take a job which allowed him to work more regular hours. But what kind of job? He was a trained detective, and he was good at it. And he couldn't think of anywhere else that his particular skills would be of value. Besides, he *was* his work – and his work was *him*. He had no idea what kind of man he would become if he left the police – or whether that kind of man could be a good father to Louisa.

You're rationalizing, you selfish bastard! he thought angrily. You're trying to cover up the fact that you want to have it all ways – the perfect life in the perfect world. But as Charlie Woodend pointed out, it doesn't work like that.

Though he hadn't seen the uniformed sergeant approaching, he suddenly noticed that the man was standing beside him, and clearly had something he wanted to say.

'Yes?' the inspector asked automatically.

'The lads aren't happy about continuin' the search under these conditions, sir,' the sergeant told him.

'What?' replied Rutter, who was still half trapped in the world of his own dark thoughts.

'They're not happy about carryin' on the search, sir. The floodlights mean that it's bright as day in some places, but there are a lot of shadowed areas as well, an' they're afraid they might overlook somethin' important.'

The sergeant had a point, Rutter thought. It would be futile – and possibly even dangerous to the investigation – to continue the search any longer.

'Call the men off,' he said. 'But make it clear to them that, at first light, I want exactly the same officers back at the exactly the same spots where they ended the search tonight.'

'Understood, sir,' the sergeant said.

'And that's not all,' Rutter told him. 'I want all the park gates securely locked. And we'll need at least six men on permanent park-perimeter patrol all through the night.' He paused. 'There shouldn't be any problem in arranging that, should there, Sergeant?'

The other man shook his head. 'None at all, sir. The lads will appreciate the chance to earn a bit of overtime. Besides...'

'Yes?'

'We all really want to catch this perverted bastard, sir – and we'll do what's necessary.'

'I know you will,' Rutter said. 'We'll all do what's necessary – at whatever the personal cost.'

It would have been wonderful to find a clue in the park right away, Rutter thought, a clear pointer to the guilty man. But investigations were rarely as easy as that. Most of the time it was a case of picking up a splinter of information here and a splinter of information there, and praying that they all eventually fused together to form a solid plank of a case.

He lit up a cigarette – and wondered how Woodend and Monika were getting on.

Peter Mainwearing was around the same age as Cedric Thornton, but there any resemblance between the two men ended. Mainwearing's hair was blond, clean, and neatly cut. His teeth were regular and cared for. His blue overalls, though marked with old oil stains, had obviously been well washed and neatly pressed before he'd put them on that morning.

But it was his attitude, more than anything else, which distinguished him from Cedric Thornton and the rest of the stream of deviants who had trickled their slimy way through the interview room that afternoon. Mainwearing had none of the stink of fear that the others carried with them. Nor did he seemed weighed down by resentment and a sense of grievance, as several of them had been.

Instead, he looked Woodend squarely in the eyes, and said, 'You're only doing your job by pulling me in, Chief Inspector. I want you to know that I understand that.'

'Do you?' Woodend asked sceptically. 'Do you really?'

'I don't blame you for being suspicious of everything I do and everything I say,' Mainwearing told him. 'Sexual offenders are a very cunning and very manipulative breed. And nobody knows that better than me – because I've been one myself.'

'*Have* been,' Woodend mused. 'Are you tryin' to tell me you're not one now?'

Mainwearing smiled weakly. 'If I was telling you that, then I was wrong to,' he admitted. 'An alcoholic never stops being an alcoholic, he just stops being a drunk. And a sex offender never stops being a sex offender – he just accepts that having been a victim himself is no excuse for making victims of others.'

'I was wonderin' just how long it would be before you started claiming to be a victim yourself,' Woodend said.

'But I *am* a victim,' Mainwearing said calmly. 'And you don't just have to take my word for it. It's all documented in my criminal record, which I'm sure you've already pulled from the files.'

'You might be right about that,' Woodend conceded. 'But why don't you tell me why *you* think you're a victim?'

'I was sexually abused as a child,' Mainwearing told him. 'From the age of six! By my own father! Dear old Dad!' He sniffed, and a single tear began to run down his cheek. He brushed it angrily away with the back of his hand. 'I'm sorry,' he said. 'I should have more control than that.'

Woodend risked a surreptitious glance at Paniatowski. By now she should have waded into the interrogation, playing the role of the bad bobby to Woodend's more reasonable one. It was a part she had already played successfully several times that afternoon. But instead of showing her claws, she was just sitting there – pale as a stone statue, as wooden as a church pew carving.

The chief inspector cursed himself for his own stupidity. Paniatowski, as he was only too well aware, had herself been abused as child – though by her step-father, rather than her natural one. The damage the experience had done to her was not noticeable most of the time, but there were occasions – and this was obviously one of them – when, despite her best efforts, that damage rose to the surface.

'An' I should have seen it comin',' Woodend told himself. 'I should have bloody well seen it comin'.'

'Are you all right, Sergeant?' Mainwearing asked – and he sounded genuinely concerned.

'Don't worry about her,' Woodend said roughly. 'You've got enough problems on your own plate at the moment, not the least of which is convincin' me that you're on the wagon as far as little boys are concerned.'

'I had counselling in prison, and I've had counselling since I came out,' Mainwearing said. 'It's been a struggle, but I've got it under control. If I ever thought I *couldn't* control it, I'd submit myself for voluntary castration.'

Woodend winced at even the mention of castration, then said, 'Do you have an alibi for this afternoon?'

'Yes, I do.'

'Let's hear it, then.'

'I was an accountant before I went into prison, but while I was serving my sentence I trained as a motor mechanic, and after I was released I decided I'd rather tinker with engines than with figures.'

'I didn't ask for your life story, I asked for your alibi,' Woodend said, glancing at Paniatowski again and seeing that she was starting to come out of the trance into which her own painful memories had drawn her.

'I have my own garage,' Mainwearing continued, unruffled. 'It's a very modest business, but I'm quite proud of it. That's where I was when your officers picked me up.'

'An' that's where you were all afternoon, is it? Workin' on a motor, no doubt. All by yourself!'

A slight, amused smile came to Mainwearing's lips. 'If I had been working alone in my garage, that wouldn't be much of an alibi, now would it?' he asked. 'As a matter of fact, I'd only just got back to the garage when your men came for me. For the previous four hours, I'd been working at the municipal bus station on one of the double-deckers that was having some rather complicated engine trouble. You can check on that, if you like...'

'Don't worry, I will.'

'...but it will be a waste of police time. I was working side by side with two of the bus company's own mechanics, and because it was such a rush job, we didn't even stop for lunch. All we had to eat was sandwiches, and we munched away at them while we were working on the engine.'

Mainwearing was either the best liar he'd ever met, or he was telling the truth, Woodend decided. He was almost convinced it was the latter – though he'd still make sure he had the alibi checked out.

'Do you want us to catch whoever abducted this young girl, Mr Mainwearing?' he asked.

'But of course,' Mainwearing replied, looking

shocked that the question even needed to be posed.

'Then help us out,' Woodend suggested. 'Give us some sort of lead to latch on to.'

'Like what?'

'Tell us the name of somebody we should be takin' a closer look at.'

'I wish I could, but I've no idea who the guilty party could be,' Mainwearing told him. 'Alcoholics often band together. I suppose that's because as long as all the people around them are drinking as heavily as they are, they can convince themselves they're normal. Sex offenders aren't like that. Theirs is very much a solitary obsession.'

Yes, by and large it *was* a solitary obsession, Woodend thought. He'd said as much to Paniatowski earlier. And the very fact that it *was* solitary was the whole bloody problem!

'Alcoholics have a knack of recognizin' kindred spirits even when other people don't,' he said, giving this line of questioning one last chance. 'Are you tryin' to tell me you couldn't spot another sex offender?'

'I probably could spot some of them,' Mainwearing admitted. 'But not all of them, by any means. As I've already said, they're a very cunning breed. And just as a recovering alcoholic steers well clear of pubs and parties where he knows there'll be booze, I steer well clear of playgrounds – and anywhere else there might be children. So much as I might wish to, I'm afraid I can't give you the name of a single sex offender living in the Whitebridge area, Chief Inspector.'

Woodend nodded defeatedly. 'You can go now, Mr Mainwearing,' he said. 'But if you're contemplatin' leavin' Whitebridge for any length of time, you must let us know where you're goin'.'

Mainwearing stood up. 'Why should I want to go anywhere else?' he wondered aloud. 'What would be the point, when wherever I went I could never escape myself?'

Woodend waited until Mainwearing had left the room, then turned to Paniatowski again. The colour had returned to the sergeant's cheeks, he noted, and she was not sitting as quite as stiffly as she had been earlier. But she still looked very troubled.

'Are you all right, Monika?' he asked.

'All right? Why wouldn't I be all right? Of course I'm all right,' Paniatowski replied in an aggressive tone which showed she clearly wasn't.

Six

It was a long-standing tradition that, at the end of a day spent investigating a major case, Woodend's team would congregate around their special table in the public bar of the Drum and Monkey. It was at this table – over pints of best bitter for the men, and glasses of vodka for Monika Paniatowski – that theories were exchanged, and imaginative leaps in detection made. It was at this table that finding the solution to complex crimes often began.

That night the team arrived at the pub just before closing time, and as they sat down it was plain to all of them that the magic – the usual electricity which leapt from one to the next – was notable only by its absence.

'The problem is that there's nothing for us to get our teeth into in this case,' Bob Rutter said dispiritedly, as he sipped without enthusiasm at the pint Woodend had just bought him.

Yes, that was *exactly* the problem, the chief inspector agreed silently.

Most violent crimes were relatively simple to solve, because the victim had some direct connection with his or her attacker.

A wealthy man is murdered – take a very close

look at the people who stand to benefit from his estate.

A victim's body displays signs of a frenzied attack – find out who had a deep grudge against him.

Greed and anger – these were the two main driving forces behind most killings.

But this case was different. It was more than likely that Angela Jackson had no connection *at all* with the man who had abducted her. He had snatched her simply because she was a young girl – and the chances were that any other young girl who'd happened to be around would have served his purpose just as well.

So how did you get a lead in a case like this one?

How could you possibly uncover the sick bastard's motive – when it was tightly locked away in his head?

'So what have you got?' Woodend asked the rest of the team, and when none of them seemed eager to be the first to speak, he added, 'Let's start with you, Colin.'

Beresford shrugged hopelessly. 'We think there were at least thirty vehicles in the car park in the half-hour before Angela Jackson went missing. But that is only a rough approximation. We can account for sixteen of them, because they belonged to people we questioned in the cafe. That leaves fourteen – more or less. We know the make and model of some of them. For instance, there was a green Ford Cortina parked there – but how many green Cortinas are there in the Whitebridge area?'

'Must be hundreds of them,' Rutter said.

'Hundreds,' Beresford agreed. 'Tracking down the one that was actually there could take us days.'

And days is just what we don't have, Woodend thought. Besides, even if we do find it, the chances are its owner merely parked it there while he went about his perfectly legitimate business.

'Put out a general appeal for people who left their vehicles in the car park to come forward,' he said aloud.

'That's already been done, sir,' Beresford said. 'There's been an announcement on the local news, and the uniformed branch are sticking up posters all over the city centre. But until we start to get results, we're at a bit of a dead end.'

'Bob?' Woodend asked his inspector.

'Nothing from the park yet, sir,' Rutter said. 'Have you had any luck?'

'Me an' Monika have been talkin' to slime all day,' Woodend told him. 'The only thing is, we both think it's the wrong *kind* of slime.'

The pub lights flashed, and the landlord called out, 'Will you please empty your glasses, ladies and gentlemen.'

There was absolutely no need to leave at that moment, Woodend reminded himself. The other customers would soon be shown the door – in strict accordance with the licensing laws – but the team could stay on if they chose, as they'd done so many times in the past and no doubt would many times in the future. Yet what would be the point of staying on, when – without any new development – they had nothing more to say to one another?

He saw the landlord looking at him question-ingly, and shook his head. 'Tomorrow's another day,' he told the team. 'And maybe tomorrow we'll get just the lucky break we need.'

It was twenty minutes past eleven when Rutter reached his home and found Janet, the new nanny, waiting for him in the hallway.

'You're rather later than I expected you to be, Mr Rutter,' she said reprovingly. 'The other parents I've worked for have always told me in advance what time they'll be home. And if they were going to be later than they'd said, they've rung up to let me know.'

'You could have gone to bed once you'd settled Louisa down for the night,' Rutter point-ed out.

'I suppose I could,' Janet agreed, looking very far from mollified by the thought.

'And in case you haven't noticed, we've got a big crisis on at the station,' Rutter snapped.

'I *have* been watching the news, and I *do* feel sorry for the girl who's gone missing,' Janet told him. 'But even so...'

She said no more, simply stood there, waiting for Rutter to make the next move.

He was handling things very badly, Rutter told himself. He was tired and irritated and frustrat-ed, but that was still no excuse.

'Look, you knew when I hired you that I worked irregular hours,' he said. 'That was why I agreed to pay you more than the going rate.'

Janet's chin was set firm. 'Money's not the point,' she said.

'Then what is?'

'Consideration. I may be your employee, but that doesn't mean I'm your slave. I'm entitled to a certain amount of respect.'

'You're right, of course,' Rutter agreed wearily. 'I appreciate having you here, and you are entitled to respect. I'll try to keep you better informed of my movements in future.'

Janet melted a little – though it was clear she was prepared to freeze up again, given the slightest reason. 'Would you like me to make you a cup of tea, Mr Rutter?' she asked.

'That would be very kind of you,' Rutter replied, laying on the consideration and respect with a trowel.

As he followed her into the living room, the first thing that caught his eye was two brightly wrapped packages.

'How did these get here?' he asked.

'They were delivered earlier, by private messenger,' Janet told him, as she headed for the kitchen.

Rutter tore the wrapping paper off the nearest, and when he opened the box he found an expensive-looking teddy bear staring up at him through dark glass eyes. He opened the second, and found a doll which appeared, at first glance, to be made of a plastic which looked like imitation china, but, on closer examination, turned out to be the real thing.

A china doll! Rutter thought. Who, in this day and age, could afford a *china* doll?

'You seem to have some rich friends,' Janet said, seeing the toys when she returned with the tea.

'Yes, I do, don't I?' Rutter agreed.

The Invisible Man was back in the crumbling terraced house – positioned at his peephole and watching the girl.

She had been filled with fear when she'd first regained consciousness, he thought.

But not with fear alone. Oh no! Disbelief and hope had been present, too.

Disbelief because she still could not quite bring herself to accept that this was anything more than a bad dream.

Hope because, like a bad dream, there had to be an end to it eventually, an end which would see her safely back home with her loved ones.

That had been then. That had been before she'd gained some inkling of just what was in store for her.

Now, the disbelief and hope had gone.

Now, all that was left was the fear.

And it would get worse, that fear. Soon it would no longer concern itself with what was happening to her at that moment, but would focus on what would happen *next*.

And even that would only be one more stage in her journey. Another step would come when she ceased to fear death – when she began to welcome it as a release.

As an escape from the sheer hell she found herself in.

And when she reached that stage, she would no longer be any fun to play with, and it would be all over.

No, that was not quite true, the Invisible Man corrected himself. She would die, certainly, but not in the swift and merciful way she sought. Instead, her death would be the final stage in the game – an exquisitely agonizing end, which would leave her as no more than an empty vessel. And standing over this shell would be the man who had brought about her end, feeling as powerful as any god that had ever held sway over the fate of mankind.

This feeling would not last. The Invisible Man knew that. Soon the cravings would start again, and another victim would have to be found. And another. And another. On and on, until the end of time. Or until he was caught.

Monika Paniatowski sat alone in her bland, impersonal flat, her gaze alternating between the blank television screen and the vodka glass that she held tightly in her hand.

There was no doubt that Mainwearing's comments about child abuse that afternoon had unnerved her and transported her back to one of the blackest periods in her life. But she could have shrugged all that off by now – if she'd had the mental space to do so. The problem was that such mental space had *not* been available, because of the other thing which had knocked her off balance – spending the early evening with little Louisa.

She was such an open and affectionate child. Paniatowski thought she could see some of her dead mother in her, but also something of her father. Yet mostly she was simply herself – a perfect little girl in her own right. Anyone would have found it hard to resist her, but resisting was even more difficult when you were a thirty-year-old unmarried police sergeant, who had been told by any number of doctors that you could never have any children of your own.

There was no point in brooding about what you couldn't have, Paniatowski told herself. Far better to count your blessings.

She had a job she adored. She had a boss who, while he could be tough and demanding, was nurturing and understanding. And if she never knew true love again, she had at least known it once, which probably put her well ahead of the game.

So she really *did* have a lot to be thankful for.

She raised her glass to her mouth, and knocked back the vodka in a single gulp. And even as the fiery liquid was making its way burningly down her throat, she was already using her free hand to reach for the bottle.

Despite the fact that she was physically exhausted, Sergeant Rosemary Stevenson's eyes were alight with excitement when she walked into her living room, stripped off her blue serge jacket, and flung it onto the nearest chair.

Her husband looked up from the book he'd been reading. 'You could have hung your uniform up,' he said mildly. 'It wouldn't have taken a second.'

'They haven't caught him yet,' his wife said. 'More to the point, they've no idea how to *go about* catching him.'

Stevenson shook his head. 'The poor girl,' he said.

'Don't you see what a fantastic opportunity this is for me – for both of us?' Rosemary asked.

'I'm not sure this Chief Inspector Woodend of yours would even listen to me,' Stevenson told her.

'Haven't you been hearing a word I've said?' Rosemary demanded. 'He's so desperate that he'd listen to a talking duck if he thought it might help. Do you think you *can* help?'

'I've certainly been giving the matter some thought,' Stevenson said cautiously.

'And?'

'There's a great deal of difference between the theoretical and the practical, which is a point that I think you sometimes miss. I can stand up in front of my students, confident that they'll believe everything I tell them, because there's nothing to challenge what I say. But to put my beliefs to the acid test – and to such an *immediate* acid test...'

'You're scared!' Rosemary Stevenson.

'Perhaps a little,' her husband conceded.

'You're shitting your pants, in case all the studies that you've built your reputation on turn out to be a load of crap.'

'I wouldn't put it as strongly as that,' Stevenson said.

'Do you think you can help Cloggin'-it Charlie or not?' his wife asked.

'Yes, I think I can help him,' Stevenson said. 'I really do.'

'So you'll go and see him in the morning?'

Stevenson nodded. 'Yes.'

A broad grin spread rapidly across Rosemary's face. 'That's my boy,' she said.

When Elizabeth Driver was forced to venture out into what she thought of as 'the uncivilized provinces', she liked to compensate herself for the inconvenience by never settling for anything but the best of what was available, and because she was her newspaper's most successful crime reporter, her editor was normally willing to indulge her.

That night she was in York, where she'd gone to cover a double murder so thin on facts that she'd been forced to make up several of her own. She was staying at the Grand Hotel, and as she picked up her bedside phone, she was – most unusually for her – completely alone.

She dialled a Whitebridge number, and when the phone was picked up at the other end, she said, 'Hello, darling, it's me.'

'Hello,' said Bob Rutter.

Elizabeth Driver frowned. Though Rutter *did*

75

sometimes call her 'darling', it was by no means automatic, and she would have to work on that.

'Did you get the presents I had delivered?' she asked. 'The ones I sent for little...' She paused. What the bloody hell was the kid's name? she wondered.

'For Louisa?' Rutter supplied.

'For Louisa,' Elizabeth Driver agreed.

'They must have cost a small fortune,' Rutter said.

They bloody had, Elizabeth Driver confirmed silently. That china doll had been so expensive that she'd only been able to use her expense account for half the purchase price, and the rest had come out of her own pocket.

'Who's counting the cost?' she asked aloud. 'I just wanted to do something that would help her to settle in to her new home.'

'That was very kind of you,' Rutter said.

Kindness had nothing to do with it, Driver thought. Absolutely nothing at all! Rutter was helping her to write the book which – though he didn't know it – was going to expose the White-bridge Police for all its failings (both real and imaginary), make her own reputation and her fortune, and quite destroy the career of one Detective Inspector Bob Rutter. And if, in order to get that book written, she had to cosy up to Rutter's snotty-nosed brat, then she was per-fectly willing to do it.

'I can't wait to meet little Louisa,' she gushed. 'The story I'm covering should be wrapped up in a day or so, and the moment it is, I'll jump into my Jag and drive straight down to White-bridge.'

There was a pause at the other end of the line. 'That ... er ... may not be very convenient,' Rutter said finally.

Elizabeth Driver pouted. 'Not convenient? Don't you want to see me? Don't you want me to meet Louisa?'

'Well, I think it might be better to leave it a week or two before I start introducing her to new people,' Rutter said cautiously. 'But that's not really the main problem.'

'Then what is?'

'We're handling a sod of a case at the moment. A thirteen-year-old girl's gone missing. We think she's been kidnapped by some pervert.'

'How terrible!' Elizabeth Driver said, mustering all the sincerity she could. 'Do you think you'll get her back unharmed?'

'We're praying that we will, but I can't honestly say that we're holding out too much hope.'

'Who's covering the story for my paper?' Elizabeth Driver asked, suddenly starting to feel resentful that she was stuck in York while some other lucky bastard was covering such a juicy story.

'What was that?' Rutter asked, as if he could not quite believe what he'd just heard.

'Who's the *Gazette* sent to Whitebridge?'

'I don't know. And to tell the truth, I'm far too wrapped up in the investigation to care.'

'Of course you are,' Driver said soothingly. 'It was thoughtless of me to even ask.'

'I could find out, if you want me to,' Rutter said.

'I wouldn't dream of it. You've already got far too much on your plate as it is,' Driver assured him. Besides, she thought, I've only to pick up tomorrow morning's *Gazette* to get the information for myself. 'When this case is over...' she said tentatively.

'Yes?'

'Can I come and see you and little Louisa then?'

'Of course you can.'

'I miss you,' Elizabeth Driver said, and after another slight pause, Rutter said, 'I miss you, too.'

Driver hung up and checked her watch, wondering if she'd left it too late to pick up a man for the night.

Beside him, his wife, Joan, was snoring peacefully, but sleep would not come to Charlie Woodend. His mind was travelling back in time. To London, shortly after the War – and to the Ellie Taylor abduction in Southwark.

She'd been just twelve years old.

'We'll get her back,' the newly promoted Sergeant Woodend had assured her grandfather, George, who'd lost a leg fighting for Queen Victoria's now-vanished Empire. 'Don't you worry – we'll get her back.'

It hadn't worked out like that at all, and from the moment an unidentified girl's body had been spotted floating in the Thames, Woodend had *known* that it wouldn't.

He and the old man had stood side by side on the wharf where George had once worked, and watched as poor Ellie Taylor's naked body was retrieved from the river.

When she was alive, she probably considered herself to be a young woman, Woodend had thought, but looking at her at that moment – her breasts just beginning to develop, her legs still almost matchstick thin – it had been blatantly obvious to him that she'd been no more than a child.

'You should leave now,' he'd told George Taylor.

'I want to stay,' the old soldier had said firmly. 'I want to see exactly what that monster did to her.'

And Woodend had agreed to let him, because – whatever the regulations said – he thought the grandfather had a right to be there.

It had been a gruelling experience for both of them. Trails of caked blood ran down the girl's legs from both her anus and vagina. Her front teeth had been knocked out, too – for reasons that were only too clear to Woodend, but which he prayed the man standing next to him would not understand.

'You promised you'd get her back for us, Sergeant,' George Taylor had said bitterly.

'And I thought there was a very good chance that I could,' Woodend had replied.

But that wasn't quite the truth. What he'd meant when he'd made that promise was that he *wanted* to believe there was a good chance.

It had been a young Woodend who had made the promise; a Woodend who, though he had been through all the horrors of war, had not quite yet abandoned the belief that there was a limit to human cruelty. It was a much older Woodend who had finally persuaded George Taylor to leave the scene and go with him to the nearest pub, where they had both knocked back stiff drinks, only stopping when they realized the alcohol was having no effect on them at all.

For a while after that day, Woodend had hoped that he could cast out the image of what he had seen, and so leave some space for the young Woodend to return to. But it had never happened. The day Ellie Taylor had died, a little part of him had died, too.

'For Heaven's sake, do try and get some sleep, Charlie,' Joan mumbled at him from the other side of the bed.

'In a minute, love,' Woodend replied. 'As soon as I've got my thoughts in order.'

Angela Jackson would be another Ellie Taylor, he told himself. He just *knew* she would.

Seven

The early morning of the day following the abduction was just about as depressing as any early morning at that time of year could be.

There was no sign of the autumn sun, which should, by rights, have been beaming down its watery regrets that it could no longer warm the earth as much as it had done in the hazy days of summer. In its place, there were only heavy grey clouds, which hovered menacingly, seemingly unaware of – or indifferent to – the fact that there was not supposed to be any threat of snow at that time of year.

Conditions were no better on the ground. Puddles had iced over, and a sheen of frost covered the roads. Plants were dying in gardens, weeds were withering in the cracks between paving stones. In trees and on bus-stop roofs, wild birds huddled and shivered.

On his drive into Whitebridge, Woodend passed the aftermath of three crashes – and tried not to think of them as an omen.

When the chief inspector finally arrived at his office, he found Bob Rutter already there, doggedly sifting through the piles of reports which had been written the previous evening.

His inspector looked just about as bad as he himself felt, Woodend thought, lighting up a cigarette and slumping down in his chair.

'How long have you been here?' he asked.

'Since six o'clock,' Rutter replied, not looking up from the reports. 'I couldn't sleep.'

'Me, neither,' Woodend said. 'How's Louisa settlin' in?'

'I wouldn't know about that,' Rutter told him. 'If you're really interested, you'll have to ask her nanny.'

It was a little early in the morning to have touched a nerve, Woodend thought. 'Why don't you slip home an' see her now,' he suggested.

'Because somebody has to keep going through all this crap in the hope it will throw up a lead...'

'True, but...'

'...and I'm the best man for the job.'

Rutter was right about that, Woodend thought. Watching him go through reports was like watching a bloodhound follow a scent which was undetectable to anyone but him. Bob had a flair for reports, just as Monika had a flair for conducting investigations on the ground.

'So have you found anythin'?' he asked.

'There's some questions I'd like answering, but that doesn't mean they're going to get us anywhere,' Rutter said bluntly.

There was an unexpected knock on the open office door. Woodend looked up and saw a man standing in the doorway.

At first sight, the visitor was not impressive.

He had light sandy hair and pale eyes. He was dressed in a tweed jacket, cavalry-twill trousers, and brown suede shoes. He looked as if he thought he had no right to be there – and as far as Woodend was concerned, he was bloody spot on about that.

'In case you didn't realize it, sir, we happen to be involved in a very serious investigation at the moment,' the chief inspector snapped. 'An' even if we weren't, this part of the buildin' is not open to the general public.'

'It's because of the investigation that I'm here,' the man said hesitantly. 'I'm Martin Stevenson. *Doctor* Martin Stevenson.'

'I don't care if you're Genghis Khan an' you've got your entire bloody Horde in tow,' Woodend said. 'You still have no right to be here.' Then a vague bell rang in his head, and a connection was made. 'Are you any relation to Sergeant Rosie Stevenson?' he continued.

'I'm her husband,' Stevenson said. 'She thought I might be of some use to you.'

'What kind of doctor are you?' Woodend asked.

'I'm a psychologist, specializing in criminal psychology.'

Rutter released a very audible sigh. 'A shrink!' he said in disgust. 'That's just what we bloody need right now.'

'You'll have to excuse my inspector,' Woodend told Stevenson. 'He's what you might call "an old-fashioned" type of bobby.'

The old-fashioned type of bobby? *Me!* Rutter

thought. *You're* the one who some people call a bit of a dinosaur. I'm the young one. The modern one. The up-to-date one.

He searched the chief inspector's face for any signs of sarcastic intent, and found none.

So just what was Cloggin'-it Charlie up to?

'I'm sure you could be of great help to the current investigation, Dr Stevenson,' Woodend said. 'But before we can talk to you, we will need a few minutes to discuss matters among ourselves.'

Stevenson nodded. 'So what should I do? Wait in the reception area until you're ready to see me?'

'If you wouldn't mind.'

Stevenson nodded again, then turned and walked back down the corridor with the air of a man who'd just been granted a reprieve.

'What was that all about?' Rutter asked, as the doctor's footfalls receded into the distance.

'It was about the fact that we're well an' truly out of our depth on this case, lad,' Woodend said. 'It was about the fact that, as you yourself pointed out last night in the Drum, we've no way of gettin' into the kidnapper's mind. But, you see, the good doctor probably has.'

'He's nothing but a mumbo-jumbo merchant,' Rutter said grumpily. 'They all are. The difference between us and them is that they deal in theories, while we deal in facts.'

'Have you ever heard of James Brussel or George Metesky?' Woodend asked mildly.

'No, I haven't.'

Woodend lit up a cigarette. 'From your reaction just now, I didn't think you had,' he said. 'Back in the 1950s – when you were barely out of short trousers – George Metesky planted a series of bombs in New York. For nearly six years, he had the whole city terrified. The main problem for the police was that there wasn't any pattern to it, so they had no idea where he was goin' to strike next. The first bomb was in a telephone box, but the ones that followed it were planted in places like theatres an' railway stations. None of his bombs actually *killed* anybody, but the last one – set off in a cinema – seriously injured three people. An' the New York bobbies were convinced it was only a matter of time before somebody *did* die. But they still had no real leads on him, even after all that time, an' it was desperation that made them finally consult Dr Brussel, who was New York State's assistant commissioner for mental hygiene at the time.'

'And this Dr Brussel was a great help to them, was he?' Rutter asked sceptically.

'As a matter of fact, he was. He studied the letters the bomber had written to both the police department an' the newspapers, he examined the photographs of the crime scenes, an' he came up with what he called a *profile* of the feller. He said that the bomber would be a heavy, middle-aged man, who wasn't married an' was probably livin' with his brother or sister.'

'Well, in a big place like New York City, that must certainly have narrowed it down,' Rutter sneered.

'He went on to say that the man would be a skilled mechanic...'

'The police probably already knew that, from the way he'd constructed his bombs.'

'...that he was a Roman Catholic immigrant, who had loved his mother almost to the point of obsession, an' also hated his father. He added that when the police did catch up with the bomber, he'd probably be wearin' a double-breasted suit – fully buttoned.'

'And was he right?'

'As near as damn it. He was a Catholic immigrant, all right, an' he was livin' with his two spinster sisters.'

'And was he wearing a double-breasted suit?'

'Not at the time they arrested him in his home, no.'

'Well, there you are, then. If you make enough guesses, some of them are bound to be right, just as some of them are bound to be wrong.'

'He was arrested in an early mornin' raid, so naturally enough, he came to the door in his dressin' gown. Once the arrest had been made, however, the police said they'd allow him to get dressed before they took him down to the station. What he chose to put on, when given that opportunity, was a double-breasted suit. An' he had it fully buttoned.'

Holding the meeting with Martin Stevenson in Woodend's own office would have given the doctor a semi-official status which the chief inspector was not – as yet – prepared to grant him. Talking to him in one of the interview rooms would have made the whole business seem much more like an interrogation than a consultation. So, as a compromise between the two courses, Woodend decided to hold their discussion in the police canteen, a long, tiled room presided over by two thick-stockinged ladies of indeterminate age who were both permanently inflicted by the snuffles and who served mugs of tea so strong that the thick brown liquid seemed almost on the point of melting the spoons.

Once they were sitting down at one of the long Formica tables, Woodend pulled out his packet of Capstan Full Strength and offered it to his guest. 'Smoke?'

Stevenson shook his head. 'No thanks, I don't.'

'Very wise,' Woodend said, lighting up his own cigarette and drawing on it with obvious pleasure.

Stevenson looked around with frank curiosity. 'So this is the famous Whitebridge police canteen, where much of the real work seems to be done,' he said. 'I've often wondered what it looked like. In fact, thoughts of it have quite tantalized me.'

'If that's true, then I'm surprised that you've never been in here before,' Woodend said.

'Perhaps I would have been – if I'd been invited,' Stevenson replied. He saw the questioning look come to Woodend's face, and continued, 'Although our working lives might seem to be somewhat complementary, my wife likes to make sure they are kept firmly apart.'

'An' why is that?' Woodend wondered.

'I suppose it's because – like Inspector Rutter here – she feels that she is a real criminologist, and that I am no more than a dilettante, playing my academic games on the fringes of real life.'

Rutter looked so uncomfortable that Woodend found it very hard to suppress a grin.

'But even if your wife *does* think that you're a dilettante, it was her who suggested that you come here today, wasn't it?' the chief inspector asked.

Stevenson smiled. 'Yes, it was,' he admitted.

'Why do you think she did that?'

Stevenson's smile widened. 'Would you, as a policeman, ever contemplate investigating your own wife?'

'Definitely not!' Woodend said, with a shudder.

'Nor will I, as a psychiatrist, analyse mine,' Stevenson said. 'She *says* she feels that in this particular case I may be of some use, and I'm prepared to take her at her word.'

Woodend nodded. What Stevenson really meant – but was too polite to say – was that his wife had told him the investigation was in the doldrums, and that if he could assist it in any way, some of the credit might rub off on her. And she was right on both counts!

'Shall we talk about the case?' Woodend asked.

'Of course,' Stevenson agreed. He took a sip

of his tea, and then tried to hide the grimace it induced in him. 'I'd like you to give me all the details you have on the abduction,' he continued. 'And I do mean *all* of them, however insignificant any particular detail might appear to you.'

Woodend grinned. 'You sound like a detective,' he said.

'I suppose that, to a certain extent, that's exactly what I am,' Stevenson agreed. 'In many ways, the human brain is as much a crime scene as the corporation park.'

Woodend told Stevenson everything they knew, and was more than conscious, as he was outlining it, of how pathetically little that really was.

When he'd finished, Stevenson nodded his head sombrely and said, 'It would seem to me that your perpetrator is almost definitely the kind of man who falls within the scope of my research. And that being the case, I'm very much afraid that it could be some time before you find the girl – and that when you do, she will already be dead.'

'Oh, yes?' Rutter said, almost contemptuously.

'Yes,' Dr Stevenson replied, and if he'd noticed Rutter's tone, he didn't show it. 'The straightforward rapist *needs* to rape, but he wants to get the whole business over and done with as quickly as possible. If he attacks his victim where he finds her, he will leave the scene immediately after he has carried out the attack. If he abducts his victim and takes her to somewhere he feels secure, he will want to remove her from this safe haven as soon as the violation has occurred. The fact that the girl you're concerned with has been missing for more than half a day means you are dealing with a different kind of man altogether, and that he has either already murdered her, or – what is much more likely – that he intends to kill her once he has no further use for her.'

Woodend nodded. The way Stevenson had argued his case seemed to indicate that he really *did* know what he was talking about, and even Rutter – who had started this meeting determined to be unimpressed – appeared to be taking the doctor a little more seriously now.

'What's he likely to do to her before he actually kills her?' the chief inspector asked.

'Something that will cause her a great deal of pain and humiliation,' Stevenson said gravely. 'He will show no mercy. He will feel none of the normal limits or restraints that you or I might feel. To him, she will not be a person at all, merely a way of achieving his aims. So he is capable of doing anything – however abhorrent and horrific it might seem to other people – as long as it will enhance his own sense of power. When you've recovered the body, I might be able to tell you more, but given the limited data available, I'm afraid I can't be any more specific than that for the moment.'

'What sort of person is he likely to be?' Woodend asked.

'Again, without more data, it is difficult to say.

The one thing I can be reasonably certain of is that he will blend well into his community.'

Woodend thought of the long line of perverts he had grilled the previous afternoon. They had been – almost without exception – men who would be shunned by normal society.

'What brings you to that conclusion?' he asked.

'My own research, and that of others working in the same field,' Dr Stevenson said. 'This research is, admittedly, limited in its scope and nature, but even so, a clear pattern is already emerging.'

'What kind of pattern?'

'I believe that you can classify this kind of killer into two main groups – the organized and the disorganized. The disorganized ones kill on impulse, when the opportunity arises. They may have certain rituals which they feel the need to carry out – mutilation or cannibalism, for example – but they will not normally perform them until after their victim is dead. These killers generally have low IQs, and are often social misfits.'

'An' the organized killer?'

'The organized killer, on the other hand, is much more intelligent. He will plan the whole operation well in advance, including how he will dispose of his victims once he's finished with them. Your man seems to be a good case in point. He didn't just *happen* to have the toy kitten on his person, you see – it was all a part of his well-laid-out plan.'

'Tell me more,' Woodend said.

'Unlike the disorganized killer's rituals, he will normally require the victim to be alive when he practises them. He will take pride in his "work", and will follow the course of the police investigation with real interest. He will not give the impression of being socially inadequate. He will have friends – perhaps even lovers – and when he is arrested, his neighbours and associates will express amazement that he could ever have been involved in anything so horrific.'

'You're paintin' a very dark picture,' Woodend said.

'Yes, I am,' Dr Stevenson agreed. 'But then it's a very dark world these people inhabit.'

Eight

Beresford was standing in the central reception area of the Whitebridge Venereal Disease Clinic. He was well aware of the fact that several sets of curious eyes were focused on him, and was trying his very best not to look like a man who'd woken up one morning to discover that something rather strange and certainly unpleasant had happened to his todger.

A woman in her mid-forties, and wearing a long white clinician's coat, opened the door of one of the offices which faced the reception area, and said in a loud voice, 'I'll see you now, Mr Beresford.'

'That's *Detective Constable* Beresford,' he replied, equally loudly, just in case someone who'd heard might know his mother, and – not appreciating the real nature of his business at the clinic – go telling tales to her.

Not that it would really matter if anyone did, he thought, in a sudden bout of gloom. If this hypothetical informer caught his mother on one of her good days, she might actually remember who he was for a moment and be shocked that he seemed to have fallen so low, but what she'd been told would soon fade from her mind, as everything else seemed to.

'As the sole administrator of this busy clinic, I have a lot on my plate today, much as I have every other day,' the woman said, still talking loudly enough for everyone in the vicinity to hear. 'So if you don't mind, I'd like to get this over with as soon as possible, Constable Beresford.'

Constable Beresford! Now *that* was better, Beresford thought, following her into her office.

The administrator took her seat behind her desk, and reached across for a cardboard file.

'I understand you wish to make inquiries about one our patients, a Mr Cedric Thornton,' she said crisply.

'That's right, we'd like to know—'

'You do understand, don't you, Constable Beresford, that our *medical* records are sacrosanct, and that I cannot give you any details of whatever ailment Mr Thornton is suffering from.'

You don't need to – he's got *VD*! Beresford thought. He wouldn't have come here if he hadn't.

But aloud, he said, 'All we're interested in is Thornton's movements yesterday afternoon.'

The administrator consulted the file. 'He signed in at half-past one, and signed out again at a quarter to four.'

'And there's no chance that he could have nipped out for an hour in the middle?'

'If he had done so, my staff would have noticed it and reported it to me immediately,' the administrator replied. 'I run a very tight ship, you know. The doctors are not here to be at the beck and call of the patients. Rather it is for the patients to make themselves available for when the doctors can find the time to treat them. And once he's signed in, no patient is allowed to leave the building before he's had his allotted treatment.'

Well, that was clear enough, Beresford thought.

If he'd been invited to sit down when he'd entered the office, he would have stood up at his point and held out his hand to the administrator, but since no such offer had been made – and he was consequently still standing – he simply said, 'Well, thanks for your help.'

He was almost at the door when the administrator said, 'There's one more thing, Mr Beresford.'

Beresford turned. 'Yes?'

'Since you're already here, why not take advantage of the fact and let me arrange for you to have a check-up?'

'That won't be necessary,' Beresford said, with frosty dignity.

The administrator made a disapproving clucking noise with her tongue.

'You men!' she said, almost contemptuously. 'You all think you're so clever, don't you? That's probably why it comes as such a shock to you when you find out that you've been infected.'

'The *reason* that it won't be necessary is because I'm a vir—' Beresford began. Then he stopped himself, horrified at what he'd very nearly confessed to the woman. 'The *reason* it won't be necessary is because I'm always very careful,' he amended.

'That's what they all say,' the administrator told him.

Beresford beat a hasty retreat, and only really slowed down when he was clear of the clinic altogether. He took a list out of his pocket, and placed a tick next to Cedric Thornton's name.

'One down, seven to go,' he told himself.

Since Bob Rutter had announced the previous evening that he intended to immerse himself in witness statements the next day, it had fallen to Monika Paniatowski to take over the job of supervising the uniformed constables who were searching the corporation park. As a result, she had been forced to drag herself from her bed at an ungodly hour, and had driven to the park while still suffering from a hangover of gigantic proportions, which the brooding – and solitary – excesses of the night before had brought on.

The hangover was still with her now, two hours later, and when she lit up a cigarette to see if it might somewhat assuage her pain, she discovered it tasted like dried buffalo dung.

She had very little hope that this extensive search would produce anything of real value, she told herself, as she attempted to ignore the pounding in her head. After all, how likely was it that a man who was smart enough to abduct a girl from a park in broad daylight – *without being seen* – would also have been stupid enough to leave something behind that would connect him with that abduction?

It was at that moment – almost as if fate had been reading her mind and decided to have some fun with her – that one of the constables searching in the bushes called out, 'Sergeant Paniatowski!'

'Yes?'

'I think I've found something!'

The constable was standing a few feet away from where the scuff marks in the earth indicated that the struggle between the girl and her kidnapper had taken place, and when Paniatowski approached him, he pointed – with great excitement – at one of the bushes.

'Under there,' he said.

Paniatowski crouched down. There was

definitely something lying among the roots. She could not get a very clear view of it, because of the obstruction caused by the leaves, but she could tell that it was dark brown and possibly rectangular. And one thing was clear – whatever it eventually turned out to be, it certainly wasn't natural.

As she pulled on her gloves, she noted that her heart was suddenly beating faster, and that her headache had all but disappeared. She stretched her arm through the foliage, and felt her finger-tips brush against the object. She took careful hold of it, between her thumb and forefinger, and slowly withdrew the arm.

What she was holding, she discovered, was a man's leather wallet. It looked expensive, and from the condition it was in, it was clear that it had not been lying under the bush for long.

The corporation bus depot was a three-minute drive from the Boulevard, the Boulevard itself being the point at which most of the service buses started and ended their routes. The depot consisted of a large hanger-like building, in which most of the buses were parked after they'd finished their service for the day, and a patch of concrete on which vehicles were park-ed between rush hours. One end of the hanger contained the cleaning tunnel, and at the other end was the garage.

Beresford found the whole complex slightly scruffy – and not a little depressing. But at least he was unlikely to meet anyone there who'd accuse him of having venereal disease, he consoled himself.

There were three mechanics on duty. They were all small dark men with bald spots, and Beresford found himself wondering if being tall and blonde was a disqualification for crawling under a bus.

'So you want to know about Peter Mainwearing, do you?' one of the mechanics said in answer to Beresford's question.

He was speaking loudly – almost shouting. He had to, in order to be heard over the noise of the radio, which was playing at full blast and echoing all around the whole garage.

'Yes, Peter Mainwearing,' Beresford agreed, shouting himself. 'Could you turn the noise down a bit?'

'Why?' the mechanic screamed back. 'Is it bothering you?'

'No, not really, but I think it's about to burst my eardrums,' Beresford told him.

The mechanic shrugged, walked over to the radio, and switched it off. For a moment or two, Beresford's ears compensated for the sudden loss of sound by hissing loudly. Then they settled down.

'Yes, Peter was here yesterday,' the mechanic said, when he returned to the spot where Beresford was standing. 'We had this problem with one of our buses, you see. The bugger just wouldn't start, and we had no idea why. Peter sorted it out. What that man can do with an engine has to be seen to be believed.'

'And he was here *all* afternoon?' Beresford asked.

'Not *all* afternoon, no,' the mechanic said.

Beresford felt a sudden tingle of excitement. If he could break Mainwearing's alibi, he told himself, it would more than make up for the humiliation he had felt in the VD clinic.

'How long *was* he here?' the detective constable asked.

The mechanic thought about it. 'He arrived at around eleven o'clock,' he said finally.

'*Around* eleven o'clock?' Beresford repeated. 'Can't you be more precise than that?'

The mechanic shrugged. 'Afraid not. But it can't have been more than ten or fifteen minutes before or after.'

'And what time did he leave?' Beresford asked, almost holding his breath in anticipation.

'Three o'clock,' the mechanic said.

'Give or take ten or fifteen minutes one way or the other?' Beresford suggested.

'Three o'clock,' the mechanic repeated firmly. 'On the dot.'

'You seem very vague about the time he arrived,' Beresford said. 'Why is that?'

'Simple,' the mechanic replied. 'Since we had no idea of how to go about the job before he turned up, we thought we might as well sit back and have a game of cards. Then, when he did get here, we packed away the cards and set to work.'

'And you didn't check your watch to see what time it was?'

'Wear a watch on this job, and you'll ruin it. Mine goes into my locker the minute I get to work.'

'And yet, despite the fact that your watch was still in your locker, you're certain that he left at *exactly* three o'clock. How is that possible?'

'Simple again. The afternoon play was just coming on the wireless. It's my favourite programme, and I remember saying to Peter that I was glad we'd got the job finished, because that meant I could listen to it in peace.' The mechanic paused. 'Here, I haven't got Peter in trouble, have I?'

'No,' Beresford promised, 'you haven't got him in trouble.'

He was telling the truth. The girl's watch had been smashed at two minutes past three, and even if it had been wrong by a few minutes, that still put Peter Mainwearing in the clear – because there was no way he could have reached the corporation park before twenty past three at the earliest.

'There's times when I've thought about being a bobby myself,' the mechanic said.

You'd have to grow at least another three inches first, Beresford thought, but all he said aloud was, 'Oh yes?'

'I mean, from what I've heard, it's an easy life.'

'Easy?' Beresford repeated.

'Well, for a start, the pay's not bad, is it? And you don't have to get your hands dirty, do you?'

Why did other people always seem to think

that bobbies had such a cushy time of it, Beresford wondered.

'You're right that *most of the time* we don't have to get our hands dirty,' he agreed. 'Of course, there are always the occasions when you have to pull what's left of a body out of a car wreck. That can be messy. Then again, we sometimes get into fights and have blood spattered all over us – usually our own.'

But the mechanic was not about to allow his illusions to be shattered by cold hard reality.

'Still, every job's got its drawbacks, and there are big compensations in yours, aren't there?' he asked, winking broadly at him.

'I don't know you mean,' Beresford said.

'Course you do. You get called out to visit a house that's been burgled. Right?'

'Right.'

'The lady of the house is still very upset about what's happened, you comfort her as best you can, and before you know it, you're in bed together. You won't deny that kind of thing goes on, will you?'

The mechanic wouldn't believe him if he did, Beresford thought. So why even try to disillusion him?

'Yes, it's happened,' he said, feeling, for once in his life, like a real man of the world.

The mechanic licked his lips. 'How many times?' he asked.

In for a penny, in for a pound, Beresford told himself. 'Lots of times,' he said. 'So many that, if I'm honest, I've almost lost count.'

He was seeing more of that part of his wife's world outside the home in a single day than he had seen in the rest of their married life put together, Martin Stevenson thought as he approached the Crown and Anchor, a pub very close to Whitebridge Police Headquarters.

He stepped through the door into the saloon bar, and knew immediately that he would not like the Crown. It was too barnlike, too gaudy, too noisy – and though it would have been inaccurate to describe it as actually *dirty*, its standards of cleanliness fell below those of the establishments he would normally choose to patronize.

Rosemary was sitting at a table in the centre of the room. She was wearing her uniform, and had her arm deliberately stretched out so that her sergeant's stripes were clearly visible to anyone who looked. She had a cigarette balanced in the corner of her mouth, and a pint of bitter in her hand.

'Did you see him?' she asked, the second that her husband had sat down opposite her.

'This is a strange place to meet,' Stevenson said, looking around him as if to confirm his initial impressions of the bar.

'Strange? What do you mean by that? There's nothing strange about it. It's perfectly normal.'

'Then perhaps what I really meant to say was that it's an "inappropriate" place,' Stevenson told her.

'Inappropriate?' his wife echoed. 'How?'

'Well, we so rarely have the chance to get together in the daytime that I'd have thought you'd have chosen somewhere nicer.'

'This is where we drink,' Rosemary said, as if it required no more explanation than that.

'*We*?'

'Me and my lads.'

'And how long have you been smoking?'

'I only do it at work.'

'Why?'

'Because everybody else does.'

'I don't see what that has to do with—'

Rosemary interrupted him with a heavy sigh. 'Listen, Martin,' she said, 'the way to get on in the Force is to blend in – to be just like everybody else. If I didn't chain-smoke and knock back ale like there was no tomorrow, my lads would think I was being stuck-up and stand-offish.'

'Does this Sergeant Paniatowski, who you always seem to be going on about, do the same?'

'She smokes.'

'But she doesn't drink pints?'

'I sometimes think you listen far too carefully to what I say, Martin,' Rosemary said.

'Most women would be more than happy that their husbands listened to them.'

'And I often get the impression that you start analysing my words the moment they're out of my mouth.'

'That's not true. I—'

'Martin!'

103

'Perhaps I do analyse them – sometimes,' Stevenson admitted. 'It's an occupational hazard, and I'm very sorry about it.'

From the expression on Rosemary's face, it was clear that the apology had not pleased her.

'Why are you always so bloody wet, Martin?' she asked exasperatedly. 'Why must you always lie down and take whatever I decide to throw at you? Why don't you ever fight back?'

Stevenson smiled soothingly. 'In many ways, my work is concerned with producing harmony out of conflict. I help people to see life how it is, and teach them how to learn to be happy with it. So I'm not so much "lying down and taking it" as following my own advice.'

Rosemary looked at him strangely. 'I sometimes wonder why I married you,' she said.

'We married *each other* for the same reason that most other couples marry,' Stevenson said. 'We had an emptiness inside ourselves, and we both hoped the other would be able to fill it.'

'And do I fill your emptiness?'

'Oh, yes.'

Rosemary softened a little, and even smiled as much as the cigarette in the corner of her mouth would allow her to. 'You still haven't answered my question,' she said. 'Did you see Cloggin'-it Charlie?'

'I saw him.'

'And did he know that you were there because of me?'

'Yes.'

'That's good. Were you able to help him?'

'Not a great deal...'

'No?'

'...but as much as I could have reasonably expected at this stage of the investigation. As things develop, I think I'll be of much more use to him.'

'It might even be because of you that he catches the kidnapper?'

'That's certainly possible.'

'It would mean a lot to me if you *could* really help him, you know.'

'Of course I know. That's why I'm here.'

Rosemary took the cigarette out of her mouth, and the smile which followed benefited from the greater flexibility it gave her.

'Unless there's a sudden development in the case, I come off duty in four hours,' she said.

'Oh?'

'I thought we might take the opportunity to go out for a meal. Somewhere really nice. Just the two of us.'

'I'd like that.'

'And then, when we get home, we might decide to go to bed a little earlier than we usually do?'

'I'd *really* like that,' Martin Stevenson said.

Dr Shastri, the police surgeon, greeted Woodend at the door of her laboratory with a broad smile, as she invariably did. 'And how is my favourite policeman today?' she asked.

Woodend, as always, felt an almost juvenile glow at being addressed in such a warm way.

Well, who wouldn't? he asked himself silently.

Given that Shastri was undoubtedly a beautiful woman, a man would have to be made of stone not to be gratified at being offered even a few crumbs from the table of her favour.

'Your favourite policeman is hopin' that you'll have identified the drug that was used to dope Angela Jackson,' he said, a little gruffly.

'Then he will not be disappointed,' Dr Shastri told him.

'What was it? Chloroform?'

Dr Shastri laughed, and it was like the tinkling of dozens of tiny delicate bells. 'You should be ashamed of yourself, Chief Inspector,' she said.

'Should I? Why?'

'Because you have allowed yourself to be just as duped by American detective films as any member of the general public would be – and I would have expected better from you.'

'Would you mind explainin' that?' Woodend asked, trying not to feel too hurt.

'Gladly. In the films, the abductor sprinkles a few drops of chloroform on a piece of cotton and holds it over his victim's mouth for a second or two, until the victim goes quite limp. Isn't that right?'

'I suppose so.'

'In the real world, those few drops would have very little effect at all. And should the kidnapper choose to administer a much larger dose, he would run quite a large risk of actually *killing* his victim.'

'So what was used in this case?' Woodend

wondered.

'A drug called halothane. It was first synthesized about fifteen years ago, and has been used as a clinical anaesthetic for the last ten. It is not recommended for older patients because it can cause cardiac depression – but it is ideal for younger patients, because it does not irritate the airways.'

'And are these properties of the drug common knowledge?' Woodend asked.

'They are not treated as a closely guarded secret by the medical profession, if that is what you are asking. But I would be surprised if the average layman had ever even heard of halothane.'

'Well, then...'

'Still, that is no real obstacle to a determined man. After half an hour in the reference section of the library, he would have learned all he needed to know.'

Woodend nodded gravely. Dr Stevenson had told him that the kidnapper would be both intelligent and careful, and it appeared that was exactly what he was turning out to be.

'How easy would it be to get hold of the stuff?' he asked.

'Not easy at all,' Dr Shastri replied.

'Then why would he...?'

'But neither would it be easy for him to lay his hands on any of the other drugs he might have used as a substitute.'

'But he clearly *did* get his hands on it, didn't he?' Woodend asked. 'How would he have gone about it?'

Dr Shastri smiled. 'I like to think I do not have a naturally criminal mind, which makes that rather a difficult question for me to answer, Chief Inspector. But let me consider the problem.' She frowned with concentration. 'I suppose one way might be to steal it from a hospital – or perhaps bribe someone working in the pharmacology department to give you some. Another way might be to fool a drug company into thinking you represented a hospital, and get them to send it to you. I suppose, if you were a chemist, you could even attempt to manufacture it yourself.'

I could check up on all those things, Woodend thought – and I will.

But the problem was that it would take time – and time was the one thing he didn't have much of.

'Thank you, Doc, you've been very helpful,' he said.

He had almost reached the door when Dr Shastri said, 'Charlie?'

The single word stopped him in his tracks. She had *never* used his first name before. He was surprised that she even knew it.

He turned round. 'Yes?'

The customary glow had quite deserted Dr Shastri's face, and in its place was a look which could almost have been anguished.

'Find this evil man, Charlie,' the doctor said. 'Find him before it's too late.'

'I'm doin' my best,' Woodend told her.

But then, all those years ago in London, he had said exactly the same thing to old George Taylor, too, hadn't he?

Nine

The row of three-storeyed terraced houses on Kings Street had been built for professional men and their families in the Edwardian era, but since the Second World War it had been a street on which professional men worked, rather than lived. Doctors had their offices there now, as did chartered surveyors, accountants, and stockbrokers. And so it was that Kings Street became the place that the people of Whitebridge went to when they were sick, had fallen foul of the Inland Revenue, needed a mortgage, or wanted to draw up their wills.

The firm of Brunton, Wallace, and Gough (Solicitors) was located roughly in the middle of Kings Street, and when Monika Paniatowski walked in through the main entrance she found herself in a reception area which was guarded by a severe middle-aged woman who looked the kind of person who got her fun by drilling holes in lifeboats.

'I'd like to see Mr Brunton,' Paniatowski said. 'Is he in?'

'Do you have an appointment, madam?' the

receptionist asked, barely looking up at her.

'No.'

'I thought not. I'm afraid you simply cannot be seen without an appointment, and even *with* an appointment, you would not be dealt with by Mr Brunton, but by one of the junior partners.'

Paniatowski held out her warrant card. 'I'd like to see Mr Brunton,' she repeated. 'Is he in?'

The receptionist opened her mouth as if ready to deliver a stinging reply, then thought better of it. Instead, she pressed a button on the intercom in front of her, and said, 'I'm awfully sorry to disturb you, Mr Brunton, but there's a police woman here, and she says she'd like to see you.'

'What's it about?' asked a metallic voice through the speaker.

'It's about your wallet,' Paniatowski replied.

'His *wallet*?' said the secretary, who was clearly furious that Paniatowski had chosen to speak to Brunton directly, instead of going through her.

'Send her in,' the metallic voice said.

The Invisible Man took a handkerchief out of his pocket, and carefully dusted the chair next to his spyhole. He smiled as he laboured, recognizing the fact that though cleanliness was very important to him, his main reason for wiping down the chair was that it allowed him to postpone the moment when he would open the spyhole and peer through it into the other room.

Anticipation!

That was the name of the game!

Savouring what was to come.

Doubling, or even tripling, your pleasure by putting it off.

Most of life was fantasy – even the parts of it that weren't. Because what you saw, he had come to realize, was not what was actually there, but what you *wanted* to see – a vision of how you *needed* the world to be.

The chair was clean – or at least, as clean as it was ever likely to be in this derelict building.

The Invisible Man laid the handkerchief on the seat – dusty side down – and slowly lowered himself into position. He would not touch himself this time, he decided. He would force himself to be restrained – would experience his excitement only with his brain and his emotions.

He slid back the cover to the spyhole – and discovered that he could not see the girl.

She's escaped, he told himself, almost choking on the panic which engulfed his whole body. She's somehow managed to get away!

The panic drained away almost as quickly as it had appeared. She couldn't have escaped, he told himself. Given the thick walls and the steel door, that was simply impossible.

Nor could she have been rescued, because if she had been, her rescuers would have been waiting for him, and he'd be wearing handcuffs by now.

What must have happened was that she'd managed to drag herself to one of the few spots in the room where she could not be seen through the spyhole.

The little bitch!

She should be punished for that. She *would* be punished for it.

Though it had not been part of his plan to do so, he would go to her right away, and teach her what real pain – the truly *agonizing* pain, which until that point she had only had a mere taste of – actually felt like.

He realized he had lost control of himself. And that would never do, because control was the whole point of this experience. He forced himself to take slower breaths, and willed the red mist which had filled his brain to dissipate.

It began to work. His heart had slowed down, his pulse was no longer galloping.

Perhaps the girl had done him a favour by moving out of view, he told himself, because it gave him the opportunity to use his imagination again – to *picture* her desperation in ways she could never possibly live up to in the flesh.

Yes, it was definitely better the way it was.

Despite his earlier resolve, he saw that his hand was stroking his groin.

'Nothing wrong with that, is there?' he said in a hoarse whisper. 'Nothing at all wrong with spoiling yourself for once.'

The solicitor had been sitting at his desk – antique rosewood and very expensive – but he quickly rose to his feet when Paniatowski entered the room.

Edgar Brunton was in his late thirties, the sergeant guessed, and had the healthy glow of someone who took regular exercise. He had finely chiselled features which, at his current age, qualified him as handsome, but with the passing of time would grow to be distinguished.

Objectively, Paniatowski thought, she should have fancied the hell out of him, but the plain fact was that she didn't. Perhaps the reason he didn't appeal to her, she decided, was that he was a little *too* perfect for her taste – a shade too much like the leading man in a Hollywood picture.

Though he'd been expecting a policewoman of some sort to walk into the room, Brunton was clearly surprised at the one who actually did.

'Are you off duty, Constable?' he asked.

'It's sergeant,' Paniatowski told him. 'And no, I'm not.'

'Then why aren't you in uniform?'

'Because I'm in the CID.'

Brunton shook his head wonderingly. 'I really wouldn't have thought the theft of my wallet merited the attention of someone from the Criminal Investigation Department,' he said.

'It was stolen?'

'Didn't you know that?' Brunton asked. 'And if you *didn't* know, why are you here?' The expression which suddenly crossed his face said he realized he'd been rude – and in more than one way. 'Where are my manners?' he continued. 'Do please take a seat, Sergeant.'

Monika sat down opposite him. 'When was your wallet stolen?'

'Yesterday afternoon.'

'In the corporation park?'

The question seemed to puzzle Brunton. 'No. It was stolen in the Daresbury Arcade. Might I ask what this is all about?'

'It was recovered in the park,' Paniatowski explained. 'Close to the spot from which Angela Jackson was abducted.'

Brunton rocked back in his leather chair. 'Good God!' he said.

'At what time was the wallet stolen?'

'Am I a suspect?' Brunton demanded. Then a smile came to his face, and he said, 'Of course I am. It's only natural that I should be. Only right and proper, too. And in answer to your question, Sergeant...?'

'Paniatowski.'

'...Sergeant Paniatowski, it was stolen somewhere around a quarter to three.'

Paniatowski looked around the office. There were three filing cabinets in one corner, and two tables on which piles of cardboard folders were stacked.

'You seem to be a busy man, on the face of things,' she said.

'Oh, I am,' Brunton agreed. 'Very busy indeed.' He glanced down at his watch. 'In fact, I'm so busy that, if you wouldn't mind—'

'So what were you doing in the Daresbury Arcade at that time of day?' Paniatowski interrupted.

For a moment, it looked as if Brunton had decided to be annoyed, then he smiled again and said, 'As you probably know yourself, the arcade houses a number of small shops.'

'Small *expensive* shops,' Paniatowski agreed. 'Shops selling antiques, jewellery, and bits of pricey bric-a-brac that people don't even know they need until they actually see them.'

'Quite so,' Brunton agreed dryly. 'That's *just* what they deal in. And I've rather come to rely on that arcade when I need to buy presents.'

'And you needed to buy a present yesterday? What kind of present? Was it someone's birthday?'

'Close, but no cigar,' Brunton said. There was a silver-framed picture on his desk, and he turned it around so that Paniatowski could see it. In the photograph were two small boys and a rather plain woman. All of them were smiling. 'It's my fifteenth wedding anniversary the day after tomorrow,' he continued. 'Last year, I forgot about it completely, and my wife – understandably – played merry hell with me. I wasn't going to be caught out like that again.'

'So what did you buy her?'

'Nothing! Because somewhere between Waterman's the Jewellers and the Venetian Glass shop, I had my wallet lifted.'

'Did you feel it being taken?'

'Not at all. It was only when I decided to buy something from the glass shop that I even realized it had gone.'

'Did you inform the police?'

'I didn't go down to the station, if that's what you mean.'

'Why not?'

'But I did ring Superintendent Crawley, who's a friend of mine, to tell him that it had gone missing, and he, for his part, assured me he'd see to it that the proper report was filed.'

'Did you make this phone call right away?'

'As a matter of fact, I didn't.'

'Why not?'

'When I returned to the office, I was told that there was a client waiting to see me. He had some business which needed attending to immediately, so I didn't get around to phoning Stan Crawley until around six o'clock.'

'By which time, your wallet had been missing for close to four hours,' Paniatowski pointed out, 'and your chances of getting it back were considerably reduced.'

An amused grin played on Brunton's lips. 'Come on, Sergeant Paniatowski, don't try feeding me that line, as if I were a mere member of the general public.'

'Aren't you a member of the general public?' Paniatowski wondered. 'And what line are you talking about?'

'The line that there was ever much hope of getting the wallet back. I deal with criminals and policemen all the time, don't forget. I know that while you have a forty per cent chance of catching the thief, there's very little hope of recovering the property he stole. I pretty much wrote the wallet off the second I noticed it was missing, and the only reason I rang Stan at all was because it was the proper thing to do.'

Paniatowski stood up. 'Thank you for your

time, Mr Brunton,' she said. Then she added, almost as an afterthought, 'You won't mind if I ask your office staff a few questions on my way out, will you?'

Brunton gave her yet another smile, which might have been forced – but just as easily might not have been – and said, 'Of course I don't. Why would I?'

'And I might also need to talk to the client you saw yesterday afternoon,' Paniatowski added.

Brunton frowned. 'I'm not sure that's strictly necessary,' he said.

'With the greatest respect, sir, I think I should be the judge of that,' Paniatowski countered.

'Now look here—' Brunton began.

'If you don't want to tell me, I can always ask your secretary,' Paniatowski interrupted.

Brunton's frown had turned into a scowl. 'His name is Jeremy Smythe,' he said.

'And where might I contact this Mr Smythe?'

'I'm not his keeper, so I couldn't say for sure,' Brunton told her, with bad grace, 'but as good a starting point as any might be the offices of JH Smythe Engineering.'

There was no sign outside the golf club declaring that this was an establishment which only admitted the town's elite – but there might as well have been. It was, for many of Whitebridge's aspiring businessmen and politicians, the golden temple on the hill – the place where, when they walked through the door as members for the first time, they understood that they had truly arrived.

At the very centre of this sought-after earthly paradise was the members' dining room, which was not so much a place to eat in as a place to be seen to be eating in, and it was to this inner sanctum that Paniatowski was led by one of the more lowly club stewards.

'That's him, sitting there by himself at the corner table,' the steward said.

The man he'd pointed to was in his early fifties, and though his expensive suit was cunningly tailored, it did not quite disguise his growing corpulence. His hair was just starting to turn grey, but his bushy moustache, leading the dash out of middle age, was already quite white. He was holding a brandy glass in one slightly podgy hand, and a thick cigar in the other.

'Has he been dining alone?' Paniatowski asked.

'No,' the steward replied. 'Until a few minutes ago, there were a couple of young ladies with him.' The steward's nose wrinkled with disgust. 'He *said* they were his nieces.'

'Thanks for the warning,' Paniatowski said.

'Warning? What warning?' the steward asked innocently.

Paniatowski crossed the room and came to a halt at the corner table. 'Mr Smythe?' she asked.

Smythe looked up at her. 'That's me,' he agreed. 'Jerry Smythe – engineering genius, raconteur, and world-famous sexual stallion.'

He had probably had more to drink with his lunch than had been strictly advisable, Paniatowski thought – but that might actually make her job easier.

'I'm DS Monika Paniatowski,' she said. 'I was wondering if you could spare me a minute or two to answer a few questions.'

'Be glad to,' Smythe replied, waving the hand holding his fat cigar expansively through the air and leaving a thin cloud of grey smoke in its wake. 'Always willing to assist the constabulary, especially when it comes in the form of a lovely package like yourself.'

'That's very kind of you,' Paniatowski said, through gritted teeth.

'I'm one of nature's gentlemen,' Smythe told her, without any hint of irony in his voice that she could detect. 'Take a seat, Monika, and ask me anything you want to.'

Paniatowski sat. 'Could I ask you to account for your movements yesterday afternoon, sir?' she asked.

Smythe pulled a comical face. 'Don't tell me I'm in trouble, Monika,' he said. 'Not that I'd mind being arrested – as long as it was by you.'

'You're not in any trouble,' Paniatowski promised.

'Then let me see,' Smythe mused. 'I had lunch at the Dirty Duck, and then I went to see Eddie Brunton. He's a solicitor. Has an office on Kings Street.'

'And what time did your meeting take place?'

'It was supposed to start at a quarter past three, but Eddie didn't arrive back at his office until twenty past.'

What exactly was it that Brunton had told her? Paniatowski wondered.

When I returned to the office, I was told that there was a client waiting to see me. He had some business which needed attending to immediately, so I didn't get around to phoning Stan Crawley until around six o'clock.

'So it was a prearranged meeting, was it?' she asked Smythe. 'You didn't just drop in unexpectedly because you had some urgent business that needed dealing with?'

'No, not at all,' Smythe said. 'It was Eddie who wanted the meeting, and who was most insistent that it should be at exactly that time. In fact, he got rather irritated when I said it would be more convenient for me if we held it later.'

'Did he, indeed?' Paniatowski asked.

'Too right, he did. I'd half a mind to damn his impertinence, and say that since *I* was doing *him* the favour, we'd have the meeting when it suited me.'

'So why didn't you?'

Smythe grinned sheepishly. 'There's a good chance I'll be made Grand Master of the Lodge next year, provided I don't antagonize too many of my fellow Masons in the meantime,' he said in a much lower voice than he'd be using previously. His hand crept across the table and rested lightly on top of hers. 'And if that does happen, Monika, I want you to know that there'll be a special place for you at Ladies' Night.'

'So what was this favour you were doing for

him?' Paniatowski wondered, pulling her hand slowly but firmly away.

Smythe looked disappointed. 'No need to act like a frightened doe,' he said. 'I was only being avuncular.'

'What was this favour you were doing for Mr Brunton?' Paniatowski persisted.

'Oh, that!' Smythe said airily. 'He wanted me to put my name forward for the committee of some fund-raising charity he's thinking of starting. Clothe the Naked, or Feed the Hungry, I think. Something of that nature, anyway. What I still don't understand is why he needed to talk about it face to face. We could just as easily have settled matters over the phone.'

'So that was *all* that this meeting of yours was about, was it?' Paniatowski asked.

'Yes.'

'You're certain about that? You didn't touch on any of your own business matters?'

'Touch on my own business matters? Why would we have done that?' asked Smythe, looking puzzled.

'Well, after all, he *is* your solicitor.'

'Who told you that?'

Edgar Brunton had told her, Paniatowski thought. He was quite explicit about it.

'I just assumed that was the case,' she said aloud.

Jeremy Smythe chuckled. 'Eddie's a good man to go out on the town with – and some of the things we've got up to together I wouldn't even *whisper* into a delicate ear like yours. But my solicitor? No chance! Given the kind of business I'm in, I need the best legal brain that money can buy – and that certainly isn't Eddie's.'

Ten

For the previous fifteen minutes, the whole team had been hunkered down around the table in Woodend's smoke-filled office. Monika Paniatowski had been the centre of attention, as she'd sketched out her conversations with Edgar Brunton, Brunton's secretary, and Jeremy Smythe. Now, as she reached the end of her tale, the three men stopped looking at her – and began looking questioningly at each other.

It was Bob Rutter who broke the short silence that followed Paniatowski's final words. 'Brunton's our man,' he said in a tone which suggested he would tolerate no contradiction.

'Is he, indeed?' asked Woodend, surprised to hear his normally cautious inspector being so forthright. 'An' what brings you to that conclusion?'

'I would have thought it was obvious,' Rutter replied, taking a surreptitious glance at his wristwatch. 'This meeting that he deliberately set up with Jeremy Smythe could have had no other purpose than to give him a partial, almost-plausible alibi.'

'You can't just look at *one* aspect of the timing,' Monika Paniatowski pointed out. 'You also have to consider—'

'The man left his wallet at the scene of the crime, for God's sake!' Rutter interrupted her.

'Somebody left Brunton's wallet at the scene of the crime, sir – but it doesn't have to be Brunton himself,' Beresford said, speaking tentatively, as if, as the youngest and least experienced member of the team, he did not wish to appear to be directly going against one of his bosses.

'Bit of a coincidence if it *wasn't* him who dropped it, don't you think?' Rutter countered, and there was a hint of aggression in his tone which made everyone else in the room feel slightly uncomfortable.

Beresford shrugged awkwardly. 'Coincidences have been known to happen, haven't they?' he asked.

Rutter turned away from him, in what could almost have been regarded as a deliberate snub. 'Remind us again what was actually in that wallet, Monika,' he said to Paniatowski.

The sergeant glanced down at her notebook. 'Photographs of his wife and his two children,' she read. 'Several business cards, some of them his own, some of them other people's. A bank cheque-guarantee card. And thirty-five pounds in five-pound notes.'

'That's a lot of money to be carryin' around,' Woodend said.

'Brunton claims he was planning to buy a present for his wife,' Paniatowski pointed out. 'And if he *had* actually bought one, he wouldn't have come away with much change from thirty-five quid, given the prices that they charge in Daresbury Arcade.'

Rutter took another glance at his watch, then swung around to face Beresford again.

'Let's follow your line of argument to its logical conclusion, shall we, Detective Constable Beresford?' he suggested. 'According to you, the wallet was dropped by the kidnapper. Right?'

'I didn't exactly say that it had to actually be the kidnapper who—' Beresford began.

'So if Brunton isn't the kidnapper, we need another name for the wallet-dropper,' Rutter cut in. 'Does anybody here have an objection if I refer to him as Mr X?'

'No objection,' Woodend said.

He was beginning to worry about Rutter, he thought. This bullying, hectoring attitude he was now displaying was not like Bob at all, and the chief inspector wondered what had brought it on.

Perhaps it could be explained by the fact that Rutter's nerves had been rubbed raw by the very nature of this particular case, he told himself – though there was no reason why they should be rawer than any other member of the team's.

Perhaps he was so desperate to rescue the girl in time that he was prepared to ruthlessly slice through anything that got in his way.

Or perhaps – and this really *was* worrying – he just wanted to get this particular investigation wrapped up so that he could spend more time with his little daughter.

'Mr X is intending to kidnap the girl in the park,' Rutter continued. 'In order to avoid making any mistakes, he's planned it out in every tiny detail. But then – just before it's all due to happen – he multiplies the risk he's running a hundredfold by stealing another man's wallet in the Daresbury Arcade. What if he'd been caught in the act and arrested on the spot, DC Beresford? What if he hadn't actually been *arrested*, but someone had seen him take the wallet? What would have happened to his kidnapping plans then?'

'Maybe he needed the money in order to finance the next stage of the kidnapping?' Woodend suggested, more to take the pressure off Beresford than because he himself believed that was a possibility.

'Oh, I see!' Rutter said. 'He's booked the two of them – himself and the girl – into a nice cosy little bed-and-breakfast somewhere, but the problem is, he doesn't have the wherewithal to pay for it.'

'Steady now, Inspector,' Woodend said warningly.

'I'm sorry, sir, I suppose I could have been a little more tactful,' Rutter admitted.

'Aye, you could,' Woodend agreed. 'An' there is no *suppose* about it.'

'But the idea you've just put forward really is

a non-starter, sir,' Rutter continued, unrelentingly. 'The man we're looking for is a careful planner. Can we at least all agree on that?'

'Yes, we can agree on that.'

'So there is simply no way he'd have been prepared to take the chance of stealing the money at the last minute. If he'd needed to steal at all, he'd have done it days in advance.'

Woodend turned to Beresford. 'Any comment, lad?' he asked.

'What I was trying to say earlier was that there's no reason to assume that the man who stole the wallet and the man who kidnapped the girl have to be the *same* man,' Beresford pointed out.

'Oh, really?' Rutter said. 'Then could you explain to me how the wallet found its way into the park?'

'The thief took it there.'

'And he just happened to drop it very close to the spot where the girl was snatched?'

'It's a possibility, isn't it, sir? Maybe he saw the kidnapping taking place, and was so shaken by the experience that he didn't even *realize* that he'd dropped the wallet.'

Rutter sighed heavily. 'The first thing that pickpockets do after they've made the lift is to separate what they want to keep from what they don't. The money would have gone into one of his pockets, the cheque-guarantee card into another. And then he'd have ditched the wallet itself as quickly as he could, because it's recognizable, and would tie him in with the crime.

Now if you'd told me that an *empty* wallet had been found in the park, I might have gone along with the coincidence theory. But the money was still inside it, and that has to mean – it can *only* mean – that Brunton dropped it himself.'

'You're the one who's looked into this most closely, Monika,' Woodend said. 'What do you think?'

'Everything Bob has said has made perfect sense, and I'd go along with him all the way if it wasn't for the other aspects of the timing,' Monika Paniatowski replied.

'What other aspects of the timing?' Rutter demanded.

'We know that Angela was kidnapped at two minutes past three, give or take a minute or two either way. And we also know for a fact that Brunton was back in his office at three twenty...'

'Do we? Are you sure of that?' Rutter asked.

'Yes, I am. His own secretary has confirmed that that's the time when he arrived.'

'Oh, well that's all right, then. If you can't believe his secretary – the woman who's dependent on him for her wages – then who can you believe?' Rutter said sarcastically.

'I'm not relying just on her word,' Paniatowski said levelly. 'His time of arrival has been confirmed by Jeremy Smythe...'

'Who, by your own account, is nothing but a drunken lecher!'

'...a very successful businessman who'd never have got where he is today if he was as much of a fool as he sometimes acts.'

'He was drunk when you saw him today – he could easily have been drunk yesterday as well.'

'But the girls in the typing pool weren't – and they also agree that Brunton turned up at twenty past three. Besides, if he was in the Daresbury Arcade at the time he claims he was, and then walked back to his office, that's just the time he *would* have arrived.'

'But *was* he in the arcade at that time – or is he lying about it?' Rutter asked, refusing to concede an inch.

'The assistant in the Venetian Glass shop confirms that he was there at some time in the afternoon, but she can't say exactly when.'

'Well, there you are, then,' Rutter said triumphantly. 'It's yet another attempt to create a partial alibi! He goes into the shop earlier than he now claims, knowing no one will be able to pin down the time exactly, then takes himself off up to the park to kidnap Angela.'

'And is back in his office twenty minutes after she disappears?' Paniatowski asked.

'I don't see why not.'

Paniatowski sighed. 'Because he not only has to grab the girl, he has to take her to the safe place that he's prepared for her. And he simply couldn't have done all that in the time available to him.'

'I disagree,' Rutter said.

'That's because you've not thought it through, Bob,' Paniatowski said gently. 'Wherever his safe haven is, it's got to be somewhere he'd be sure he wouldn't be observed when he was

128

unloading an unconscious girl from the back of his car. A country barn, perhaps. Or some part of the town that's virtually deserted because it's in a demolition area. And there's nowhere like that anywhere near the corporation park.'

'If he was prepared to break a few speed limits...'

'Brunton didn't even have his car available. It was in the staff car park, blocked in by two other vehicles belonging to his partners.'

'He could have borrowed a vehicle,' Rutter said stubbornly.

'Now that really *would* have been taking an unnecessary risk,' Paniatowski countered. 'Say the girl had puked up or soiled herself. How would he have explained that fact to the man he'd borrowed the car from?'

'He might have anticipated her doing something like that, and put plastic sheeting underneath her.'

'And would he also be willing to run the risk of the man who'd lent him the car realizing that he'd borrowed it at exactly the same time as the girl went missing?'

'He could have borrowed it for the whole day.'

'How would he have explained the need to do that, when his own car was sitting in the car park?'

'I don't know,' Rutter admitted. 'But you can bet that he'll have thought of something.'

'We're gettin' nowhere fast,' Woodend said.

'So what do *you* think, sir?' Paniatowski and Rutter asked him simultaneously.

'I agree with Bob that the most likely reason for his wallet bein' in the park is because he dropped it there himself,' Woodend said. 'An' Edgar Brunton's profile does seem to match the profile that Dr Stevenson gave us of the likely abductor pretty closely. He's intelligent, methodical, an' nobody who knows him will believe he could do a thing like this.'

'The timing...' Paniatowski protested.

'I've heard what you've had to say on that, an' you've made some good points,' Woodend told her. 'But just because we don't yet see how he *could have* done it in the time available doesn't necessarily mean that *he* couldn't have found a way. So, while it would be a great mistake to rule out all other lines of inquiry, I think we should concentrate our main effort on Brunton.'

'You sound as if you're thinking about having him picked up, sir,' Paniatowski said.

'Well, that's certainly my inclination,' Woodend admitted.

'You'll get a lot of flak from Superintendent Crawley, and Brunton's friends at the Rotary.'

'An' let's not forget the Masons,' Woodend said, 'because, from what you've told us of your conversation with Smythe, Brunton's a member of the funny-handshake brigade as well. An' then, of course, there's always Mr Marlowe – our esteemed chief constable. I imagine he'll have somethin' to say about me arrestin' such a prominent member of the community.'

'So why not hold off until you've got something more substantial to pin on him?' Paniatowski asked.

'Because time's runnin' out for that poor little lass,' Woodend said. 'An' there are big advantages to havin' a suspect in custody. Once we've got him banged up, we can start questionin' him, and there's always the chance that he'll break down under interrogation, an' tell us where the girl is.'

'I'm the only one here who's met him, and I can assure you that even if he *is* guilty, you'll get nothing out of him,' Paniatowski said.

'Then there's the fact that once we've got him under lock an' key, we'll have greater freedom to pursue the investigation,' Woodend said, ignoring the comment. 'We can show his picture round the hospitals an' clinics, for example, to see if we can find anybody who'll admit he tried to buy anaesthetics from them. We can show the same pictures to the people who were in the park, an' that might just jog their memories. An' we can do a thorough background check on him, which might just tell us where he's likely to have hidden the girl.'

'Do you think I could have a word with you in private, sir?' Paniatowski asked.

'This *is* private,' Woodend said, looking round the office.

'I meant, just the two of us.'

For a moment, it looked as if Woodend was about to tell her to go hang herself, then turned to Rutter and Beresford and said, 'Would you mind excusin' us for a few minutes, lads?'

The other two men stood up awkwardly, and

stepped out into the corridor. Woodend waited until they'd closed the door behind them before speaking again.

'I hope you're not goin' to give me a hard time, Monika,' he said.

'That's not my intention, sir,' Paniatowski replied, 'but I would like to know why you're *really* in such a rush to arrest Edgar Brunton.'

'I've already told you, once we've...'

'Please, Charlie!'

Woodend nodded. 'All right,' he agreed. 'Maybe Brunton is innocent, as you seem to think he is. If so, I'll have done him an injustice by arrestin' him, an' no doubt he an' all his powerful friends will make sure that I pay for it. But there's another side to the coin, isn't there? He could also be guilty. An' if there's even the slightest chance of that, I want him lockin' up.'

'Why?'

'I should have thought that was obvious – because while he's in custody, he can't be doin' any harm to that little girl.'

Eleven

Edgar Brunton stared across the table of Interview Room Three at the man in the hairy sports jacket and the man in the smart blue suit.

'You do realize that this is all a very big mistake, don't you?' he asked, conversationally.

'Is it?' Woodend replied.

'Of course it is. And I'm very much afraid that you're the one who's going have to pay for making it.'

'Don't threaten me, Mr Brunton,' Woodend growled.

'I'm not threatening anyone,' Brunton told him. 'Far from it. All I'm actually doing is pointing out the facts as they stand. Take a close look at me, Chief Inspector. Do I look, in any way, like a kidnapper to you? Can you *honestly* picture me as child abuser?'

'I don't think I said anythin' about child abuse,' Woodend countered. He turned towards Rutter. 'Did *you* say anythin' about child abuse, Inspector?'

'No, I most certainly did not,' Rutter said flatly.

Brunton laughed. 'Don't try your primitive psychology on me, because it simply won't wash. You may not have mentioned child abuse, but we all know that's what this is all about. Why else would the man have kidnapped her? Because he wanted to teach her to play chess?'

'You seem to be taking a very flippant attitude to this whole matter, sir,' Woodend said.

'On the contrary, I'm taking it very seriously. If I *appear* flippant, it's only as a perfectly naturally reaction to the incompetent way you're conducting this interview.'

'Is it incompetent?'

'Very much so. And please remember that, as a solicitor, I've had a lot of experience in observing police interrogations.'

'Maybe you're right,' Woodend conceded.

'That the interrogation is incompetent?'

'That you're not bein' flippant. Maybe you're just usin' flippancy as a mask for your anger. I think that, deep down, you're a *very* angry man. I think anger is the main drivin' force in your life.'

'I'm certainly angry at this moment,' Brunton agreed. 'Who *wouldn't* be angry after being arrested by the police for something they hadn't done? My reputation has been harmed irreparably. Irreparably! Because even when you release me – and you *will* have to release me eventually – there'll be people in this town who think there's no smoke without fire, so I must be guilty.'

'You're not helpin' us, you know,' Woodend said quietly. 'An' if you're innocent, as you keep claimin' you are, I'd have thought you'd have *wanted* to help us.'

Brunton seemed to be turning the statement over his mind, then he said, 'You're right. I'm not helping.' He paused again, before continuing, 'We seem to have got off on the wrong footing, don't we? And perhaps that's partly my fault. Shall we start again?'

'If you like,' Woodend said.

'I'm a happily married man. I love my wife – if I didn't, I wouldn't be in this mess in the first place.'

'Now that is an interestin' way of lookin' at things,' Woodend said. 'Would you care to expand on it?'

'Willingly. If I hadn't loved my wife, I would never have left the office to buy her a present, and there would have been at least half a dozen witnesses who could swear that I was sitting at my desk the whole afternoon, and so couldn't possibly have kidnapped the girl.'

'Let's talk about that shoppin' trip of yours,' Woodend suggested. 'You realized your wallet had been stolen when you reached for it in the Venetian Glass shop. Is that correct?'

'Yes, it is.'

'So what I'm goin' to try an' do now is put myself in your position. I'm standin' in the shop. Right?'

'Right.'

'I reach for my wallet, an' I find that it's gone. What's the first thing I'm likely to say?'

'You tell me.'

'I imagine it would be somethin' like "Bugger!" An', given the circumstances, I'd probably say it quite loudly. Then, because it's not my habit to swear in front of shop assistants, I'd probably have said, "Sorry about that, love, but my wallet's just been pinched."' Woodend took a drag on his cigarette. 'Would you like to make any comment at this point, sir?'

'No.'

'I thought not. An' you didn't make any comment *then*, either. You see, we've spoken to the assistant, an' she doesn't remember you sayin' anythin' at all about your wallet bein' stolen. An' why? Because you still had it! Because you didn't actually lose it until you were in the park!'

'That's not true.'

Woodend sighed. 'You found a piece of glassware you wanted to buy, didn't you?'

'Did I? How do you know that?'

'Because you'd never have reached into your pocket for your wallet if you hadn't found somethin' you wanted – which would mean that you'd never even have noticed it had been stolen.'

Brunton nodded. 'You're right, of course. I did find a piece of glass I liked. As a matter of fact, it was a rather beautiful vase. I don't think I've ever seen one quite like it before.'

'In other words, it was unique?'

'I didn't say that. Indeed, I have no way of knowing whether it was unique or not, though given the asking price, I rather doubt it was. All I *did* say was that I've never seen one quite like it before.'

'Weren't you worried you'd miss the chance to buy it?'

'I beg your pardon?'

'Well, you couldn't buy it then and there, could you? Your wallet had been stolen.'

'Correct.'

'An' wasn't there a risk that if you came back later, once you'd laid your hands on more money, it might have already been sold?'

'That's certainly a possibility.'

'So why didn't you ask the assistant to reserve it for you?'

'I suppose I was so angry – both with the thief and my own carelessness – that I didn't think of that.'

'But you didn't show that anger? Nobody *noticed* you were angry?'

'I suspect that the nature of our respective professions causes us to show different faces to the world, Chief Inspector,' Edgar Brunton said. 'It is perfectly acceptable for a policeman like yourself to be belligerent – it's sadly what we've come to expect of those who enforce the law – but a solicitor is supposed to appear calm at all times, and that becomes a habit.'

'Where did you get the car from?' Woodend demanded suddenly.

'What car?'

'The one that you used to take Angela Jackson to your hideaway.'

'Since I did not kidnap the girl, your question is irrelevant.' Brunton turned his attention to

137

Rutter. 'You've been very quiet, Inspector.'

'Have I?' Rutter asked. 'Maybe that's because I was listening to what you had to say.'

'But surely, by now, it must be time for you to take on the appearance of the *good* cop.'

'I'm afraid I don't know what you're talking about.'

'Of course you do! The first phase of the interrogation involves the chief inspector throwing out accusations left, right, and centre, until he's almost foaming at the mouth. Then we come to the second phase, where you step in with a more gentle, reassuring manner. And I'm so grateful to you for this softer approach that I immediately spill all the beans that I've been holding back from bad-cop Charlie. That's almost guaranteed to work.'

'This isn't a game, you know,' Woodend said angrily.

'I *do* know that,' Brunton agreed. 'That's why I've been trying to help you in the only way that I can – which is to make it perfectly clear that you're talking to the wrong man. But you're not interested in that, are you? You *like* playing games! Playing games is what justifies your existence. So I've given up on you, Chief Inspector, and knowing – as I do – that within twenty-four hours you'll be issuing me a grovelling apology, I've decided to extract as much fun out of my present unfortunate circumstances as I possibly can.'

'And if a child *dies* while you're having your fun?'

'Then that's your fault, rather than mine, because instead of wasting your time putting me through the third degree, you should be out there looking for the real kidnapper.'

Woodend was the first to step out of the interview room and into the corridor, but Rutter was close on his heels.

'Shut the door behind you,' Woodend said.

Rutter did as he'd been instructed, then said, 'Well, what do you think about the—'

Woodend raised his hand to quiet his inspector. 'Can you give me a minute, Bob?' he asked.

'No problem,' Rutter told him.

But it was more than a minute he needed. For *five* minutes, Woodend prowled up and down the corridor like a wounded angry lion. Then, taking exception to a piece of the corridor wall which appeared to be exactly the same as every other piece of corridor wall, he threw a punch at it with so much force that the plaster around the point of impact cracked.

'Did that help?' Rutter asked sympathetically.

'No, I can't really say it did,' Woodend admitted, looking down at his bruised and bleeding knuckles.

'If you'd like me to take over the questioning for a while...' Rutter suggested.

'Brunton's such an arrogant bastard!' Woodend said, glancing back up the corridor, at the closed interview-room door. 'He's a supercilious arrogant *cocky* bastard!'

'He's certainly all of that,' Rutter agreed readily. 'But do you think he's a *guilty* bastard?'

'Oh, he's guilty, right enough,' Woodend replied. 'I'm convinced of that. I can smell it on him. I can see it written in big letters above his head. But he thinks I'm never goin' to be able to *prove* he's guilty – an' I don't know why he should be so confident of that.'

'Probably because, as you've just pointed out yourself, he's an arrogant bastard.'

'There's more to it than simple arrogance,' Woodend told him. 'There *has to be*. He knows somethin' that we don't.'

A uniformed constable appeared at the other end of the corridor. 'Dr Stevenson's arrived, sir,' he said.

'Where is he?'

'Waiting for you in your office.'

Woodend nodded. 'Good!'

Stevenson's arrival was more than welcome, he told himself. Because perhaps the doctor could succeed where he'd failed – perhaps a trained shrink like him would find a way of getting under Brunton's skin.

Dr Martin Stevenson was sitting in what was usually Monika Paniatowski's chair. Woodend, observing him through the window, thought the doctor was looking a little nervous at the idea of helping the police on such a serious case – but that he was also rather excited at the prospect.

When the chief inspector opened the door and entered the office, the doctor jumped up from the seat as if he were on a spring, and said, 'Have you made any progress?'

'You could say that,' Woodend told him. 'We've got a suspect. He's in his late thirties, a successful professional man with a family. He's highly respected in the community, an' has no criminal record we've been able to uncover. What do you think?'

'I think it's possible he may actually be what he appears to be – a pillar of the community,' Stevenson said cautiously.

'But there's nothin' in what I've just told you that would rule him out of the picture?'

'Nothing at all. It's fairly rare for the type of person I've studied to be actually married, but the psychological make-up of most of my subjects could certainly be able to *accommodate* marriage.'

'I'd like you to talk to him,' Woodend said. 'Would you be willin' to do that, Dr Stevenson?'

'More than willing. In fact, I'm sure I'd find the whole experience fascinating.'

'Well, then...'

'But I must warn you that because of my professional code of ethics, I can't even go near him without his explicit agreement. And how likely do you think it is that he *will* agree?'

'Very likely,' Woodend said. 'Especially if I promise him that an all-clear from you would be his ticket out of here.'

'Are you ... are you prepared to make – and keep – such a promise?' Stevenson wondered.

'Yes, I am.'

'Don't you ... er ... think that might be a little risky?'

'Not if you're as good at your job as I believe you to be.'

Stevenson looked troubled. 'You're putting a lot of responsibility on my shoulders, you know,' he said.

'They're broad enough,' Woodend told him.

Stevenson hesitated for a second or two, then said, 'Very well. If he's prepared to see me, I'm more than willing to see him.'

'Good man!' Woodend said enthusiastically. 'You stay here, while I go an' talk to Brunton, an' then we'll set up—'

'Wait a minute!' Stevenson exclaimed. 'Did you say your suspect's name is Brunton?'

'Yes.'

'Edgar Brunton?'

'That's the man. Do you know him?'

'In a manner of speaking,' Stevenson replied heavily. 'And I'm afraid it won't be possible for me to see him.'

'But you were willin' enough a minute or two ago,' Woodend said. 'What's suddenly changed your mind?'

Stevenson folded his arms, and kept silent.

What the hell was going on? Woodend wondered. And then, suddenly, he thought he knew!

'Tell me, doctor, is lecturin' at the university *all* you do to earn a crust?' he probed.

'No,' Stevenson said, with some reluctance.

'Then how else do you earn money?'

'I have a small – very limited – private

142

practice.'

'An' is Edgar Brunton one of your patients in this small – very limited – private practice?'

'If he was, I couldn't tell you.'

'So you're not sayin' that he's not?'

'I'm not saying anything.'

'What are you treatin' him for?' Woodend demanded. 'Is it the kind of mental condition which might lead him to kidnap an' torture young girls?'

'You're making this very difficult for me,' Stevenson said.

'It isn't exactly a picnic for me, either,' Woodend told him. 'A kid's life is at stake, an' all I'm askin' you to do is help me save it.'

'I know that.'

'So if you won't talk to Brunton directly, at least give me some kind of clue as to what to do next.'

'That isn't possible,' Stevenson said, looking more and more distressed with every second that passed.

'Since you know all about him, you'll probably have a good idea of the sort of place he'd be likely to hide the girl,' Woodend persisted. 'Isn't that right?'

'There's nothing I can say on the matter.'

'All right, then, at least give me a clue about what he's likely to do if I release him,' Woodend pleaded. 'Will he kill the girl at his first opportunity? Or is he likely to decide to keep her alive – because he'll be convinced we'll never catch him? I need answers, Doc. I *desperately* need answers right now!'

'I know you do,' Stevenson said, regretfully. 'But I'm afraid I can't give them to you.'

'Can't you, by God!' Woodend demanded, as the anger he had been keeping a fairly tight lid on finally bubbled its way to the surface. 'Well, in that case, Doctor Stevenson, I've no choice but to arrest you for obstructin' the police in the course of their inquiries. What have you got to say about that?'

Stevenson sighed heavily. 'I suppose you're only doing your duty as you see it,' he said.

'Bloody right, I am,' Woodend agreed.

'And I hope you'll accept that I am similarly bound to do mine, as *I* see it,' Stevenson continued.

Woodend shook his head. 'No, I don't accept that,' he said.

'But surely...'

'Listen to me, doctor,' Woodend urged. 'Whatever decisions I've made today, I'll be able to live with in the future. But do you really – honestly – believe that you'll be able to live with yours?'

Twelve

The police convoy was made up of three un-marked vehicles, each carrying two detectives. It entered the grounds of the Brunton house through a pair of ornamental gates, and from there proceeded up a long driveway, which was laid with expensive stone slabs, rather than being covered in 'common' asphalt. There were mature hardwood trees on each side of the drive-way, and at the end of it was a house which, even by the standards of the Whitebridge rich, was large – and perhaps even just a little osten-tatious.

Monika Paniatowski, who was in the lead car, took in the scene for a few moments and then turned to her driver. 'The Bruntons seem to place a high value on their privacy,' she said.

'Don't they just,' Beresford agreed.

'Which means our arrival will be about as welcome as a nun's in a knocking shop.'

They had reached the turning circle in front of the house. Beresford parked with the care and attention of someone who had only recently passed his driving test, and the other two cars pulled in behind him.

There were six steps leading up to a terrace

which ran the length of the house's frontage and before Paniatowski had even had time to open her door, a woman appeared at the head of them. She was wearing an elegant cashmere suit, and her elaborate hairstyle was so highly lacquered that it looked as if it might be possible to bounce billiard balls off it. The picture of her on Brunton's desk had not lied, Paniatowski noted – because for all her expensive accessories, she really was rather plain.

'The lady of the manor,' Paniatowski said to Beresford. 'Do *you* want to show her the warrant, or shall I?'

Looking up at the woman, and seeing the stony gaze she was aiming in their direction, Beresford grimaced. 'If it's all the same to you, Sarge, I'd rather you did it,' he said.

Paniatowski got out of the car, and walked towards the house. The woman on the terrace made no move to meet her halfway, but then the sergeant had never expected that she would.

It was as Paniatowski's right foot reached the third step to the terrace that Mrs Brunton held out a warning hand to indicate that this invasion of her property had gone far enough.

'What are you doing here?' she demanded. 'Isn't it enough that you've taken my husband into custody? Have you come to arrest me as well?'

'No, madam, we haven't,' Paniatowski replied evenly. She had a piece of paper in her hand, and now she held it out for inspection. 'I have here a warrant to search these premises.'

Mrs Brunton bristled. 'I simply cannot allow that,' she said.

'I'm afraid you really have no choice in the matter, madam,' Paniatowski told her.

'Your chief constable, Henry Marlowe, has dined at this house,' Mrs Brunton said, speaking over Paniatowski's shoulder and addressing her remarks not at the female sergeant with the warrant, but at the five male detective constables who were standing and waiting at the base of the steps. 'In fact, he's dined with us a *number* of times.'

'Good for him,' Paniatowski said, thinking, even as she spoke, how much she could sound like Woodend on occasion. 'But you see, madam, where Mr Marlowe chooses to feed his face is irrelevant. It wouldn't matter to me if he was your long-lost brother come back from the dead – because the plain fact is that this is a legally executed warrant, which entitles me to search the house. And that's just what I'm going to do.'

'And if I refuse to allow you to enter my home?'

'We're looking for a girl who may be dying in excruciating agony even as we stand here arguing the toss,' Paniatowski pointed out.

'I understand that – but it has nothing to do with my husband.'

'We think it does. And if you try to stand in my way while I'm executing this warrant, I'll have to have you removed. Forcibly, if necessary.'

'You wouldn't dare!' Mrs Brunton said scornfully.

Paniatowski took two more steps forward, stopping just short of the terrace.

'We're prepared to follow whatever course is necessary to get the little girl safely back to her family,' she said in a voice which had become a harsh whisper. 'And if I thought, for one second, that stuffing your head down the toilet would even slightly increase our chances of that, you'd be tasting shit right now. So, please, Mrs Brunton, don't try to tell me what I would – or wouldn't – dare to do.'

'This is an outrage!' the other woman said. 'I shall complain to the highest authorities.'

'You do that,' Paniatowski told her. 'But while you're working out which of your many influential friends you should contact first, my team will be searching the house.'

It was an hour into his renewed interrogation of Edgar Brunton that Woodend had realized he was faced with two stark choices. The first choice was to break off the session again, and step out into the corridor until he'd cooled off. The second was to stay where he was, which, he recognized, would almost inevitably lead to him wringing his suspect's bloody neck. He had wisely chosen the former option, and it was as he was pacing up and down outside the interview room that he saw the red-faced man in the muted grey suit striding angrily towards him.

'What the hell do you think you're playing at,

Charlie?' Superintendent Crawley demanded. 'Whatever could have possessed you to treat Edgar Brunton as if he were a suspect in the Angela Jackson abduction?'

'He *is* a suspect, sir,' Woodend said. 'In fact, he's the *prime* suspect.'

'And on what do you base this amazing conclusion of yours?'

'On information gathered during the course of my investigation.'

'Don't give me any of that vague official-sounding crap!' Crawley exclaimed angrily. 'You're not talking to a civilian here, remember. I'm your boss. I want all the details. And I want them now.'

Woodend outlined his evidence.

'But you've got practically nothing!' Crawley blustered, when he finished. 'It'll never stand up in court. Not for a minute!'

'By the time it finally gets to court, I'll have more,' Woodend promised. 'Besides, while I'd love to see Brunton go down for a long time, that isn't my main concern at the moment.'

'Isn't it?' Crawley asked astonished. 'Then – in the name of God – what the bloody hell is?'

'Gettin' the girl back alive.'

Crawley glanced nervously up and down the corridor, as if to make sure that their conversation had not been overheard, and his part of it misunderstood – or possibly understood only too well.

'Ah yes. Of course. Getting the girl back alive,' he said feebly. 'That's the first priority for

149

all of us. It goes without saying.'

'I'm pleased to see that we appear to be on the same side, sir,' Woodend said.

'But allowing for the fact that it *is* our main priority, I'm far from convinced you're going the right way about achieving it.'

'Then what is the right way?' Woodend wondered. 'How would you do it, sir?'

'Well, for a start, I wouldn't put as much faith in this shrink as you seem to be doing.'

'I'm convinced he's right,' Woodend said stubbornly.

'Because Edgar Brunton fits the profile he gave you?'

'Partly.'

'So if he'd described an entirely different kind of man, would you have *arrested* an entirely different kind of man?'

'Not unless there'd been other evidence pointin' to him.'

'Evidence!' Crawley said scornfully.

'Doesn't it strike you as a little strange that Edgar Brunton only reported his stolen wallet to you several hours after it had supposedly gone missing?' Woodend asked.

'He's a busy man,' Crawley said. 'Anyway, we're getting off the point again. What I want to know is whether it's true that this shrink of yours refuses to confirm or deny that Edgar Brunton is likely to be your man?'

'He's Brunton's doctor,' Woodend said. 'He feels his hands are tied.'

'Well, maybe I can persuade him to have them

bloody well *untied*,' Crawley blustered. 'Do you know where he is, right now?'

Woodend nodded. 'For the last hour an' a half, he's been in the cells.'

'He's been *where*?'

'In the cells,' Woodend repeated.

'Are you mad?' Crawley demanded. 'Have you gone completely off your bloody head?'

'No, I don't think so,' Woodend said, making every effort to sound as sane as he possibly could.

'Then just what *is* your bloody game?'

'Dr Stevenson *wants* to do the right thing, but he doesn't think his medical ethics will allow him to,' Woodend explained.

'Yes! I know! You've already made that perfectly clear.'

'So I'm hopin' that, after bein' banged up for a while, he'll manage to persuade himself that he has no choice but to tell me what I want to know.'

'And if that doesn't work?'

'Then we've lost nothin' by tryin', have we?'

'Lost nothing! The man's a university lecturer! An important figure in the community! God knows how many friends he's got in high places.' Crawley paused for a second to draw breath, before carrying on with his onslaught. 'I want him released immediately, Chief Inspector. Do you understand? Immediately!'

'I'm afraid I can't do that,' Woodend said firmly.

'What? Are you refusing to obey a direct

order?'

'An' are you willin' to take responsibility for kickin' loose a man who might be able to help us crack this case?' Woodend countered. 'Because if you are – an' if things turn out badly as a result of it – I'll make certain that everybody knows it was your decision.'

For a moment, it looked as if Crawley would behave like a man and stick to his decision. But it *was* only for a moment. Then, the political animal which inhabited most of his soul advised him to let Woodend have his way – to let Woodend take the fall, if any fall was to be taken.

'Based on your specific recommendation – which I will expect you to put in writing – I'm prepared to agree to hold Dr Stevenson in custody for a little while longer,' he said reluctantly.

'Thank you, sir,' Woodend replied.

'You'd better be right about this, Charlie,' the superintendent hissed, 'because if you're wrong – if you've ruined Edgar Brunton's reputation needlessly, or if Dr Stevenson decides to complain about the way he's been treated – I'll have you back directing traffic before you can blink.'

'I'm not wrong,' Woodend said. 'But if I was you, sir, I wouldn't go threatenin' me with somethin' that – given the job I've been landed with here – is already startin' to feel like a promotion.'

Edgar Brunton's study, with its long bookcases full of rows of leather-bound books, looked more like a film set than a place in which someone actually worked.

'However can he afford to run a place like this?' Monika Paniatowski mused.

Beresford shrugged. 'Have you employed a solicitor recently, Sarge?' he asked.

'No,' Paniatowski replied. 'Have you?'

'As a matter of fact, I have. What with Mum's condition getting worse by the day, I thought it might be best if...' He trailed off.

'I'm sorry,' Paniatowski said. 'I shouldn't have asked.'

'It's all right,' Beresford told her – though it clearly wasn't. 'Anyway, the point is that a solicitor's advice doesn't come cheap.' He grinned, as if to demonstrate that he had succeeded in putting unpleasant thoughts behind him. 'Don't get me wrong, I'm not saying that as a class solicitors are greedy – only they'll have the shirt off your back before you've even had time to sit down.'

Paniatowski smiled, and then immediately grew serious again. 'Perhaps that's true,' she said. 'But I'm starting to get the distinct impression that our Mr Brunton isn't half as successful as he likes to pretend he is.'

'Does that really matter?' Beresford asked. 'Do you think how much money he makes could have any relevance to this case?'

'Not really,' Paniatowski admitted. 'From what little I've read on the subject, sex offenders don't only just come in all shapes and sizes – they come from all income groups as well.'

'Back in the boss's office, you were arguing that Brunton couldn't have done it,' Beresford said. 'Now you're talking like someone who has very little doubt he's guilty. *Have* you changed your mind?'

'Yes, I have.'

'Why the complete turn-around?'

'Because I've been talking to the boss on the phone, and *he* thinks Brunton is guilty. Doesn't just think it – feels it deep down inside his gut. And if there's one thing I've learned while I've been working with Charlie Woodend, it's to put my trust in his gut.'

Beresford nodded, then looked around the study. 'So what are we looking for, and where do we start?'

'There's no easy answer to that,' Paniatowski told him. 'We won't *know* what we're looking for until we find it – and then it will be pretty obvious that that's what we should have been searching for all along.' She paused, then said, 'Wait a minute! There is one thing that we should *definitely* be keeping an eye open for. Property deeds!'

'You mean deeds to flats, and places like that?'

'No, not like that at all. Flats aren't anywhere near private enough. We're looking for deeds to places like lock-up garages and country cottages.'

'Places where he could have hidden the girl,' Beresford said.

'Exactly,' Paniatowski agreed.

154

A team of twenty uniformed officers had been out on the moors all afternoon. The sergeant in charge had been given a list of all the villages within a fifteen- or twenty-minute drive of Whitebridge centre, and told that his team should visit every one of them.

By the time they'd reached the fourth village, they were working like a well-oiled machine. Most of the constables were deployed to search outlying buildings – the disused barns and near-derelict cottages that seemed to ring every village. The rest of the team, the ones the sergeant considered his brightest lads, were assigned to knock on the door of every house and put a standard set of questions to whoever answered.

The first question was accompanied by a photograph of Angela Jackson. Did she look familiar? the officers asked. Had someone like her been seen in the village recently? There were no positive responses, and the sergeant had never expected there would be – but it was at least worth a shot.

The third question was whether they'd noticed any strangers in the village the previous day, but this, too, had received nothing but negative replies.

The fourth question was divided into several parts, and was the big one. Had someone bought a house in the village in the last year or so – say a man in his late thirties? If such a person had bought a house, did he visit it regularly or only put in the occasional appearance? And when he was there, did he make an effort to be sociable with new neighbours, or did he seem to want to keep himself pretty much to himself?

This question advanced the search no more than the first three had. Yes, someone had bought the cottage up the road, but they were an elderly couple. Yes, the house on the end of the row had been sold, but the new owners were very friendly, as were their four kids. Yes, someone had taken over the old bakery and converted it into a home, but the man's name was Hardcastle, and he had a number of relatives already living in and around the village.

Yes, yes, yes. No, no, no.

It had been a complete waste of a day, the sergeant thought, as he ticked another village off his list. Wherever Angela Jackson was, she certainly wasn't in one of the places that he and his men had visited.

Perhaps, he thought, they should have checked on the villages further afield – the ones that were half an hour or forty minutes away from Whitebridge centre. He'd even suggested it when he was being briefed. But Chief Inspector Woodend had been adamant that wouldn't be necessary.

'For obvious reasons, I can't give you all the details behind my thinkin', Archie,' he'd said to the sergeant.

'Of course not, sir. I understand that.'

'But you can take it from me that if she is in a village, it'll be one that's close to the town. It's all a question of logistics, you see. He simply wouldn't have had the time to take her very far.'

So they'd done it Mr Woodend's way, the sergeant thought. Because that was what he'd wanted, and because he was the boss.

But what if, on this occasion, Mr Woodend was wrong?

Thirteen

'What's happened to Inspector Rutter?' Edgar Brunton asked, when Woodend re-entered the interview room alone.

'He's off investigatin' another aspect of the case,' the chief inspector said, sitting down opposite him.

Brunton raised a quizzical eyebrow. 'Oh?'

'Don't you want to know *what* aspect?'

'Only if it amuses you to tell me.'

'We've got a search warrant for your house. We're goin' through all your private papers.'

'How very unpleasant of you,' Brunton said. 'I shall certainly sue you for that, once I'm released.'

'Inspector Rutter's very good at rootin' out grubby little secrets,' Woodend commented.

'Unfortunately for you, I don't have any *to be* rooted out,' Brunton said calmly.

'We'll find the girl soon, you know,' Woodend

said. 'We'll find her, she'll identify you, an' then you'll be buggered. So why don't you save us the trouble? Tell us where she is, an' it'll go much easier for you at your trial.'

Brunton smiled. 'If I were guilty – which I'm not – nothing I could say now would make it easier for me later. The press would call me a monster, and the judge would bow to political pressure and impose on me the maximum sentence permissible under the law.'

'Don't you think the papers would be right to call you a monster?' Woodend asked, curious.

Brunton hesitated for the briefest moment, then said, 'It's not me that we're talking about here.'

'All right, I'll accept, for the moment, that we're not talkin' about you,' Woodend agreed. 'So let me put it in a way that might make it easier for you to give an answer. Don't you think the papers would be right to call *whoever* we're talking about a monster?'

Another hesitation. 'I'm a trained lawyer,' Brunton said finally. 'I'd have to know all the facts before I could express an opinion.'

'The girl's been kidnapped, an' – according to your shrink, Dr Stevenson – will have been tortured horribly by now,' Woodend said. 'What more facts do you need than that?'

'Who told you that Martin Stevenson was my therapist?' Brunton demanded with a sudden show of anger.

'Doesn't matter,' Woodend countered. 'He is, isn't he?'

'I may have consulted him on occasion,' Brunton admitted. 'But what passed between us is my business and no one else's.'

'Did you tell him how you had fantasies about inflictin' pain on children?' Woodend asked.

'Would *you* tell *your* psychiatrist if you harboured such fantasies?' Brunton countered.

'Which means that you do have the fantasies, but you didn't describe them to him?'

'Which means nothing of the kind.' Brunton smiled again. 'You really are getting much better at this, Mr Woodend,' he said. 'There's a subtlety to your questions which was notably absent earlier.'

'It's not my main aim in life to have a man like you give me a mark out of ten for my performance,' Woodend told him.

'I don't believe you,' Brunton said. 'We all want to influence other people. We all want to impress them.'

'An' we all want to have *power* over them?' Woodend suggested.

'That too,' Brunton conceded. 'It's going to be much harder to find the girl than you seem to think it will be,' he continued.

'Because you've done such a good job of hiding her?'

'Because there are literally thousands of places – perhaps hundreds of thousands – where her abductor could have decided to hide her. You simply haven't got the manpower to search them all. And even if you had, the courts would never issue the blanket warrant that would be necessary to carry out all the searches, because while an Englishman's home is not actually his castle, he does, at least, have a reasonable expectation of refuge in it.'

'Do you know what really convinces me that you're our man?' Woodend asked.

'No, but I could take a guess,' Brunton said. 'Perhaps it's your jealousy that's making you reach such a far-fetched conclusion.'

'My *jealousy*?'

'Exactly! A jealousy fuelled by the fact that my standing in the community is so much higher than yours, and that while I am paid large *fees* for my services, you are forced to scrape by on a *wage*.'

Woodend shook his head. 'It's not that at all. It's the fact that you seem to feel absolutely no compassion at all for this poor kid that's gone missin'.'

'Come, come, Chief Inspector, aren't you being a little hypocritical now?' Brunton asked. 'Most people are not really very concerned about anything that doesn't affect them directly. They'll pretend they are, of course, especially if others are watching them. But that's all it is! A pretence!'

'Is that right?'

'You know it is. Hundreds of thousands of children are starving in Africa, even as we sit here chatting. Now, I don't wish those children any harm – if I was offered the opportunity to machine-gun a line of them to death, for example, I would quite properly refuse – but neither do I care enough about their predicament to do anything to improve it. And, if you're honest, neither do you.'

'I don't believe that,' Woodend said.

'You don't believe that you don't care?'

'I don't believe that if you were offered the choice of lettin' them kids live or killin' them off, you'd be able to resist the temptation of killin' them off – because that would *really* show your power, wouldn't it?'

'You don't understand me at all,' Brunton said.

'Wrong!' Woodend told him. 'It's you that doesn't understand *yourself*. But maybe you will, eventually.'

'Is that right?' Brunton asked, clearly – and consciously – imitating his interrogator.

'Yes,' Woodend said. 'I think there's a very strong chance of it. After all, the prison shrink will have at least thirty years to help you find the real you.'

'Brunton really *doesn't* make that much money, you know,' Monika Paniatowski said, looking up from the pile of statements, receipts, and bills resting on the desk in the study.

'What was that again, Sarge?' asked Beresford, who had spent the previous two and a half hours going through Brunton's extensive book collection in search of hidden documents, and was now so punch-drunk that though he heard Paniatowski's words, they made no sense to him.

'Brunton. He doesn't make that much money.

His social calendar is full to bursting – lunch with a town councillor, a game of golf with an important local businessman...'

'Well, there you are then, Sarge – he's rubbing shoulders with all the right people.'

'Yes, but when you compare that social calendar with his list of clients, there are not many names that appear on both. Most of his *friends*, like Jeremy Smythe, take their business elsewhere, and most of *clients* are nowhere near prosperous enough to eat where he eats, and probably wouldn't be allowed in the golf club – except through the tradesmen's entrance.'

And then there was Brunton's office, she thought – overflowing with folders from the cases he was supposedly dealing with. But *why* was it overflowing? He had plenty of clerical staff on hand, who could have filed them away. There could only be one reason for the mess. The folders were there for display. They were there because he wanted to create the impression that he was busier than he actually was!

'Maybe he's already made all the money he ever needs to make,' Beresford suggested, closing one book, placing it back on the shelf, and reaching for the one next to it. 'Maybe his work's more like a hobby to him now.'

'Maybe,' Paniatowski replied, unconvinced. She checked her watch. 'I'm getting stale,' she said. 'Let's take a five-minute break, shall we, Colin?'

'Good idea,' Beresford said, quickly slamming the book back onto the shelf and walking away from it before the sergeant had time to change her mind.

He looked around for somewhere to sit down. He wanted to be close enough to talk comfortably to the sergeant, but also in such a position that he didn't constantly catch himself staring down at her legs. The chair on the opposite side of the desk seemed perfect.

Paniatowski pulled a packet of cigarettes out of her pocket, and offered them to Beresford. 'Smoke?'

'Will that be all right?' Beresford asked dubiously.

'You mean, will the grand Mrs Brunton object to the air in this room – which should carry with it only the aroma of the finest Havana cigars – being polluted by the stench of cheap cigarettes smoked by common police officers?'

'More or less,' Beresford agreed.

Paniatowski grinned. 'I'm sure she'll object. She may even lodge a complaint. But we didn't ask to be here – the only reason we *are* here is because her husband's a pervert – and I'm dying for a smoke.'

'Me, too,' Beresford said.

They lit up, and took that first comforting drag which should in theory assuage the need, but in practice only leads to a craving for more of the same.

'Are you all right, Sarge?' Beresford asked cautiously.

'At this moment, or in general?' Paniatowski replied.

'Well, you know, in general.'

'Do you want to know how I'm coping with the idea that while I'm a childless woman living alone, my ex-lover has his daughter living with him now?'

'Well, no. Not exactly.'

'Or are you more interested in finding out how I feel about the fact that we both suspect that same ex-lover is sleeping with a slag of a journalist called Elizabeth Driver?'

'I was only making casual conversation,' Beresford said awkwardly.

'No, you weren't,' Paniatowski told him.

'No, I wasn't,' Beresford admitted. 'But listen, Sarge...'

'Yes?'

'I know that I'm so inexperienced that I'm still practically wet behind the ears, but—'

'Inexperienced in what?' Paniatowski interrupted. 'In police work? Or in life?'

'In both. And I know there are probably a hundred people you'd rather talk to than me...'

'Get on with it,' Paniatowski said.

'...but if you ever do need a shoulder to cry on, I just want you to know that mine's always available.'

Having said his piece, Beresford fixed his eyes firmly on the floor, looking awkward – and perhaps a little humiliated.

Paniatowski reached across the desk and put her hand on his shoulder. 'Thanks, Colin,' she said. 'I don't know if I'll ever take you up on your offer – but it's certainly comforting to know it's there.'

Someone coughed – loudly and unnaturally. Both Paniatowski and Beresford looked up, saw Rutter standing in the doorway, and immediately found themselves wondering just how long he'd been there.

There was a moment of embarrassed silence, which seemed to suggest he had been there for quite some time, then Rutter said, 'The boss wants you back at headquarters right away, Monika.'

'Is he assuming that I'll have finished this job by now?' Paniatowski asked. 'Because if he is, he's way off the mark. I've barely made a dent in it.'

'He doesn't expect you to have finished,' Rutter told her. 'That's why I'm here – to take over from you.'

'Any idea *why* he wants me back at headquarters?'

'He wants *you* to take over from me in the Brunton interrogation.'

Paniatowski frowned. 'It's not like him to go switching jobs around at this stage of the investigation,' she said. 'Why's he doing it now?'

'I've no idea,' Rutter said.

There had been times in the past when their relationship had made any conversation between the two of them sound strained, Paniatowski thought. But Rutter's voice was not just strained now – it was evasive.

Which meant that he had a pretty good idea of why the switch was being made, and whilst part of it might be because Rutter *was* better at following paper trails, that couldn't be the whole picture. And suddenly she saw *exactly* what the whole picture was – in all its gory detail.

She stubbed her cigarette, and stood up. 'I'll see you later, Beresford,' she said.

'See you later, Sarge,' Beresford replied.

Head down, she walked quickly to the door. She didn't speak to Rutter. She didn't even look at him. He might take it as rude, but that didn't matter. All that concerned her at that particular moment was that he didn't see that she was crying.

Edgar Brunton glanced up when the door to the interview room opened, and, for the first time since he'd been taken there, looked somewhat knocked off balance.

'What's she doing here?' he asked Woodend, across the table.

'This is Sergeant Paniatowski, Mr Brunton,' the chief inspector said mildly. 'I'm sorry for not introducing you formally, but I was under the impression you'd already met one another.'

'I know who she is,' Brunton spat back at him. 'I asked you what she was doing here.'

'She's replacing Inspector Rutter as the "good policeman" in this amusing cabaret we're putting on for you.'

'I don't want her here,' Brunton said.

Paniatowski walked across the room and sat down next to Woodend. 'Do I bother you, Mr

Brunton?' she asked. 'Now I wonder why that could be?'

Brunton folded his arms, and said, 'No comment.'

'DCI Woodend claims that the thinking behind me joining this little party is that it will free up DI Rutter to do something else,' Paniatowski continued, conversationally. 'But I don't think that's the real reason at all. In fact, I think he's lying through his teeth.'

'This is some kind of trick, isn't it?' Brunton asked.

'Why would you think that?'

'Because you're a woman who's got her career to think of, Sergeant – and unless you'd agreed to it between yourselves in advance, you'd never say that kind of thing about your boss while he was actually in the room.'

'That's a good point, Monika,' Woodend agreed, playing along in the way that he *hoped* she was expecting him to, but really having no idea where Paniatowski was going with this approach.

'The thing is, while he undoubtedly *was* lying, he was only doing it to be kind,' Paniatowski said, unperturbed. 'The reason he didn't want me to know why I'm here is because he thought it would *hurt* me to know.'

'I have no idea what you're talking about,' Brunton said.

'I was sexually abused as a child,' Paniatowski said bluntly.

'Yes?'

'And I'm guessing that Mr Woodend thinks *you* were, too – especially since he's learned that you've been visiting a shrink. So *that*'s why I'm here – because he believes that since we've both suffered in similar ways, you'll find it much easier to talk to me.'

'This is ridiculous,' Brunton said. 'I wasn't abused at all. My mother loved me. She took wonderful care of me.'

'Sergeant Paniatowski said you'd probably been abused, but I don't recall her mentionin' your mother at all,' Woodend said.

'The implication was there,' Brunton spluttered. 'The implication was *clearly* there.'

'He's got it all wrong about your mother, hasn't he?' Paniatowski asked Brunton, in a voice which was positively oozing understanding.

'He most certainly has.'

'The problem's not with your mother at all – it's with your wife!'

'My wife! What are you suggesting?'

'I'm not as clever as Inspector Rutter is at going through documents, but even someone as slow-witted as me can spot the bleeding obvious when it's staring them in the face,' Paniatowski said. 'You maintain a very expensive office and live in a luxurious house, yet even the most cursory glance through your business accounts reveals that you don't earn enough to pay for either of them. So where *does* the money come from?'

'That's absolutely none of your business!'

Brunton said, outraged.

'Why, it comes from your wife, of course,' Paniatowski said airily. 'She's a rich woman, isn't she? And that really must be very humiliating for you, knowing that – to all intents and purposes – you're a kept man.'

'My wife's family didn't *start out* rich,' Brunton said. 'When she was growing up, her parents ran a tripe stall. On the market!'

'What's that supposed to mean?' Paniatowski wondered.

'It means that she got something out of the marriage, too. She would never have scaled the heights of Whitebridge society if she hadn't been married to me. Besides,' Brunton added, almost as an after-thought, 'we are very much in love, and so the question of who has how much money never really arises.'

'Even the presents you give her – including the one you claim to have been intending to buy her yesterday – are financed out of her account,' Paniatowski continued, unrelentingly. 'It's almost as though she was giving the presents to herself – and you know that. There must have been times when you wanted to strangle her – only that would mean going to prison. There must have been times when you wanted to divorce her – except that would entail giving up the life of luxury you've grown so accustomed to. So what else could you do to make your suffering bearable? Well, I suppose you could make some other poor bloody female suffer, and half convince yourself it was your wife.'

'I want a lawyer,' Brunton said.

'You *are* a lawyer,' Woodend reminded him.

'There is an old adage in my profession that a man who represents himself has a fool for a client,' Brunton said, recovering a little of his poise. 'I want to thank Sergeant Paniatowski for reminding me of it.'

'You did a bloody marvellous job in there,' Woodend said, when he and Paniatowski had stepped out into the corridor.

'Thank you, sir.'

'But why didn't you let me know where you were going with the interrogation in advance?'

'Because that would have made you a player in the game – and I didn't want that. I knew that if I was to make progress, it would be by going head to head with Brunton.'

Woodend scratched his head. 'Now where did you get the idea from?' he wondered.

'I got it from watching the way you work,' Paniatowski told him.

Woodend grinned self-consciously for a moment, and then quickly grew more serious. 'That comment you made about me havin' you in there because you'd suffered child abuse yourself...'

'Yes?'

'That was purely for Brunton's benefit, wasn't it?'

'I suppose it was – partly,' Paniatowski conceded.

'Meanin' that partly it *wasn't*?'

170

'You're an instinctive bobby, sir,' Paniatowski said. 'And there's nothing wrong with that. I'm inclined that way myself.'

'That's a nice way of avoidin' answerin' the question,' Woodend told her.

'Thank you, sir.'

'But I don't *want* you to avoid it. You've got somethin' on your mind, so why don't you just spit it out?'

Paniatowski sighed heavily. 'You may not even have realized that it was my childhood experiences that made you decide to put me in that room with Brunton,' she said. 'But that *was* almost certainly why you did it.'

'An' if you're right, what kind of feller does that make me?' Woodend wondered.

'The kind whose first reaction is to try and protect whoever he sees as most in need of that protection. In the past, that's been me. And I still need your protection – but not as much as Angela Jackson does.'

'So what *am* I?' Woodend asked worriedly. 'A saint or a sinner?'

Paniatowski grinned, and passed her hand across her face to brush away the tears she hoped her boss hadn't seen forming.

'I suppose you're a bit of both,' she said. 'We all are. But, on balance, I think you tilt slightly on the side of the angels.'

Woodend looked embarrassed, but did his best to cover the look by glancing back at the door of the interview room.

'Brunton's asked for a lawyer, an' so we'll

171

have to get him one,' he said. 'But if we go back in there now, I wouldn't be surprised if he cracks before the bugger ever arrives.'

'Neither would I,' Paniatowski agreed.

There was the sound of footsteps coming down the corridor, and they turned to see that Rutter was approaching them.

'Finished goin' through Brunton's stuff already, Bob?' Woodend asked. 'That must be a record – even for you.' Then he noticed the expression on Rutter's face and added, 'Something's happened, hasn't it? Something bad.'

Rutter nodded gravely. 'They've found a girl's body,' he said.

Fourteen

The girl's body had been discovered on a piece of waste land in Stainsworth, which was one of Whitebridge's more dilapidated districts, and had been scheduled for urban clearance if and when the government ever got around to making the money available. A dozen narrow terraced streets fed into the land – streets which had once been home to mill workers like Charlie Woodend's dad, and now housed families living mainly off unemployment benefit and other handouts from the state.

Whenever Woodend drove through the area,

he looked at the crumbling buildings and almost invariably found himself harking back to a period which had been poorer and harder, yet also seemed to him to have been more honest and more decent. But no such thoughts entered his head that night.

By the time Woodend and Rutter arrived at the scene, several official vehicles – patrol units and unmarked CID cars – were already parked on the road next to the land. There were street lights every few yards, but none of them was working, and the only illumination at the roadside came from the rotating light on the waiting ambulance, which cut an eerie and ever-shifting orange swathe through the darkness.

Further away, in the centre of the patch of waste land, there *was* light – a small island of it, provided by hastily erected police emergency lighting.

A spotlight on failure, Woodend thought miserably. On *my* failure!

He stepped out of the car, and noticed immediately how cold the air had suddenly become. He turned up the collar of his jacket, then looked around him. A number of dark menacing figures with pointed heads were standing at intervals around the periphery of the land, and he walked up to the nearest of them.

'Where's the path, Constable?' he asked.

'It starts just past the next lamp post, sir,' the constable replied.

It wasn't much of a path – barely a couple of feet wide – but the beam from Woodend's torch showed that it was free of weeds, which indicated it was fairly heavily used.

The walk from the pavement to the point at which the emergency lighting had been erected was a short one, but to Woodend's leadened legs, it felt as if it were an epic journey.

A sheet had been laid on the ground, in the centre of the circle of light. It had been placed there to cover the girl – perhaps to give a little of the privacy in death that she had been denied in the last moments of her life – but from the indentations on its surface, it was possible to see exactly where she lay.

'She looks so tiny,' Woodend thought bitterly.

A number of flattened yellowish objects lay crushed into the ground around her, and it took Woodend some seconds to identify them as chips – or 'French fries', as the Yanks he'd known in the War had called them. He wondered what they were doing there, then wondered *why* he was wondering, then recognized that he was simply putting off the moment when he looked at the girl.

But it could not *be* put off!

Beresford, his face set in a grim mask, was maintaining a vigil next to the body.

'The ambulance men are ready and waiting to take her away the moment you've seen her, sir,' he said. 'But if I was you, I'd leave your examination until she's been cleaned up.'

'An' why's that?' Woodend demanded. *'You've* seen her, haven't you?'

'Yes, sir.'

174

'Well, then?'

'But I don't have a daughter.'

'I don't want to look at her,' Woodend admitted. 'But I'm in charge of this investigation, an' I bloody *have* to, don't I? So let's get it over with.'

Beresford bent down, and gently pulled away the sheet to reveal the girl's head.

Woodend let out an involuntary gasp. Though he had not admitted it, even to himself, he had been praying this would turn out to be some *other* girl.

A girl he knew nothing about.

A girl he had not tried – and failed – to save.

But it wasn't some other girl!

It was unquestionably Angela's face – the mouth contorted with the terror she had felt as she died, the eyes looking up at him with sightless rebuke.

'I need to see the rest of her,' he said.

'You're sure?' Beresford asked hesitantly.

'Just bloody do it!' Woodend told him.

Beresford stripped the rest of the sheet away, and beside him, Woodend heard Rutter moan, then say, 'Dear God!'

The body was naked, and caked in a mixture of blood and dirt.

It had been slashed!

And stabbed!

And burnt!

It was hard to estimate how many times the poor child had been wounded, though some unfortunate soul – probably Dr Shastri – would have to count all those wounds eventually.

'Cover her up again, Colin,' Woodend said. 'Cover her up – an' make it quick!'

Beresford rapidly pulled the sheet over the girl again, but though the corpse was no longer visible to the eye, the image of it had been burned deeply into Woodend's brain.

'There was a note, sir,' Beresford said.

'A note!'

'On a piece of cardboard which had been torn off a baked-beans box. It was written in block capitals, and it ... it was pinned...'

'Steady, lad,' Woodend said.

Beresford gulped in a fresh supply of chill night air.

'It wasn't *pinned* to anything,' he said. 'It was *nailed* to her leg. I ... I ... removed it, and had it sent down to the lab for analysis.'

'You just did right,' Woodend assured him. 'Can you remember exactly what it said?'

Beresford shuddered. 'Oh yes, I can remember. It said, "This is a gift from the Invisible Man to all my fellow sufferers everywhere".'

A gift? Woodend repeated silently. This poor mutilated child was, in the eyes of the man who had tortured and then killed her, a gift!

And what the hell did he mean by calling himself the *Invisible Man*?

The bastard was even sicker than he'd thought – sicker than he could ever have imagined.

He looked around him. At the edge of the circle of light which bathed the girl's body stood half a dozen constables.

'Who found her?' he shouted. 'I want to talk to whoever it was that found her.'

'It was a couple of local lads, sir,' one of the constables said. 'I've put them in my car.'

'Bring 'em here now,' Woodend said. 'No, not now! Wait until the body's been taken away.'

The ambulance men lifted the corpse onto a stretcher, and when they'd removed it, the constable shepherded the two boys forward.

One of the boys was around nine years old, the other one closer to eleven, Woodend guessed. They had thin pale faces, and runny noses. It was a long time since the clothes they were wearing had been new, and now they were almost threadbare. Both boys were shivering, but the chief inspector soon decided that it was not the cold which was having such an effect on them – though the cold was certainly bad enough – it was being ushered into the frightening presence of the big stranger in the hairy sports jacket.

Woodend forced a smile to his lips. 'You look as though you think you might be in some kind of trouble,' he said. 'Well, you're not. It's not every lad who would have reported what he'd found, like you two did. There's many that would have just run away an' tried to forget it. So you've been very brave. In fact, I think both of you deserve a medal for what you've done.'

The boys nodded gratefully. 'Thank you, mister,' the older one said.

'What's your names?' Woodend asked.

'I'm Pete, an' this is Brian,' the bigger boy said.

'An' what were you doin' here, on this path?'

'Dad said he'd had a bit of luck on the horses today, an' he was goin' to treat us to fish an' chips,' Pete told him. 'This is the quickest way to the chip shop from our house.'

That would certainly explain the flattened chips on the ground around the body, Woodend thought.

'And how did you happen to find the ... the girl?'

'Brian ... Brian fell over her,' Pete mumbled.

'It was dark!' his brother said, as if he still felt he needed to find an excuse for making the discovery. 'I didn't see her.'

'Was it dark when you *went* to the chip shop?' Woodend asked.

Pete shook his head. 'No, but it was startin' to *go* dark.'

'If she'd been here on your way there, you'd have seen her, wouldn't you?' Woodend said.

'Couldn't have missed her,' Pete replied.

'An' how much later was it that you came back?'

'Hours,' Brian said. 'Hours an' hours.'

His brother grinned. 'About fifteen minutes,' he told Woodend.

Not long, the chief inspector thought. But long enough.

'Did you notice anybody strange hangin' about when you were on your way to the chip shop?' he asked.

The boys thought about it.

'No *people*,' Pete said finally.

'Then what?'

'There was a car parked over there,' Pete said, pointing towards the kerb at the edge of waste land.

'An' was anyone inside it?'

'Yes, there was a man inside. He was smokin' a cigarette. You could see it glowin'.'

'What did he look like, this man?'

'I don't know.'

'Was he as old as me, do you think? Or was he younger, a bit closer in age to the gentleman standing next to me,' Woodend said, pointing to Bob Rutter.

Pete shrugged his thin shoulders helplessly. 'Like I said, it was nearly dark, mister. I couldn't really see.'

'Do you know what kind of car it was? Was it like the one that your dad drives?'

Pete giggled. 'Dad doesn't have a car. He says that honest workin' men like him—'

'Our dad doesn't work,' Brian interrupted.

'...that honest workin' men like him can't afford such a grand luxury,' Pete continued, ignoring his younger brother's naive honesty. 'He says we'll all have to wait till the revolution comes before we get to drive around in big cars like the bloated boor ... bour...'

'Bourgeoisie?' Rutter supplied.

'That's right,' Pete agreed. 'Boor-jw-zee.'

If Pete had been a doctor's or a dentist's son, he'd have known about cars, right enough,

Woodend thought – would have been counting down the years before he was behind the wheel of one himself. But why should these kids take an interest in something they'd been told by their own father that they'd never have any chance of owning themselves?

'What colour was this car?' he asked.

'I think it was brown,' Pete said dubiously. 'Or it might have been black. Or dark blue.'

'How big was it?'

'Not *too* big, if you know what I mean.'

'I'm not sure that I do.'

'But not too *small*, neither. To tell you the truth, mister, I didn't really notice.'

It was hopeless, Woodend thought. He was never going to get a decent description out of these kids.

He closed his eyes and pictured the scene as it must have been an hour earlier.

The boys cross the waste land. They are hurrying – because fish and chips is such a feast to them that they can already taste it.

In the car – which may be brown, black, or blue – the man sits, smoking a cigarette and watching them. He waits a while once they've gone – to give the boys plenty of time to get away from the area, and to allow darkness to fall – then gets out of his vehicle and walks around to the boot. He does it in leisurely manner, as if he hasn't got a care in the world, because it is always possible that someone is watching him, and he doesn't want to raise their suspicions.

Once he is at the back of the car, he removes his key from his pocket, and looks carefully around him. There is nobody there. He's not really surprised at this. In the houses which surround the waste land, the television will be churning out its usual mindless pap, so why should anybody be out on the street?

He knows that the next part of his plan must be carried out quickly, so he takes a deep breath before opening the boot.

The dead girl is inside it. Perhaps he has wrapped her in a carpet or tarpaulin, on the off-chance that he will encounter someone before he has time to dump the body. Or perhaps she is as naked and vulnerable as she was when Pete and Brian found her.

He picks her up and throws her over this shoulder, then walks quickly towards the rough path. Ten or twelve steps, and he is halfway across the waste land. He drops the girl un-ceremoniously – for why should he be gentle with her now, after all that he has done to her in the previous few hours? – turns, and trots back to his vehicle. Once inside the car, the man inserts his key in the ignition, fires up the engine, and drives away.

The whole operation has taken just a couple of minutes.

Why do you keep calling him 'the man', Charlie? Woodend found he was asking himself, as he lit up a cigarette with shaking hands. Because he wasn't just 'the man', was he? He was the killer!

Which meant – because it simply *had to* mean – that the *other* man, the man he'd got locked up in a cell at headquarters and who he'd been convinced was responsible for all this, couldn't be the killer at all!

Fifteen

There was a layer of ice on the puddles in front of the morgue, and several sets of tyre-skid marks were clearly visible in the thick frost which had settled overnight.

Woodend had woken up shivering, that first morning after the discovery of the body, but – as in the case of the boys the previous night – he doubted it had much to do with the external temperature.

His coldness was deep, deep inside him.

Cold anger.

Or perhaps cold sorrow.

Dr Shastri was waiting for him in her lab. She looked totally exhausted, and did not even attempt to summon up one of her customary cheery greetings.

'This is a very bad business, Chief Inspector,'

she said. 'A very bad business indeed.'

'It is,' Woodend agreed. 'What can you tell me about the body?'

'The direct cause of death was suffocation,' the doctor said flatly. 'But before she died, the poor child was tortured in a most horrible and merciless manner. I counted a hundred and twenty-seven wounds on her broken body, and most of them were inflicted pre-mortem.'

'When did she die?' Woodend asked.

'Since she was abandoned naked, on cold ground, and while the temperature was dropping, it is difficult to pinpoint the time with any great deal of accuracy,' the doctor said.

'So what's your best guess?'

'Some time between four and six o'clock yesterday afternoon.'

In other words, somewhere between half an hour and two and a half hours before her body was dumped, Woodend calculated.

'I'm surprised the killer suffocated her,' he said.

'And why is that?'

'Because suffocation's a relatively painless death, an' this whole thing was about makin' her suffer.'

'You have a point,' Dr Shastri agreed.

'How many of the wounds were made post-mortem?' Woodend asked.

'As nearly as I can tell, around thirty of them.'

'An' that puzzles me too,' Woodend admitted. 'Surely he would have got more pleasure out of inflictin' them while she was still alive.'

'Perhaps there is some ritual that he has convinced himself he must follow, and this ritual involves both pre-mortem and post-mortem wounding,' Dr Shastri suggested. 'But I am doing no more than speculating here. In truth, I can say very little on the subject, because I am far from being an expert.'

The phone on the wall rang, and Dr Shastri answered.

'Yes,' she said. 'Yes, he is.' She turned to Woodend. 'It's for you. The chief constable.'

Woodend took the phone from her.

'I've been ringing round everywhere, trying to find you,' the chief constable growled. 'What are you doing at the morgue?'

What did he *think* he was doing at the morgue, Woodend wondered. Shopping for the family groceries? Trying to get a sun tan?

'I've been talking to Dr Shastri, sir,' he said.

'About what?'

'About the dead girl.'

'Forget that for now,' Marlowe told him. 'I want you back at police headquarters right away. You're going to meet the press.'

'I'm not sure I'm prepared to give them a briefing on the investigation at the moment, sir,' Woodend said.

'Did I mention a *briefing*, Chief Inspector?' Marlowe demanded. 'Did I even mention your *so-called* investigation?'

'No, sir, but...'

'This has nothing to do with the investigation at all. You will be reading out a statement to the

184

press that I've already drafted for you. You can put it in your own words, but you'll stick to the spirit of the text or – by God – I'll have your head on a silver platter.'

'A statement?' Woodend repeated. 'What kind of statement?'

'What kind of statement do you *think*?' Marlowe asked.

The maintenance staff at police headquarters had over-compensated for the drop in temperature by turning the heating up to maximum. Now the whole building felt uncomfortably sticky, and this feeling was at its worst in the press room, where the television crews had set up their lighting well in advance of the briefing.

Woodend stepped onto the podium. He wanted to loosen his tie, but with all those eyes in the room clearly fixed on him – and countless more watching him through the miracle of the goggle box – he knew it would be a mistake.

He cleared his throat, and stared into the bright lights.

'I would like to make a statement which is only indirectly connected with the cowardly attack on – and subsequent murder of – Angela Jackson,' he said, noting as he spoke how wooden and hoarse his voice sounded. 'Some of you will no doubt be aware of the fact that for the greater part of yesterday we had a man in custody, and were questioning him about Angela's disappearance. That man has since been released.'

'Who is he?' called out one of the faceless reporters from behind the lights.

'Normally we would not give out that detail, and we are making an exception to the rule in this case only because the individual concerned has requested that we do so,' Woodend ploughed on. 'His name is Edgar Brunton, and many of you will know that he has practised as a solicitor in Whitebridge for a number of years.'

He paused, and looked around the room. Standing at the back, and thoroughly enjoying the spectacle of his humiliation, were the chief constable and Superintendent Crawley.

'The reason Mr Brunton wanted his name released was to scotch the rumours that have been circulatin' around Whitebridge since his arrest,' Woodend continued. 'I think it is a wise decision on his part, an' I would like to make one thing clear as of this minute – I no longer believe that Mr Brunton had anythin' to do with the dead girl's abduction. He has assured me he is innocent, an' I accept that assurance unreservedly.'

And that's the truth, the whole truth, an' nothin' but the bloody truth, he told himself.

'I would just like to add that I offer my sincere apologies for any distress I have caused to Mr Brunton an' his family,' he concluded.

'So who's the real killer?' another reporter shouted out.

'I can't comment on any other details of the investigation at the moment,' Woodend said.

'Is there still an investigation to comment *on*?'

a third reporter demanded. 'Or did you drop all other lines of inquiry the moment you thought you'd caught your man?'

'Of course we didn't drop all other lines of inquiry,' Woodend said contemptuously, moving off the prepared script. 'Durin' the entire time we were questionin' Mr Brunton, we were also pursuin' other leads. An', in case you've forgotten, we were still doing all we could to try an' return Angela to the safety of her family.'

'In which you failed,' the reporter countered.

'Like I said, we did all we could – all that was humanly possible.'

'Really?' the reporter asked. 'Isn't it true that a number of officers – quite a *large* number of officers – were involved in building up the case you were intending to bring against Mr Brunton?'

'Yes, that's quite true.'

'And wouldn't they have been better employed in following up leads which could have helped to catch the real killer?'

'You're talkin' with the advantage of hindsight,' Woodend said. 'The way it looked at the time...'

'Isn't it true?' the reporter insisted.

'Yes,' Woodend said heavily. 'It's quite true.'

Chief Constable Marlowe and Superintendent Crawley were sitting behind Marlowe's desk, and Woodend – like an errant schoolboy – was standing in front of it.

'Well, that press conference was certainly a

most satisfactory exercise,' Marlowe said. 'It served to both clear the air and lay the blame where it should rightly have been laid.'

'I told you you were making a mistake to arrest Edgar Brunton,' Crawley said smugly.

'The evidence all pointed to Brunton,' Woodend said.

'And the evidence – what little of it there was – was completely wrong,' the chief constable pointed out. 'So what do we do now?'

'We go back to square one,' Woodend said. 'Except that now we've got a fresh crime scene, we just might be able to—'

'I wasn't talking to you!' Marlowe said harshly. He turned to Superintendent Crawley. 'What *do* we do now, Stan?'

'Well, sir, our first step should be to examine the area where the body was found, in the hope that will provide us with some fresh clues.'

'I just said that,' Woodend pointed out.

'And who do you think should be in charge of the case, Stan?' Henry Marlowe asked, ignoring him.

'I think I should supervise the overall running of the case, although, of course Chief Inspector Mortlake would be handling things on the ground.'

'Wait a minute! This is my case!' Woodend said.

'It *was* your case,' the chief constable said. 'Now it belongs to Superintendent Crawley and DCI Mortlake.'

It was the worst possible choice Marlowe

could have made, Woodend thought. Crawley was not so much a policeman as a wheeling-dealing politician *pretending* to be a policeman. And as for Mortlake? The man was a joke – an over-fussy, over-complicated parody of a detective, who seemed to model his methods more on the elaborate goings-on described in 1920s country-house mysteries than on the gritty reality of modern-day police procedure.

'So where does that leave me?' he asked Marlowe.

'As of this minute, you are being transferred to other duties,' the chief constable told him.

'What other duties?'

'That is yet to be decided, but you will be notified in the fullness of time. And if I were you, Chief Inspector, I would keep my head down until that reassignment comes through. The reporters are baying for your blood – and I can't say that I blame them.'

'This isn't just another stage in the runnin' battle between you an' me, you know,' Woodend said. 'This is a murder case. There's a killer out there – an' he might strike again, soon.'

'You're probably right,' the chief constable conceded. 'That is why it is important that we catch him as soon as possible.'

'An' I'm the best man to do that.'

'Really?' Marlowe asked. 'Judging by your track record on this investigation so far, I would have said you're the very *worst* man to put in charge, which is why I'm placing the case in the hands of someone much more competent.'

'But, sir...'

'You're dismissed, Chief Inspector Woodend,' Marlowe said coldly.

Sixteen

It was lunchtime. Woodend and Paniatowski were sitting at their usual table in the public bar of the Drum and Monkey. Woodend had all the appearance of a man who has had a coal wagon dropped on him from a great height, and Paniatowski of a woman who wanted to do something to ease her boss's distress, but had absolutely no idea what that something might be.

'Any idea of what job you're likely to be posted to next, sir?' Paniatowski asked.

Woodend shrugged. 'Crawley threatened to have me transferred to Traffic yesterday, but it won't be that.'

'How can you be so sure?'

'Because it's such an obvious demotion.'

'And don't they *want* it to be obvious?'

'Yes, but they can only push things so far. Put me into Burglary an' they're sayin' it was *somethin'* of an error of judgement on their part to ever give me the kidnappin' case in the first place, because it was just beyond the threshold of my competence. Put me into Traffic, on the other hand, an' they'll be sayin' I was out of my depth *long before* I was put in charge of the investigation – in which case, *they're* the bloody fools an' I'm just the bumblin' idiot.'

'So you think it will be Burglary?' Paniatowski asked.

'I don't know – an' frankly, at the moment, I don't give a damn,' Woodend replied morosely. 'What's got me worried is that the bastard who killed Angela Jackson is still out there. I want to see him collared, an' I don't think either Crawley or Mortlake are up to the job. But there's nothin' I can do about that, is there? Because I'm out, an' they're in.'

A man in a tweed jacket and brown trousers, who had been watching them for some time, chose that moment to walk over to their table and say, 'Could you spare me a few minutes for a word in private, Chief Inspector?'

Woodend looked up at him. 'I really don't want to talk to you, Dr Stevenson,' he said.

'Please!' Stevenson said.

'I could always go and powder my nose, if you wanted me to, sir,' Paniatowski said tactfully.

Woodend sighed. 'Aye, you might as well,' he agreed, and when she'd stood up, he said to Stevenson, 'Take a seat, Doc.'

Stevenson sat. 'You must hate me,' he said.

'To tell you the truth, I haven't quite made up my mind about that, one way or the other,' Woodend admitted. 'You could have told me that you didn't think Brunton was guilty, you know. You could have pushed your code of medical bloody ethics to one side for a second, an' at least given me a hint. If you'd done that, I could have let him go, an' we just might have found the girl in time.'

'I doubt it,' Stevenson said. 'I think the girl was doomed from the moment she was kidnapped.'

'You could *still* have told me,' Woodend persisted. 'You could have given me a fightin' chance.'

'It was more complicated than you seem to think, Chief Inspector,' Stevenson said awkwardly.

'Was it? How?'

'Edgar Brunton has this problem, and, on a purely personal level, it's a serious one.'

'He hates his wife. An' – by extension – he hates women in general,' Woodend said.

Stevenson looked as if he'd just been struck by a brick. 'He told you that himself, did he?' he asked.

'No, I worked it out. Or rather, my sergeant did. This trick-cycling game's not as difficult as you fellers with a personal stake in it would have us believe. I'm right about his problem, aren't I?'

Stevenson glanced around, as if he expected to see the committee of the General Medical Council lurking in the corner, taking notes.

'I'd go so far as to say that Brunton strongly *resents* women,' he admitted, 'but I'm not sure I'd be able to claim – with any degree of certainty – that he actually *hates* them.'

'Still, you knew enough about him to know he

couldn't be the murderer – but you still said nothin' to me.'

'That's the point! I *didn't* know!' Stevenson protested. 'I suppose it's true that I thought the prospect was highly unlikely, given what he'd said to me during the sessions we've had together.'

'Well, then...?'

'But I couldn't be absolutely *sure*. Some patients manage to completely fool their doctors. Not many, but enough. How was I to know whether or not *he'd* been fooling *me*? I asked myself if I could take the chance of you releasing a dangerous psychopath back onto the streets, purely on my say-so. And I decided I couldn't. I kept hoping and praying that you'd uncover a piece of evidence which would clear matters up, one way or the other.' Stevenson raised his hands to his face. 'Oh God, I was such a coward, wasn't I?'

'I'm not here to judge you,' Woodend said, feeling a sudden – and unexpected – pity for the man.

Stevenson lowered his hands again. 'It's very kind of you to say that,' he told the chief inspector. 'But it doesn't really help much.'

'Doesn't it?'

'No! Because ever since the moment you had me locked up, I've been judging *myself*, and finding myself wanting.'

The words made Woodend uncomfortable – as did the reminder of Stevenson's incarceration.

'I apologize for arrestin' you,' he said.

'You only did what you thought was right,' Stevenson told him.

'Yes, I did think it was right – at the time,' Woodend admitted. 'But lookin' back on it, it seems to me that at least a part of the reason I did it was because I was furious with you – an' wanted to make you suffer.' He paused to light up a Capstan Full Strength. 'What time did they eventually let you go?'

'Just before midnight.'

'What!'

'Everybody had forgotten about me. But that's perfectly understandable – after the discovery of Angela's body, you all had a lot on your minds.' Stevenson gave Woodend a thin smile. 'Don't worry, I'm not going to sue the police for false arrest.'

'Superintendent Crawley *will* be relieved,' Woodend said, then, realizing how ungracious he must have sounded, he added, 'Thank you. I appreciate it.'

'Think nothing of it,' Stevenson replied.

There was a short, awkward silence, then Woodend said, 'I still think you have somethin' to contribute to this case. But I'm not sure that you'll be allowed to.'

'But surely if that's what you really do think, then you'll give me another chance to—'

'It isn't my case any more.'

'What?'

'I've been taken off it. It's been assigned to somebody else.'

'But that's terrible!' Stevenson told him. 'If

anyone can track this man down, it's you.'

'We could sit here all day, exchangin' compliments an' makin' each other feel better,' Woodend said awkwardly. 'Or you could just listen, while I tell you what I think you should do next.'

'I'm listening,' Stevenson told him.

'Contact DCI Mortlake. Use all your powers of persuasion to convince him that you have somethin' of value to offer.'

Stevenson nodded. 'I'll do that.'

'An' just so you'll be prepared for anythin' he might throw at you, I suppose I'd better fill you in on the details of what we found on the waste ground.'

'Yes,' the doctor said. 'That might be a good idea.'

Woodend told Stevenson about the condition the body had been discovered in, and the note that had been found nailed to her leg.

'If we don't catch him, do you think he'll kill again?' the chief inspector asked, when he'd finished.

Stevenson nodded sombrely. 'I'm almost certain that he will.'

'Soon?'

This time, Stevenson shook his head firmly. 'No, not soon.'

'How can you be sure of that?'

'From the very nature of the note, which almost seems like an announcement of his arrival on the scene, I would guess that this is his first killing.'

195

'That was my thought, too,' Woodend said.

'And in virtually all cases, there's quite a long gap before the killer decides to strike for a second time.'

'What do you mean by "long"?'

'Normally, it will be between six months and a year. But remember, that's the gap between the first and the second killing. As his obsession expands and develops, the space between the killings will grow shorter and shorter, until it finally reaches the point at which the urge is so overpowering that he will kill every single time he has an opportunity.'

So DCI Mortlake and Superintendent Crawley had around six months to get a result, Woodend thought.

And would they be able to?

He wanted to say that they would – wanted to convince himself that, with the entire resources of the Central Lancs Police Force behind them, even a couple of incompetents like Crawley and Mortlake were bound to catch the man before he struck again.

He *wanted* to say it – but, looking at the situation objectively, he very much doubted whether it would be true.

The Invisible Man sat at the table, with the morning's national and local newspapers spread out in front of him.

Most men in his position would have bought all the papers from the same place, he thought with smug satisfaction, but then he was *not* most men.

He was far too canny to have made that kind of elementary mistake. He had realized – as the average killer would not have done – that such an action would have left a clear trail. And it only needed one policeman to be clever enough to go around the newsagents, asking if any customer had shown undue interest in the news, for the whole game to be up. So, bearing that in mind, he had driven all over town, buying two newspapers here and one newspaper there, until he had the complete collection.

In many ways, he was most gratified by the coverage that the killing had received, though it annoyed him that there was no mention of the note left with the body, nor of the name he was using.

The police were probably holding back some of the information deliberately, he thought. He had read they often did that, so that when they made an arrest they could trick the suspect into revealing himself through the fact that he had information which the general public didn't.

As if that kind of cheap trickery would work on him!

As if *any* of their clumsy ruses would work on *him*!

Even so, it was still a disappointment that his message to the world – to all the *men* in the world – had been suppressed.

But it didn't really matter, he told himself. Not when you took a long-term view of things. The police would have to release his name eventually – if not after the next killing then at least after the one which followed it.

He was not yet sure when the next killing *would* take place. He felt, in many ways, like a painter or sculptor who has just finished his masterpiece, and is quite content, for the moment, to simply rest on his laurels.

But this feeling would not last forever. He was certain of that. Eventually he would feel the urge begin again. At first, it would be no more than a minor irritation, a little like an annoying itch. But slowly it would grow, until it built up into a great surging river which would burst its banks if he failed to satisfy it.

Yes, the urge would most certainly return. It might not be for as long as a year. It might be considerably less than that.

But it *would* return.

PART TWO:

The Visible Men

Seventeen

Woodend was lying on his back, a few yards below the crown of a gently sloping Yorkshire hill. A soft spring breeze was blowing softly around him, and as he gazed idly up at an almost cloudless sky, he gave his thoughts free rein to wander wherever they wished.

'Are you asleep, Charlie?' asked a woman's voice, half accusatory and half amused.

He raised himself on one elbow. 'Asleep? Me? Certainly not!'

'Well, you *looked like* you were asleep.'

'I was doin' no more than absorbin' the peace an' tranquillity that we're surrounded by,' Woodend said, with as much injured dignity as he could muster – but even as he spoke the words he was already beginning to admit to himself that perhaps he had dozed off for a *few* minutes.

He looked down the hill. In the near distance, a small flock of sheep were munching contentedly at the lush grass. Beyond them, he spied several baby rabbits running around – revelling in the new freedom that emergence from their dark burrows had given them. There were daffodils swaying sedately in the soft spring breeze, and deep-blue bugle flowers resting regally on top of their large spikes.

At this time of year, there was nowhere better on God's green earth than the Yorkshire Dales, he told himself.

'By, but this has been a really grand day out, hasn't it, love?' he asked the woman.

'Perfect in every way,' Monika Paniatowski agreed contentedly.

Woodend reached into the pocket of his hairy sports jacket, and extracted his packet of Capstan Full Strength. But even before he opened it, he could tell by the feel of the packet that it was empty.

'Damn it, I seem to have run out of fags, Monika,' he said. 'Can I borrow one of yours?'

'They're filter tips, Charlie,' Paniatowski said.

Of course they were! He should have remembered that she smoked the same kind of poncey cigarettes as Bob Rutter did.

He sighed theatrically and said, 'Well, I suppose I'll just have to lower my standards for once.'

Paniatowski laughed. Then she took two cigarettes out of her packet, put both of them in her mouth, lit them, and handed one to Woodend.

His relationship with Monika had changed so much since their failure in the Angela Jackson case had resulted in them no longer working together, Woodend thought.

He'd worried, when they'd first been split up as a team, that they'd also grow apart as people, but the reverse had proved to be true. They were closer now than they'd ever been. He was grateful for that, and tried to avoid remembering, *too* often, that their increased intimacy was due, in no small part, to the way that Bob Rutter had behaved.

He checked his watch. 'Joan and Louisa seem to have been gone quite a long time,' he said, slightly concerned.

Paniatowski laughed again. 'You worry far too much,' she said. 'The way you fret over that child, you'd think you'd never brought up one of your own.'

But he had fretted over Annie, too, when she was growing up, he thought. He *still* fretted over her. It was just a thing that men with daughters did.

Besides, it was not really Louisa he was worried about at that moment – it was Joan. Ever since she'd had her mild heart attack in Spain, two years earlier, he simply hadn't been able to stop himself from thinking of that heart of hers as little more than a ticking time bomb.

'When's Bob back?' he asked, to take his mind off his wife's condition.

'Tomorrow,' Paniatowski replied.

'It's really very good of you to look after little Louisa while he's away,' Woodend said.

Especially, he added silently, when we both know – though neither of us would ever admit it to the other – that Bob's spending his time with that bloody Driver woman.

'It gives the nanny a break from her duties,'

Paniatowski said. 'Besides it's no hardship at all for me to take care of Louisa. She's a lovely little kid.' She took a drag on her cigarette. 'How's work?'

'Bloody,' Woodend admitted. 'I didn't join the police force to spend my days pushin' paper around. I don't like it – an' I'm not very good at it.'

'Perhaps they'll move you into something more interesting soon,' Paniatowski said.

But they both knew that was not going to happen.

'I've been thinkin' of takin' early retirement,' Woodend said.

'Seriously?' Paniatowski asked, alarmed.

'Seriously,' Woodend agreed. But then he chuckled and continued, 'The only problem with doin' that is, it would give Henry Marlowe more satisfaction to see me go than any man's entitled to in one lifetime.' He took another drag on the filter-tip cigarette, and decided he would never get used to them. 'How's your new job goin'?' he asked.

'Quite well,' Paniatowski told him.

'Really?'

'Really. The Domestic Violence Unit's doing pioneering work, and I think I'm making a valuable contribution to it.' She paused. 'Only...'

'Only, it's not the job you were born to do?' Woodend suggested.

'Only, it's not the job I was born to do,' Paniatowski agreed.

They heard the sound of a little girl giggling

loudly, and turned to see Joan and Louisa coming slowly over the crest of the hill.

'My Joan really shouldn't be pushin' herself like that,' Woodend said.

'Stuff and nonsense,' Paniatowski told him. 'She's having the time of her life. Louisa's like a granddaughter to her, and the longer she's with her, the younger she looks herself.'

And there was some truth in that, Woodend conceded – but he still didn't want to be the widower of a young-looking corpse.

Joan and Louisa drew level with them.

'You should have come with us, Uncle Charlie,' the little girl said excitedly. 'We saw an elephant's footprint. Didn't we, Auntie Joan?'

'We saw somethin' that I said certainly *looked* like an elephant's footprint,' Joan replied cautiously. 'But I'm not too sure there *are* any wild elephants in Yorkshire.'

She was short of breath, Woodend thought. She was trying to hide it from him, but she was definitely short of breath.

'So what have you two been talkin' about while we were off explorin'?' Joan asked Woodend and Paniatowski. 'Old times, I'll bet.'

'Not really,' Woodend said.

'Well, I am surprised.'

And so, in a way, was Woodend. There'd been a time when he and Paniatowski couldn't have been together for more than five minutes without talking shop, but he supposed that now those days were gone – and never coming back – they'd both decided to almost pretend that

205

they'd never existed.

'We should be setting off for home, or we'll be missing Louisa's bedtime,' Paniatowski said.

'You're probably right,' Woodend agreed.

And he was thinking to himself that it was almost heart-breaking to see how attached Monika had become to the little girl.

Because – sooner or later – it was bound to end in tears.

Mary Thomas had lived in Whitebridge for a little more than two months, and though it had initially been a big wrench to leave all her old school friends behind in the Valleys, she had quickly decided that there had also been quite a lot of advantages to the move.

For a start, since this town was much bigger than the one they'd come from, she no longer had to attend the same school as her dad taught in. And in Whitebridge, there was so much more to do with your free time than there ever had been at home in Wales – more church youth clubs to attend, more flashy big stores to go window-shopping in front of, more municipal parks to walk in, and more good-looking boys – also walking in the parks – to conduct a mild flirtation with.

There were many more opportunities to make a bit of extra pocket money for herself, too. That very morning, for example – the third day of the half-term holiday – she'd been babysitting for one of her teachers, who had gone off to play in a hockey match. It was easy work, looking after kids, and she'd enjoyed it. And as she walked home for her lunch, jingling the money the teacher had paid her in her pocket, she was more than happy with the way her life was going.

She was passing one of the old derelict mills, a short distance from the new estate where she now lived, when she noticed the man. He was old – about her father's age – and rather smartly dressed. He was standing by his car, with a large map opened in front of him, and he looked very perplexed.

When he saw her approaching, he smiled and said, 'Excuse me, miss, but could you tell me the way to Buckley Street?'

Mary smiled back, and shook her head. 'I'm a bit of a stranger to Whitebridge myself,' she said. 'There's a lot of the town I haven't even got around to seeing yet.' Then she noticed the look of disappointment come to the man's face, and she added, 'But you've got a map, haven't you?'

The man grinned lopsidedly. 'Yes, I have,' he agreed. 'The problem is, I can't seem to make much sense of it. I was never very good at reading maps, even at school. I expect you're much the same way yourself.'

'You're wrong about that,' Mary said. 'I'm absolutely brilliant with them!'

The man smiled again. 'Really?'

'Really! You would be, too, if you'd been brought up by a dad who's a geography teacher.'

'Oh well, if I've got an expert on hand...'

The man held out the map to her. Unfolded as it was, it was like being handed a large, opened newspaper.

Mary took it in both hands, and held it a couple of feet from her face. 'Shouldn't take a minute,' she said.

Or it wouldn't have, she told herself, if this had actually *been* a map of Whitebridge.

But it wasn't.

Her first thought was that the man was playing some kind of joke on her. Her second was he was *so* bad with maps that he didn't even realize this wasn't a town map at all, but one of the whole of Scotland.

There was no time for a third thought, because Mary felt the map being pushed, with some force, into her face. There was no time to struggle either, because she was only just starting to understand what was happening to her when she felt a blow to her head, and everything went black.

'Ladies and gentlemen, as a result of favourable tail-winds over the Atlantic, we are slightly ahead of schedule, and should be landing at approximately five o'clock, local time,' the pilot said over the tannoy.

'That's just typical!' the man sitting next to Dr Martin Stevenson snorted in disgust.

'What's wrong with being early?' Stevenson wondered.

'Nothing. Nothing at all! As long as they tell us well enough in advance that we're *going* to be early. But they didn't, did they? My wife won't turn up until at least six o'clock because – so she says – she doesn't like to be kept waiting around. So I'll be the one who'll be waiting, won't I?'

'I suppose so,' Stevenson agreed.

He had already suspected that his fellow passenger was the kind of man who, if he found a ten-pound note lying in the street, would complain that it wasn't a twenty – and what he'd just heard merely confirmed it.

'I expect you're in the same boat yourself,' said the man, who had noticed Stevenson's wedding ring, and was plainly searching for common ground on which they could share annoyance.

'The same boat?' Stevenson repeated.

'Your wife won't turn up until later, either. Well, that's women for you, isn't it?'

'Actually, I wasn't expecting my wife to pick me up anyway,' Martin Stevenson said.

'No?' the other man said. 'Can't she drive or something?'

'As a matter of fact, she's a very good driver,' Stevenson told him. 'Probably better than me, in fact. But she's working, you see.'

'And I suppose she just couldn't be bothered to take the day off,' the man said sympathetically.

'It's not a question of being *bothered*,' Stevenson replied. 'The reason that my wife won't be there to pick me up is because she happens to take her work very seriously.'

And that was no more than the truth, he thought to himself.

Since there was a phone free in the baggage hall, and since his own luggage had not yet arrived on the carousel, Martin Stevenson decided to ring his wife, on the off-chance she was home.

She was.

'But you've only just caught me in,' she told him, the excitement clearly evident in her voice.

'I'm glad you seem so pleased to have me back,' he said.

'What?' Rosemary Stevenson answered, as if she had no idea what he was talking about.

'And since you ask, the conference went very smoothly,' Stevenson continued. 'My paper was extremely well received, and there were a couple of university department chairmen there who even hinted at the possibility of offering me a visiting professorship next year.'

'I don't think I'll be at home when you get back,' Rosemary said. 'In fact, you won't be seeing much of me at all for the next few days.'

'Have you heard a word I've said?' Stevenson wondered.

'The thing is, I've just been assigned to my first big case. In fact, it couldn't be bigger.'

Stevenson sighed. When his wife was in this mood, he knew from experience, there was no way on earth she was going to pay any attention to what he wanted to tell her. On the other hand, if he didn't pay attention to what *she* wanted to say, she would very likely cut up nasty. And after the hectic few days he'd had, the last thing he wanted to have to handle was a row with his wife.

'Couldn't be bigger,' he repeated. 'What is it? A murder?'

'Not yet. But there's a fair possibility it could end up as one.'

She was teasing him, he thought. Teasing him about a serious crime!

She was so wrapped up in herself and her own doings that she imagined it was all he was interested in, too. Still, for the sake of domestic tranquillity, he supposed he had better continue to play the game.

'What is it, then?' he asked. 'An armed robbery that went wrong?'

'Not even close,' she told him. 'Would you like a clue?'

He suppressed another sigh. 'I suppose so.'

'You don't sound very keen!'

'I am. I promise you I am. It's just that I'm rather tired, because I haven't really stopped...'

'The clue is that when Monika Paniatowski finds out I've been assigned to this case, she'll be really pissed off,' Rosemary said.

And then she hung up.

Eighteen

Woodend was in the living room of his hand-loom weaver's cottage, sitting in the battered old armchair he'd treated himself to on the day he'd been promoted to the rank of inspector. In one hand he held a copy of Charles Dickens' *Bleak House*, and in the other was the inevitable Capstan Full Strength. He looked at peace with the world, and – for the moment at least – he was.

In the kitchen, Joan Woodend was preparing the supper. She had left the door open while she worked, because she knew – though she would never let her husband *know* she knew – that Charlie sometimes got an almost childlike pleasure from watching her cook. Now, with the meal in its last stages of preparation, she turned towards the living room and said, 'I really enjoyed that day out, Charlie.'

'Good,' Woodend said. He spoke abstractly, since half of his mind was still immersed in Dickens' prose.

'She's a lovely little girl, that Louisa,' Joan said.

'She is,' Woodend agreed.

'An' Monika's such a nice young woman.'

'She's a real champion.'

Joan glanced over her shoulder to check on the progress of the meal, then said, 'You know, I used to worry about you an' her.'

'Me an' who?'

'You an' Monika?'

'An' why ever would you have done that?'

'Well, she's a good-lookin' young woman...'

'She is.'

'...an' there are girls, or so I've heard, who are rather attracted to older men.'

Woodend chuckled. 'She'd never have me, lass, don't you worry. She's far too good for that.'

'An' what does that make me?' Joan asked, starting to sound aggrieved. 'Just good *enough*?'

'Oh, *you're* far too good for me an' all,' Woodend told her. 'Always have been, an' always will be. But you see, your problem is that like it or not, you're stuck with me.'

Joan smiled affectionately at her husband. 'The local news is on in a minute,' she said. 'Why don't you turn the telly on?'

'Might as well,' Woodend agreed. 'Not that there'll be any *good* news – because there never is.'

By the time the television had warmed up, the local news programme was just starting, and a grim-faced announcer was staring into the camera.

'First, the headlines,' the announcer said. *'There is growing concern in Whitebridge over the apparent disappearance of a school girl.'*

'Oh God, no!' Woodend groaned.

What was it Dr Stevenson had told him when he'd asked how much of a gap there usually was between the killings?

Six months to a year!

And this was just seven months!

'The police are as yet unwilling to either confirm or deny whether they believe this case to be connected with the abduction and brutal murder of schoolgirl Angela Jackson, late last year,' the newsreader continued, *'but some non-police sources have already begun to point out the similarities.'*

A new image appeared on the screen. It was of a place that Woodend was more than familiar with.

Superintendent Crawley was standing on the podium in the press-briefing room, looking distinctly uncomfortable. Flanking him were DCI Mortlake and the recently promoted Detective Sergeant Rosemary Stevenson.

'Mary Thomas is thirteen years old, and has only recently moved to Whitebridge,' Crawley was saying. 'She is, by all accounts, a quiet, well-behaved girl, and we are treating her disappearance with the utmost seriousness. I urge anyone who has seen her today, or even thinks they *might* have seen her today, to contact Whitebridge Police Headquarters immediately.'

'Is it the same murderer?' one of the reporters called out.

Crawley glared at him. 'We don't know that there has even *been* a murder,' he pointed out.

'In fact, we must all hope and pray that there has not, and that Mary will turn up at home – safe and well – in the near future. In calling this press conference, all we are doing is taking precautionary measures.'

'Don't tell them that, you bloody fool!' Woodend bawled at the television screen. 'Don't – for God's sake – allow them to walk away with the idea that what's happened to her might not be serious!'

He reached for the phone on his side table, and dialled a number he knew by heart.

'Monika?' he said, when the woman at the other end of the line had picked up.

'I heard it, too,' Paniatowski said.

'The Drum an' Monkey, in half an hour,' Woodend told her.

'I can't.'

'You *can't*!'

'I'm still looking after Louisa, remember.'

'When's she due to go to bed?'

'I'm starting to get her ready now.'

'Have you got vodka in the house?'

'No,' Paniatowski said. 'I'm trying to cut down. Besides, with Louisa staying with me...'

'Read her one of the shorter bedtime stories tonight,' Woodend said. 'I'll call in at the off-licence for vodka an' beers, an' I'll be round at your flat as soon as I can be.'

He looked up, and saw Joan standing in the kitchen doorway. There was a blank expression on her face – so blank that he couldn't tell whether she was merely resigned or starting to get angry.

'So you won't be wanting your supper, then?' she said, her voice as flat as her look.

Woodend shook his head. 'Not now. Put it in the oven on a low heat, an' I'll eat it later.'

'You won't,' Joan said.

'You're right,' Woodend agreed. 'I won't.'

Joan shook her head slowly from side to side. 'I know you don't enjoy workin' in administration, but *I've* quite liked the fact that you've been home quite a lot for these last few months,' she said.

'I know you have,' Woodend said. 'I've liked it too. In a way.'

'This new case has nothing to do with you, you know,' Joan said, and now he was starting to think that the anger definitely had the upper hand over the resignation. 'It has absolutely nothing to do with you at all. It would have had once – but not any more.'

'A kid's gone missin',' Woodend said, standing up and walking over to the coat rack. 'A *thirteen-year-old* kid. An' Marlowe's given a couple of numbskulls the job of findin' her. I can't just stand by an' let that happen.'

'You don't have any choice,' Joan told him sharply. 'They're not goin' to put you back in charge, you know.'

'Of course I know that,' Woodend replied, slipping on his coat and walking towards the front door.

'So what can you an' Monika do on your own?' Joan asked him, in a voice which had almost risen to a scream. 'Do you seriously think that you can solve it by yourselves – without any backin' from the rest of the force?'

'I don't know,' Woodend admitted. 'But we've certainly got to try.'

Then he opened the door and stepped out into the night.

The Invisible Man was back in his chair in the derelict house. It had been a busy day for him – but also a very rewarding one.

He had not really anticipated the need to take another girl so soon. Though he had always warned himself that it might happen earlier, his *belief* had been that it would be a year – or perhaps a little longer – before the craving gripped him again. That he had turned out to be so wrong was probably, he suspected, due to the pressure of external circumstances on him – circumstances over which he had no real control. But he did not really want to go into that now.

He was, he thought, like a man in a small boat, being carried along by a huge wave. His main objective was not to speculate about how the wave came into being, but simply to stay afloat.

The urge to look through the spyhole was almost overwhelming, but he wanted to resist it as long as he could.

Think about something else, he ordered himself. Think about the latest football scores.

'Manchester United 2 – Nottingham Forest 1. West Bromwich Albion 1 – Wolverhampton Wanderers...'

It was no good. He had never been very interested in football – or any other sport, for that matter. He was simply not a team player. His pleasures had always been of a much more personal and private nature.

Well then, if not football, what? Something connected to the periphery of his obsession – something he could think about without getting *too* excited.

Other sex offenders – if that was what you wanted to call them – might perhaps provide just the diversion he was seeking.

There were some who would always claim they'd only done what the girl had wanted them to.

He had heard them himself.

In court and *elsewhere*.

Sometimes their heads would be bent and their voices would be full of whingeing self-pity at the predicament they found themselves in. Sometimes they would hold their heads erect, and speak with obvious pride.

But always they would say the same thing – 'I'd never have forced myself on her.'

As a defence, it was most common among paedophiles – a group of sad pathetic little men.

But others, who took their pleasure in far more exciting ways, would sometimes use it, too. It was even used – and he found this almost in-credible – by men who shared his own urges. He knew this for a fact, because one of them had told him – had actually confessed as much to him.

Not that the man in question had considered it a confession at all, he thought. No, it had been more a boast – meant to demonstrate that he knew, better than most people, how things really were.

'She liked the pain I was causing. I could see she liked it,' he'd said in a low, thick voice.

The Invisible Man had said nothing to contradict him. In fact, he'd nodded his head, as if to indicate that had been his experience, too.

But he was thinking, Oh yes! Absolutely! Spot on! Girls *love* being slashed with sharp razors. They like nothing better than having an electric current pass through their genitalia!

And yet he'd been sure that this man – like others he'd read about, heard, and talked to – really *did* believe what he was saying.

The Invisible Man despised such weakness and self-delusion. *He* never told himself that the girl enjoyed it. Indeed, it would have quite spoiled things for him if she had – for where was the sense of control over your victim, if all you were doing was pleasing her?

There was nothing even vaguely godlike in that.

It was doing what she *feared* – what made her *soil* herself to even think about – that brought the rush of blood to the head. And to ... to other places.

It was the pain and suffering she emitted which released a truly Olympian feeling of power.

He'd meant to distract himself, and he failed.

No matter – he'd held out long enough. He slid back the cover to the spyhole, and pressed his eye tightly against the lens.

The girl was huddled in the corner, as the previous one had been. But this one would be better than Angela Jackson. Much more satisfying.

He did not know *how* he knew this. Only that he did.

If they ever caught him, they would call him a madman, he thought. And perhaps they would be right. Perhaps he *was* mad. But perhaps the reverse was true. Perhaps he was one of the few sane people left on earth – one of that chosen band who knew what they wanted and went out and got it.

The girl looked frantically around the room. She didn't know about the spyhole – how could she have done? – yet she could still sense that she was being watched.

That was good. That was *very* good.

'It won't work,' Paniatowski said flatly, taking a sip of the vodka that Woodend had brought with him.

'What won't work?'

'Any of it.'

'So we do nothin', do we? We just sit on our hands while the man kills this girl – an' the next, an' the next.'

'Look, I want this bastard caught as much as you do,' Paniatowski said. 'Ever since I first heard about this new kidnapping, I haven't been able to look at Louisa without imagining a time when she's grown up and at the mercy of a man like that.' She glanced quickly across at the bedroom door, beyond which the child was sleeping peacefully. 'But we can't carry out a proper investigation from a distance. It simply can't be done, sir.'

He'd been expecting just this kind of resistance to the idea, Woodend told himself.

But he was encouraged by the fact that she'd stopped calling him Charlie – that now he was 'sir' again. That was a clear indication, he argued, that though she was saying they could not work together on this case, she was acting as though they already were.

'We're a couple of very smart bobbies,' he said. 'We won't get our hands on as much information as Mortlake an' Stevenson will have access to, but we can make more from the crumbs that fall off their table than they can make from the whole bloody feast.'

'Assuming that any crumbs *do* fall,' Paniatowski pointed out.

'An' then there's what we learned during our investigation into Angela Jackson's disappearance,' Woodend argued. 'They can't take that away from us, however much they might want to.'

'True,' Paniatowski agreed. 'What we know is ours for ever – but then we don't know *much*, do we?'

'That's where you're wrong,' Woodend told her. 'We stopped thinkin' about what we'd learned because we'd been taken off the case – an' because we'd lost our main battle, which was to find Angela alive. But the fact that we were no longer lookin' for leads doesn't mean there weren't any to be found. I'm honestly convinced we've already got the key to crackin' this case – it's just that we haven't recognized it for what it is yet.'

Paniatowski looked sceptical. 'You're saying that we missed something, are you?'

'We're bound to have done.'

'Like what?'

Yes, that was the problem, Woodend agreed. *Like what?*

'We always knew – because of the timin' – that the killer's hideaway couldn't be that far from Whitebridge,' he said, 'but from what we learned just before we were taken off the case, we now know it has to be actually *in* the town.'

'And you base this theory on...?' Paniatowski asked.

'On where Angela Jackson's body was found. The killer wasn't goin' to dump her far from where he murdered her, was he?'

'Why not?'

'Because the longer she was in the car, the more he was at risk. And he'd have known that! If he only transported her dead body half a mile or so, the chances of anythin' goin' wrong were minimal. But if he had to drive her halfway across the country, there was always the danger that he could be involved in an accident, or stopped by a motor patrol doin' a random check, or—'

'You're clutching at straws,' Paniatowski interrupted.

'An' there's the wounds,' Woodend ploughed on.

'What about them?'

'The point of torture is to inflict pain, isn't it?'

'Of course.'

'But a lot of those wounds were made when the poor kid was already dead. How do you explain the killer behavin' in that way?'

'Didn't you tell me that Dr Shastri thought it was part of some kind of ritual?'

'No, I didn't. I said she *suggested* it as a possibility – no more than that. But I wasn't convinced at the time, an' I'm even less convinced now.'

'So what *do* you think?'

'I think he had a plan – a timetable, if you like. On the first day he was goin' to do this to her, on the second he was goin' to do that, an' so on. But somethin' happened to disrupt that plan. Somethin' happened to make him kill her earlier than he intended to. An' so what he did to her after she was dead was what he'd *wanted* to do while she was still alive. Now if we could work out what that somethin' that forced him to act prematurely *is*, we'd be halfway to catchin' him.'

'What other ideas have you got?' Paniatowski asked.

'We could use the shrink again.'

'And do you really think he'd be willing to help us – especially when his own wife is on the team investigating the second kidnapping?'

'Yes,' Woodend said firmly. 'I do. The impression I get of Martin Stevenson is that he's a thoroughly decent feller. Of course, he's not blind to the fact that it wouldn't do his reputation any harm if he helped to catch the killer, but I think there's more to him than that – I think he genuinely wants to be of use.'

'But why would he want to be of use to *you*? Why wouldn't he want to help his wife instead?'

'Because he's got faith in me.'

'Oh, come on, sir, you're not saying that because it's true, you're saying it because it's what you need to *believe*!'

'You didn't see his face, that day in the Drum an' Monkey, when I told him I was bein' taken off the Angela Jackson investigation. Trust me, Monika, the man looked devastated.'

Paniatowski took another sip of vodka, sucked greedily on her cigarette, and then shook her head wonderingly.

'So, to sum up,' she said, 'what you have on offer is a vague theory that the killer's hideaway is in the centre of Whitebridge, an unsubstantiated belief that he killed the girl before he'd been planning to, and a desperate hope that Martin Stevenson will be idealistic enough to help us, even though it may damage his wife's career?'

'That's about it,' Woodend admitted.

Paniatowski suddenly smiled. 'Well, we've solved cases before with less than that to go on,' she said.

Nineteen

The Drum and Monkey opened its doors for business at eleven o'clock in the morning. Even at that hour, there would be a couple of potential customers pacing impatiently up and down outside, and by a quarter past eleven there would be a fair number of drinkers in the pub – the unemployed and the under-employed; shift-men who had finished their day's work and shift-men yet to start it; bank clerks out on their break, who were looking guilty about drinking so early in the day and always carried a packet of strong peppermints in their pockets; and the criminal fringe which didn't look guilty of anything, even though it usually was.

And today there was the addition of the big bugger, the blonde, and the smoothie, the land-lord thought, glancing across at the table in the corner. He hadn't seen the three of them to-gether for quite a while.

'Are you sure you want to get involved in this, Bob?' Woodend was asking Rutter.

'Why *wouldn't* I want to be involved?' Rutter countered.

Woodend shrugged. 'Well, you know, we will be stickin' our necks out a bit – an' there's always the chance we'll lose our heads as a result.'

'There's nothing new about that, is there? We've done it often enough in the past.'

'True, but circumstances have changed, haven't they? You've got Louisa livin' with you now. An' you've got a cushy job in crime prevention, which means you work regular hours, an' usually get home in time for tea.'

'What is this?' Rutter demanded angrily. 'Are you trying to exclude me from the investigation as a punishment for seeing someone who neither of you happens to approve of?'

'No, it's not that all,' Woodend told him soothingly. 'It's just that we thought you might prefer to play it safe.'

'There's a poor bloody kid out there who desperately needs the help of the best team available,' Rutter said hotly. 'And that's us, isn't it?'

'Yes,' Woodend agreed.

'Well, then?'

Woodend nodded. 'All right. If that's your decision, you're in,' he said. 'Has anybody got any new ideas?'

'I have,' Paniatowski said. 'Or rather, it's not so much a new idea as an old one we never got to follow through.'

'Go on,' Woodend said.

'The killer used a drug on Angela Jackson that isn't readily available to members of the general public. If we can find out where he got it from, it might give us a lead on him.'

'I've got the perfect excuse for looking into that,' Rutter said. 'I'm a *crime-prevention officer.*'

Despite the seriousness of the situation, Woodend found himself grinning. 'The way you say it, you make it sound more like an insult than a job description,' he told the inspector.

'Yes,' Rutter agreed. 'I do, don't I?'

'The other idea that the boss and I have agreed on is that the murderer's likely to have dumped his victim no more than a mile or so from the bolthole where he killed her,' Paniatowski said to Rutter. She pulled a map out of her handbag, and spread it on the table. 'So this is the area we need to look at,' she continued.

She'd drawn three circles on the map, and she was indicating the points at which the circles intersected.

'Why *three* circles?' Rutter asked.

'One has as its centre the spot where Angela Jackson's body was found,' Paniatowski said. 'The centre of the second one is where she was kidnapped, and the centre of the third is where Mary Thomas was snatched – because if he didn't want to drive far with a dead victim, we can be almost sure he didn't want to drive far with live ones.'

'It's good thinking, and by employing it you've certainly cut the search area down a lot,' Rutter admitted, 'but there are still an awful lot of buildings to look at, and people to question.'

'There are,' Woodend agreed. 'But it's not quite as formidable as it might at first appear.

The hideout would have to be somewhere comparatively quiet – somewhere the neighbours would be unlikely to see him carryin' the girl.'

'And somewhere they were unlikely to hear her screams,' Paniatowski said sombrely.

'So there's already whole streets in this area we should be able to rule out,' Woodend continued.

'Shouldn't we suggest to Superintendent Crawley and DCI Mortlake that they carry out the search?' Rutter wondered. 'They're the ones who've got the manpower for it.'

'That's why I'm hopin' they come up with the same idea independently of us,' Woodend said. 'But if *we* suggest it, they're likely to ignore it – precisely *because* we suggested it.'

'You're right, of course,' Rutter said. 'It sickens me to admit it, but that's exactly what they're likely to do.'

'We'll split the area we need to search into three parts,' Woodend said. 'But not equal parts. I'll take the biggest one, because cloggin'-it is my speciality, an' because you'll both have other things to do.'

'Hang on a minute,' Paniatowski said. 'I know Bob's going to try and trace the source of the drug, but what other things have *I* got to do?'

'You'll be consortin' with the enemy,' Woodend said.

'I beg your pardon, sir?'

'Sorry, I meant "consultin' with our colleagues". We need to know how the official investigation's goin', an' since they're unlikely to tell us if we ask them a direct question, you're just goin' to have to be sneaky.'

'Is there any particular *way* you'd like me to be sneaky?' Paniatowski wondered.

'Aye. I'd like you to cosy up to the newly promoted Detective Sergeant Rosemary Stevenson.'

'You must be joking!' Paniatowski said.

'Not at all. You've got a lot in common. You're both women sergeants in a police force where most of the officers are still men, half of whom believe that a woman's place is the kitchen, an'—'

'And Rosemary Stevenson absolutely hates my guts,' Monika Paniatowski interrupted.

'*Did* hate your guts,' Woodend corrected her. 'Hated them when you were a detective an' she was still in uniform. But the situation's changed, hasn't it? Rosemary's the top dog now...'

'Top *bitch*,' Paniatowski said.

'If you like,' Woodend agreed easily. 'She's part of an important investigation team – an' you're not. I'm sure she'd more than welcome the opportunity to be really condescendin' to you. An' if you eat a little humble pie, you'll be givin' her all the chances she'll need.'

'I'd rather rip my own tongue out,' Paniatowski said.

'I'm sure you would,' Woodend replied. 'But that wouldn't help *our* investigation, whereas brown-nosin' will.'

'All right,' Paniatowski said, with a look of distaste on her face. 'I'll do my best to cosy up to Rosemary Stevenson – but I don't have to like it.'

'No, you don't,' Woodend agreed. 'Truth to tell, you'll probably bloody *hate* it.'

They all left the Drum and Monkey at half-past eleven, and by twelve o'clock Woodend was parking his old Wolseley in the visitors' car park at the University of Central Lancashire.

It was the first time he'd ever visited the university, and as he walked across the campus, he was trying to work out exactly why it should be making him feel so uneasy.

His own schooling had never gone any further than Sudbury Street Elementary – which he had left at age fourteen to go to work in the mill with his dad – but that was not to say that he had anything against advanced education. In fact, he wished anyone who was lucky enough to receive it nothing but the best. So it was not the *idea* of a university he found unsettling, he decided, but the actual place itself. He felt – though he couldn't quite say why – that there should be more ivy and gargoyles around. Somehow, all this steel, glass, and concrete did not sit well in his mind with learning and research. No doubt Monika Paniatowski would have said he was old fashioned if he'd expressed this idea to her, he thought – but then Paniatowski said he was old fashioned about most things.

The psychology building was in the centre of the complex. It was three storeys high, and had a wavy roof which reminded Woodend of a piece of cardboard left out in the rain. The porter on the desk directed the chief inspector to the second floor, where Dr Stevenson had his office.

Woodend climbed the stairs and knocked on the doctor's door. After a moment, a voice from the other side of it called out, 'Come in.'

Martin Stevenson was sitting behind his desk. The last time they'd met had been in the Drum and Monkey, and Stevenson had been wearing a tweed jacket and brown cavalry-twill trousers. This time, the doctor was dressed in a sharp blue suit that Bob Rutter would probably have immediately lusted after. But there was nothing sharp about his face. He looked tired – and perhaps a little stressed.

'I'm sorry to turn up like this, without callin' first,' Woodend said apologetically.

'It's not a problem,' Stevenson assured him. 'Knowing that I'd be suffering from jet-lag, I've deliberately made no appointments for today.'

'So you've been travellin', have you?' Woodend asked.

'Indeed. I was in San Francisco. I only got back last night.'

'But you'll have heard about...'

'The awful thing that happened while I was away? Yes, of course I've heard about it. I've got an inside source, remember.'

'Your wife,' Woodend said.

'My wife,' Stevenson agreed.

'It's because of your wife that I had my doubts about comin' here today,' Woodend admitted.

231

'Oh?'

Oh! Was that it? Woodend wondered. He was in a difficult situation here – as he thought he'd just indicated to Stevenson – so why couldn't the man help him out a little?

Because, he supposed, given the obvious purpose of his visit, Stevenson was in a bit of a difficult situation himself.

And because the man was a bloody *shrink* – and bloody shrinks always seemed to believe that you should do most of the talking, however difficult that might be for you.

'I was never very happy about not bein' able to complete my investigation into the Angela Jackson murder,' he said, approaching the subject obliquely.

'I know you weren't,' Stevenson said.

'And it only makes it worse that, because I didn't catch the killer, he's been able to snatch another poor bloody girl.'

'You're weighed down by feelings of guilt,' Stevenson said, quite matter-of-factly.

'I wouldn't put it quite like that.'

'Wouldn't you? Then don't you think you might perhaps be deluding yourself?'

'I didn't drop the case – the case dropped me!' Woodend said angrily.

'Now you're starting to try to justify yourself,' Stevenson told him. 'And that simply won't work.'

'Will it not?'

'No – because you're the kind of man who rarely makes excuses for himself. So even though others don't hold you responsible for what happened or didn't happen – and even if you can understand, on an intellectual level, that there's nothing more you could have done – the guilt stays with you. And it will continue to stay with you until you have – in your own terms – made amends.'

'I didn't come here to be analysed,' Woodend said.

'No, you didn't,' Stevenson agreed. 'You came here to ask for my help. But now you are here, you're afraid that my loyalty to my wife will prevent me from providing it.'

'An' will it?'

'*I* wasn't happy about your being taken off the Jackson case, either,' Stevenson said. 'Killers like the one who murdered Angela are notoriously difficult to catch until they make their big mistake. And some don't make that mistake – ever! Even the ones who do eventually slip up can often get away with five or ten – or even twenty – murders before they're eventually apprehended. But I thought you had a very good chance of catching this one before anything as terrible as that was allowed to happen.'

'Better than DCI Mortlake has?'

Stevenson smiled. 'He's my wife's new boss,' he said. 'She wouldn't appreciate me casting any aspersions on his ability, would she?'

'No, I don't suppose she would,' Woodend agreed.

'But if, without it being seen as a criticism of Mr Mortlake, I can help you in your "unofficial" investigation, then I'll be glad to do.'

'Thank you,' Woodend said.

Elizabeth Driver sat at her desk. Lying in front of her was the manuscript of the book which Bob Rutter believed was going to be a tribute to his murdered wife.

As if that was ever going to happen!

As if she could ever be bothered to write a book about blind, plucky little Maria, which, while it might bring a tear to the eyes of a few sentimental idiots, would never sell more than a couple of thousand copies!

Rutter was essential to the book she was *actually* writing. She'd realized that from the start – even before her literary agent had made it abundantly clear to her. Rutter was the one who could provide her with the mundane details which would make her wilder claims *sound* authentic, even if they had been cooked up after a few gin and tonics. And she was far from convinced that he would stay the course, because though she'd finally slept with him – after a show of reluctance which would have had her countless lovers rolling around the floor in fits of laughter – she sensed she was losing her grip on him.

Part of the reason, she suspected, was that he'd not yet seen any of the book she was *supposed* to be writing, so perhaps she'd have to buckle down and produce a few pages of saccharine-laden prose which would fool him into believing she was serious about the project.

But another problem was the brat. Louisa didn't like her, and made that plain on every possible occasion. And since Rutter had a mawkish attachment to the child, it was beginning to sour his relationship with her.

And then there was Charlie Bloody Woodend. He was to be one of the centrepieces of her book – a moderately famous policeman who turned out to be bent; a popular idol discovered to have feet of clay.

Her decision to destroy Woodend had been based on the fact that, looked at objectively, it would make a good story, but there had been the added bonus that after all their clashes over the years – most of which she had lost – she would finally emerge triumphant.

But how could she bring Woodend down now, when he'd *already* been brought down?

How could she expose the crime-busting copper for what he really was, when he wasn't a crime-buster at all, but merely a pencil-pusher?

As much as she hated the idea of helping him, there was no choice in the matter, she decided. To bring Woodend down, she was going to have to build him up again first. She didn't yet know how she would go about it, but no doubt something would occur to her, as it always did. And in the meantime, she'd better write something to appease Rutter.

She threaded a sheet of paper into her typewriter, and began to hit the keys. It wasn't easy going, but after five minutes, she at least had something.

To know Maria was to understand the triumph of the human spirit. How many women, who lost their sight in their early twenties, would have found they had the backbone to build a new life – a life in perpetual darkness? And how much more incredible is it that not only did she bravely build a new home for her husband, but also took the courageous decision to have a child?

Truly disgusting! Driver thought, reading it back to herself. Absolutely vomit-worthy.

Still, that bloody moron Bob Rutter would lap it up.

Martin Stevenson had insisted that any further conversation between them took place away from the psychology building.

'You're not one of my students, and you're not one of my patients, so it would be inappropriate to use either my office or my consulting room for what we have to say to each other. Anyway, I think we'd *both* be more comfortable if we held our discussion on neutral ground.'

'I quite agree,' Woodend had replied.

And so they had gone to the student-union bar.

It was a dark, semi-subterranean place. The walls were painted in garish colours, and plastered with left-wing political posters. Hidden speakers – and there seemed to Woodend to be hundreds of them – pumped out eardrum-bursting rock-and-roll music. The tables looked as if they had been rescued from the wreck of the *Titanic*, and the chairs had clearly not been designed for anyone who thought that – even in the dim and distant future – they might start suffering from back problems. All in all, the bar was the chief inspector's worst nightmare of a place in which to drink.

Stevenson himself seemed quite at home, despite the fact that his smart blue suit made him stand out like a sore thumb against the faded blue jeans that most of the other customers were wearing. He waved to several of the students, and stopped to have a brief word with a couple more.

'You seem to be a very popular feller,' Woodend said, as Stevenson led him to a corner table where the noise of the music was a little more bearable than it was in the rest of the bar.

'Yes, I do,' Stevenson agreed, without even a hint of complacency in his voice.

'How do you manage that?'

'There's no real trick to it. I have a real enthusiasm for my subject, and work hard to communicate that enthusiasm to those I'm paid to teach. Besides, I genuinely like and respect my students – so why wouldn't they feel the same about me?'

They both ordered beer, and when it arrived, Woodend was surprised to find that it was a rather fine pint.

'So how can I help you?' Stevenson asked, when they'd both had a few swallows of ale.

'I've got this idea,' Woodend said, and outlined his theory that Angela Jackson's post-mortem injuries had originally been intended to be inflicted *before* she died.

'It's possible,' Dr Stevenson admitted cautiously, when he'd finished. 'But it's also equally possible that your police doctor – Dr Shastri, is it?'

'Yes.'

'That Dr Shastri might have been right when she suggested that the post-mortem injuries were part of a predetermined ritual.'

'But if *I'm* right, an' he killed her before he was intendin' to, what could have been the reason for it?' Woodend persisted.

'He may have suddenly lost his temper with the girl, and killed her without actually meaning to.'

'An' what would have made him do that?'

'The first thing you must train yourself to understand is that, to him, the girl is not important in herself,' Stevenson said.

'I understand that already,' Woodend replied.

Stevenson frowned. 'I'm not sure you do,' he said. 'At least, not fully. To get a clear picture of what the predator is like, it's necessary to go back to what he probably did in childhood.'

'All right,' Woodend agreed.

'There are a number of documented cases of killers who started to torture when they were no more than children themselves,' Stevenson continued. 'They typically began with ants and flies. They'd burn the ants by holding a magnifying glass between them and the sun, and they'd pull the wings of flies and watch, fascinated, as the fly spun around and around, totally helpless.'

'I knew kids at my school who did that,' Woodend said.

'Yes, it is remarkable how much cruelty lurks in even the most benign of us,' the doctor said. 'There is a difference, however, between the boys you knew and the man who eventually became our predator. He will have graduated from insects to small creatures like frogs and birds, and then to domestic animals – dogs and cats. And though he might have gained greater pleasure from killing the bigger creatures – mainly because they were better able to make clear to him their awareness of what was being done to them – his attitude to all the creatures he tormented would have been essentially the same.'

'Jesus!' Woodend said.

'The reason it will have remained the same is that they were all nothing but objects to be used for his pleasure. And his attitude will not have changed when he progressed to human victims. That is why he could do things to Angela which would have turned any normal person's stomach.'

Woodend shuddered. 'You're right, I don't think I did quite understand before,' he admitted. 'But I'm certainly gettin' the picture now.'

'But if the girl in herself is unimportant, the killer's *perception* of what she is – or what she represents, which is often the same thing – is vital,' Stevenson continued. 'He wants her to react in a particular way. He *expects* her to react in a particular way. And if she doesn't, he is very likely to view it as her wilful attempt to spoil his fun. That is when he may lose his temper to such an extent that he kills her before he planned to.'

'But Angela was smothered,' Woodend pointed out. 'That doesn't seem like the act of an angry man.'

'He may have seen smothering her as a disciplinary measure,' Stevenson said. 'Taking her to the brink of death and then pulling her back, as a way of teaching her a lesson. But the problem with going to such extremes is that it is easy to get it wrong. And that could be what happened. He may simply have misjudged it.' The doctor paused for a moment. 'This is all pure speculation on my part, you realize. I would need to study the man before I could say more.'

'Now that you know exactly what was done to Angela, do you still think that the image he presents of himself to the outside world will be of a perfectly normal, well-balanced man?' Woodend asked.

'Oh yes,' Stevenson replied. 'What he did to Angela only *reinforces* my original impression. He is a man wearing a mask, you see. But detecting the mask is made more complicated for you by the fact that at least part of the mask is *real*.'

'How do you mean?'

'He doesn't just *act* normal – he *is* normal in many respects. But deep inside, he is a wounded animal, who suffered a trauma – or series of traumas – during the course of his childhood from which he has never recovered.'

There was one more question that Woodend was finding it difficult to ask, though he knew that he must.

He swallowed deeply, and said, 'How much time have we got?'

'I beg your pardon?'

'How long will it be before he kills Mary Thomas?'

Dr Stevenson pressed his fingertips of his right hand against the fingertips of his left, and the expression on his face said that he was finding it as difficult to answer the question as it had been for Woodend to ask it.

'Even if you're wrong about Angela's death occurring earlier than was intended – even if he killed exactly when he planned to – I don't think it will be as quick this time,' he said finally.

'Could you explain to me *why* you think that?'

'Tell me, Chief Inspector, do you remember the first time you made love to a woman?'

'Of course I do! It's not somethin' you're likely to forget, is it?'

'It was all over very quickly, wasn't it?'

'Well, I suppose you could say...'

'You were so eager, now that you were finally getting what you'd wanted for so long – what you'd dreamed about for so long – that you rushed blindly into it, and found yourself ejaculating almost before you'd got started. Am I right?'

'Close enough,' Woodend said uncomfortably.

'The second time was much better for you, wasn't it? You had more idea of what to expect, and forced yourself to take it much slower – to really relish the experience. Yes?'

'Yes.'

'That's what I think our killer will be doing with his second victim. Taking his time. Relishing the experience.'

Twenty

The moment Rutter walked through the main entrance of the Pendleton Clinic, he felt that something was wrong. At first he could not pin down the source of the feeling, because, on the surface at least, the clinic looked to him to be perfectly fine. And then he put his finger squarely on the problem. It was not that the place looked *perfectly fine* – it was that it looked *perfect*!

There was no sign of wear and tear in the foyer. Nothing seemed used. It was almost as if the building had only opened its door for business the second before he had arrived.

And the people were perfect, too. The nurses crossing the foyer in their tailored uniforms could have been modelling them on the catwalk. The doctors had the clean-cut muscular look of Olympic athletes.

All in all, the clinic did not resemble any working hospital Rutter had ever seen. Rather, it presented itself as an almost Hollywood-inspired picture of how a top-flight hospital *should* look – and if Dr Kildare had suddenly walked into the foyer, he would have been only slightly surprised.

Rutter showed his warrant card at the reception desk, and said he'd like to talk to whoever was in charge.

The almost-too-pretty receptionist who was manning the desk favoured him with a radiant smile, picked up the phone, chatted briefly to someone called Sonia, and then pressed a button in front of her.

A good-looking porter in a smart blue uniform appeared at the desk almost immediately.

'Take this gentleman to the administration suite, please,' the receptionist said. 'I've just made him an appointment with Mr Derbyshire.'

The porter led Rutter down a long corridor which was as new and shining as the rest of the hospital seemed to be.

'Are you ex-job?' Rutter asked.

'I beg your pardon,' the porter said.

'A lot of people involved in this kind of security work are ex-bobbies,' Rutter explained.

The porter laughed. 'Not me,' he said. 'I'm an actor. I'm just resting at the moment.'

'"Resting"?'

243

'Between roles.'

Now why aren't I surprised? Rutter asked himself.

The director of the clinic was called Lawrence Derbyshire. He was a roundish, pinkish man with a shiny bald head and a complacent expression which stretched all the way from his chubby forehead to his double chin. When they shook hands on the threshold of Derbyshire's plush and fussy office, Rutter suspected he wasn't going to like the man, and after five minutes of listening to him drone on about how wonderful the clinic was, that first impression had been more than confirmed.

'Here at the Pendleton Clinic, we try to cater for the better class of patient,' the director was saying at that moment.

Rutter wondered what Woodend would have replied to that. Probably something like, 'The better class of patient, eh? What does that mean, exactly? That they have more exclusive illnesses?'

But he was not Cloggin'-it Charlie, and so contented himself with saying, 'In other words, fee-paying patients.'

'Well, of course,' the director agreed, sounding surprised that such a clarification was even needed. 'It is quite enough for our patients to have to deal with their illnesses. The last thing they need is to find themselves trapped in an environment with people who do not aspire to the same tastes or attitudes. That is why we engender an atmosphere here which is both comforting and familiar, stable and—'

'Very impressive. I must remember to put my name down on your waiting list,' Rutter interrupted. 'But the reason I'm here at the moment is to check on your security.'

'There is no need for that,' the director said. 'Our security is perfect. It has to be. Some of our patients are quite famous, you know.' He turned to indicate an array of photographs of people on the wall behind him, some of whom Rutter vaguely recognized. *'Really* quite famous,' he added for emphasis. 'And if they thought that we were lax enough to allow every grubby little pressman with a camera to come sneaking in here whenever he—'

'How secure are your drugs?' Rutter asked.

The director blinked. 'Our drugs? Who mentioned drugs?'

'I did. Just now,' Rutter said. 'Why do you ask? Has anyone mentioned them before?'

'No, of course not. Our control system has always been second to none. In fact, we've recently improved it.'

'If it's second to none, why did you *need* to improve it?' Rutter wondered aloud.

The director had started to sweat, and the globules of moisture were beginning to roll down his fat cheeks.

'We are constantly striving to improve our already excellent standards,' he said.

'So you've had no drugs go missing in ... shall we say ... the last six or seven months?'

'No,' the director croaked.

Lying toad! Rutter thought.

The man sitting opposite DCI Mortlake and DS Stevenson in Interview Room Three was wearing a brown suit and a tie with horses' heads on it.

'It says here that you're a mechanic, Mainwearing,' Mortlake said, looking down at his notes.

The big bugger who pulled me in last time might have been rough with me, but at least he had the courtesy to put a 'mister' in front of my name, Peter Mainwearing thought. 'I *am* a mechanic,' he said aloud.

'You know, it's a couple of months since I last took my car into a garage, but I could have sworn that when I did, the mechanics were all wearing overalls,' Mortlake said.

'That's how I remember it, the last time I was there, too,' Rosemary Stevenson agreed.

'Yet here we have a man, picked up from his *place of work*, dressed in a suit that wouldn't look out of place at a wedding. Strange, isn't it?'

'Very strange,' Rosemary Stevenson said. 'I wonder what the explanation could be. Perhaps he's such a bad mechanic that nobody sends him cars to work on any more.'

'I've got plenty of work on,' Mainwearing said. 'I just saw no point in starting it today.'

'I see,' Stevenson said. 'That explains the lack of overalls. But what it *doesn't* explain is why, when the officers arrived to bring you in, they

246

found you all dressed up with nowhere to go.'

'I had somewhere to go,' Mainwearing said.

'Where?'

'Here. I knew you'd bring me in for questioning. That's why I saw no point in starting work. And since I wasn't going to be working, I saw no point in putting on my overalls, either.'

'Now that is interesting,' Mortlake said.

'Very interesting,' Stevenson agreed.

'What made you so sure we'd pull you in?' Mortlake demanded. 'Was it because you knew we'd already talked to witnesses who'd seen you in the act of kidnapping the girl?'

'There are no witnesses to it,' Mainwearing said.

'That's what *you* think,' Mortlake told him. 'But you're wrong. Three people saw you. Get that, Mainwearing? Three!'

'There are no witnesses because I didn't do it.'

'Says he didn't do it,' Mortlake told Stevenson.

'Well, he would, wouldn't he?' Stevenson replied.

'Where's the girl?' Mortlake shouted.

'I don't know.'

'Do you have an alibi for yesterday afternoon?'

'Yes.'

'Let me be quite clear on what I mean by that, Mainwearing,' Mortlake said. 'When I ask if you've got an alibi, I don't expect you to produce one which involves any of your perverted, seedy friends. If you're to convince me it's genuine, the people who vouch for you will have to be of unquestionable respectability – and I'll expect there to be at least three of them.'

'Like the three witnesses who saw me snatch the girl?' Mainwearing asked, with an amused smile on his lip. 'Well, I'm sorry to disappoint you, but there aren't three. In fact, there's only one.'

'How very convenient for you! Who is he? Your bookmaker? A limp-wristed barman of your acquaintance?'

'My probation officer.'

'Your *probation* officer!'

'I have to see him once a week. It's one of the conditions of my parole.'

'Oh,' Mortlake said, clearly disappointed.

The dispensary of the Pendleton Clinic was as neat, shining, and perfect as the rest of the institution, and Rutter found it easy to imagine the fat director leading his rich clients through it as if they were on a conducted tour of a stately home.

The man in charge of it introduced himself as Tom Wade. He, too, was good-looking – the director aside, that seemed to be a requirement of the job – and though he was in his early thirties, he seemed to have somehow retained the wide-eyed innocence of a much younger man.

'There are three members of my staff always on duty during the working day,' he told Rutter.

'And at night?'

'Just one man. We don't need any more, once the operating theatres have closed down.'

'The director tells me you've recently tightened up on security in here,' Rutter said.

Wade frowned. 'Have we? If we have, nobody told me about it. And as far as I can see, we use the same procedures we always have.'

'So there've been no changes at all in the last six or seven months?'

'I suppose it depends on what you mean by changes. One of my staff – a chap called Norman Willis – was sacked.'

'By you?'

Wade laughed. 'No, not by me. Hiring and firing isn't one of my responsibilities. He was sacked by Mr Derbyshire.'

'And what was the reason given for his dismissal?'

'Mr Derbyshire said he didn't fit in. And perhaps he was right. Perhaps Norman felt that, too – because he certainly didn't kick up any fuss when he was given the elbow. In fact, he gave me the distinct impression that he couldn't get out of the clinic fast enough.'

'When was this?' Rutter asked.

Wade frowned with concentration. 'Let me see. It was just after the bi-yearly stock-taking, so it must have been about seven months ago.'

'Who does this stock-taking?' Rutter asked. 'Is it you?'

'No, I've got more than enough work on my hands already, without having to do the bean-counting myself,' Wade said. 'Mr Derbyshire gives that job to an outside agency.'

'Now that is interesting,' Rutter said pensively.

Twenty-One

The area where Monika Paniatowski's three circles intersected had looked small enough to be perfectly manageable when seen on the map, Woodend thought, but when you were actually walking around that same area on foot, it seemed to be almost never-ending.

He hadn't realized before – although perhaps he should have done – just how much of his home town had fallen into decay. Corner shops, where he had spent his precious pocket money on gob-stoppers, were now gone. Pubs he had drunk in as a young man had long ago called 'last orders' for the final time. Chip shops had stopped frying, pawnbrokers had ceased to accept pledges. There were whole streets he had wandered through on his childhood expeditions which were now boarded up, and waiting in creaking emptiness for the demolition ball.

Perhaps it was all for the best, he told himself. People were no longer content to live in a two-up, two-down cottage, with the only tap located in the back yard, and the kettle perpetually on the boil, heating up water for the tin bath in front of the open fire. They had endured a bloody depressing Depression and a depressingly bloody World War. Now they expected better – and who could blame them?

He met very few people on his journey through this wasteland – and not a single one of them had been a policeman.

And why was that?

Because Superintendent Crawley and DCI Mortlake had either dismissed the idea of a search as pointless, or – what was even worse – had never even considered the possibility at all!

'You stupid bastards!' he said. 'You stupid, stupid bastards!'

He had spoken more loudly than he'd intended, but that didn't matter, since there was no one there to hear him.

He reached Gladstone Street, which was yet another row of old terraced houses. There had once been an ironmonger's shop on the corner, which stocked everything you could possibly need and possibly imagine, Woodend remembered. Now that had gone, too. The frontage had been ripped out, and a large metal door – currently closed – had replaced it.

He read the sign above the door.

Mainwearing's Automobile Repairs
Quality, efficiency, speed
All our repairs carry a full guarantee

Woodend looked up the street. There was not a single house which looked to be still occupied.

This was just what he'd been out searching for, he thought – the perfect place for a sadistic killer to hide his latest victim.

But the killer wasn't Mainwearing. At the time Angela Jackson had been kidnapped, he'd been busy at work in the corporation bus garage, and had three witnesses to confirm it.

'You stupid bastards!' he said again.

But what if they weren't? nagged a voice in his head. What if Crawley and Mortlake were right in their assumptions, and the girl was being held somewhere else entirely?

Who was the stupid bastard then?

Despite the fact that his alibi had checked out, Peter Mainwearing had still been detained for two hours in one of the cells, which, he supposed, was a peevish punishment for his having an alibi in the first place.

When the police did finally get around to releasing him, he felt in such need of a drink that he headed straight for the Dog and Duck, which was a pub that he would not normally have been seen dead in, but did have the one virtue of being close.

The public bar of the Duck had a local reputation for being a rough place. And even in the lounge bar – which was at least a *little* more genteel – Mainwearing's smart brown suit was a beacon for comment. As he stood at the counter ordering his drink, he could already hear several crude and unflattering comments being made behind him – but it was not until he'd actually been served that things started to go seriously wrong.

The trouble took the form of a large man with a scar on his cheek, who prodded Mainwearing's shoulder – harder than was strictly necessary – and demanded, 'Don't I know you?'

'I don't think so,' Mainwearing told him.

'I think I do,' the man insisted. 'I did some buildin' work for you once. My name's Wally Decker. Remember me?'

'No,' Mainwearing said weakly – and unconvincingly.

'An' your name's Mainwearin', isn't it?'

There seemed no point in pretending any longer. 'That's right,' Peter Mainwearing said.

'Course, when I was workin' for him, I didn't know who he was – or what he'd done,' Decker said, addressing the bar in general. 'It wasn't till after I'd finished the job that my mates started raggin' me about what a good time I must have had with the pervert. If I *had* known, I'd never have gone anywhere near him – however much he was payin'.'

'I served my time,' Mainwearing said wearily, but with a growing tremble in his voice. 'That's all behind me now.'

'Behind you?' Decker repeated. 'You know a lot about bein' behind, don't you? It was bein' *behind* young kids that got you into trouble in the first place, wasn't it?' He laughed loudly at his own wit, then the humour drained away and he glared at Mainwearing and said, 'It's not funny!'

'I ... I never thought it was,' Mainwearing protested.

Decker was not known to be the most intelligent of men. When a new thought came to him, it generally took its time, but it was plain from the expression on his face that one had just arrived.

'What are you doin' here?' he demanded.

'I ... I came in for a drink,' Mainwearing said.

'But where were you *before* you came in for a drink?'

'That's really no business of yours,' Mainwearing said weakly.

'No business of mine?' Decker repeated. 'It is if I say it is. I think *I* know where you've been. The cop shop! Am I right?'

'I ... I really don't want to discuss it.'

'They'll have been askin' you questions about that missin' girl, won't they? Did you tell them what you've done with her?'

'I don't know what you're talking about.'

'Course you didn't tell them! You wouldn't have the guts to come clean, would you? An' because most bobbies are nancy-boys themselves, they wouldn't have had the balls to beat it out of you.'

'I think I'd better go,' Mainwearing said.

'You'll leave when I tell you that you can leave,' Decker bawled at him.

Defying a man like this one would be a big mistake, Mainwearing told himself. But his legs refused to listen to his brain, and began moving him towards the door.

He had not taken more than a couple of steps when he felt Decker's fist slam into his stomach. He let out a great 'whoosh' and doubled over, only to spring back again when Decker followed through with a blow to his face.

'Where is she?' Decker yelled. 'What have you done with her?'

Blood was bubbling up in Mainwearing's mouth. 'I don't know,' he sobbed. 'You have to believe me. *I don't know.*'

And then he was on the floor, his hands clutching his head in a desperate attempt to protect it, while the other man's boot went to work, with ruthless efficiency, on his ribs.

The director of the Pendleton Clinic was going redder by the second and – cradled in his executive leather chair as he was – was starting to resemble a fat lobster in a cooking pot.

'This is a private clinic,' he said, glaring at Rutter across his desk. 'You had absolutely no right to question my staff.'

'And you had no right to conceal the fact that a criminal offence has been committed on these premises,' Rutter told him.

'What criminal offence?' Derbyshire asked unconvincingly. 'I have no idea what you're talking about.'

'Why did you sack Norman Willis?'

'I don't know. I'll have to look it up in his record.'

'Maybe we can *both* look it up in his record,' Rutter suggested,

'That won't be necessary,' Derbyshire bleated. 'I do remember now. I terminated his employment here because his ... because his work proved unsatisfactory.'

'Where did you get that particular piece of information from?' Rutter wondered. 'Did it come from the head of your dispensary?'

'Yes ... I mean, no.'

'Which is it?'

'I'm sure that the head of the dispensary would have told me if he'd *noticed* his poor performance.'

'So let me see if I've got this straight,' Rutter said. 'You're claiming that the man supervising Willis had no idea how he was doing his job – but you did?'

'Well, yes.'

'And *when* did you notice he wasn't doing his job? Was it just after you'd carried out a stock-taking?'

Derbyshire took a silk handkerchief out of his pocket, and mopped his brow. 'You must understand my position, Mr Rutter,' he said. 'The clinic's reputation is of paramount importance, and if there was even a hint of—'

'He was stealing drugs, wasn't he?' Rutter interrupted.

'There was possibly some discrepancy in stock,' Derbyshire admitted reluctantly.

'He was stealing drugs!' Rutter repeated.

'Only on a very minor scale. Any other hospital would have let him off with a warning, but here at the Pendleton Clinic...'

'What drugs?'

Derbyshire shrugged. 'The usual kind that people like him decide to steal, I suppose. Amphetamines, barbiturates...'

'And halothane?'

'I'm not a medical man by training, Inspector, so I don't really feel I'm in a position to...'

Rutter stood up and leaned across the desk, so that his face was almost touching the fat man's.

'And halothane?' he repeated coldly.

'I believe one small bottle of halothane *did* go missing,' the director conceded.

Twenty-Two

Monika Paniatowski sat perched on a stool at the counter of the public bar of the Crown and Anchor. There was a mirror running the full length of the wall behind the counter, and in it she could see a reflection of DS Rosemary Stevenson and her 'lads', who were sitting at a table behind her.

Ten minutes earlier, when she'd walked into what was virtually enemy territory, Paniatowski had been fully expecting to be greeted by a hail of jeering and mockery, as befitted someone who'd become virtually a pariah since the Angela Jackson case. But there had been no such torrent of abuse. In fact, Rosemary Stevenson's team had hardly seemed to notice her.

The reason for this passivity was immediately obvious. A heavy cloud of gloom – invisible but still palpable – floated over Stevenson's table, and those afflicted by it had little interest in anything but getting drunk.

Paniatowski recognized the mood. There had come a point in almost every investigation her own team had been involved in when it seemed as if – whatever they did – they would never crack the case. But then one of them – sometimes Woodend, sometimes Rutter, sometimes herself – would produce a slight flicker of hope, and the rest would rally round it until that flicker became a bright burning flame.

There was no evidence of such a thing happening soon in Stevenson's team. None at all. DCI Mortlake wasn't even there to give them the lead – and Stevenson herself was clearly not up to the job.

Rosemary Stevenson rose shakily to her feet, and tottered off in the general direction of the toilet. Paniatowski waited for a minute, then put her vodka glass down on the bar and followed.

By the time Paniatowski reached the loo, Stevenson was leaning against one of the basins and gazing, with bleary eyes, into the mirror.

'Well, look who it is!' Stevenson said, seeing Paniatowski's reflection behind her own. 'It's my old mate Sergeant Monika Pania ... Pania...' She turned around with some difficulty, and grabbed onto the washbasin for support. 'What are you doing here, Monika? Come to spy on me?'

Yes, that's precisely why I'm here, Paniatowski thought.

She forced a smile to her lips and said, 'Spy on you? Why ever would I want to do that. I've come for a pee.' She paused. 'But if you want to talk, I can hold off for a little bit longer.'

'Why should I ... why should I want to talk?' Stevenson asked, slurring her words.

'I just thought you might,' Paniatowski said lightly. 'But if you don't, that's fine with me, too. And even finer with my bladder!'

'You used to think you were somebody, didn't you?' Rosemary Stevenson demanded aggressively. 'Well, look at you now. And look at *me*, now? Don't you just *wish* you were me, Monika?'

'Not really,' Paniatowski said. 'It's been rough being me now and again, but I've never wanted to be anybody else.'

Stevenson nodded drunkenly. 'No, no, you probably haven't,' she agreed. She sniffed. 'Where do you find the strength from, Monika?'

'From inside myself, I suppose,' Paniatowski said. 'You'll find it inside *yourself*, too, if you bother to look.'

'Tha's ... tha's the best advice I've ever been given,' Stevenson said, swaying slightly again. 'You're my best mate, Monika. My very best mate in the whole wide world.'

'What's been upsetting you so much?' Paniatowski asked. 'Is it the investigation?'

'The investigation?' Stevenson repeated. 'What investigation? They say the first twenty-four hours are crucial, don't they? They say that if you don't get anywhere in the first twenty-four hours, you'll never get anywhere ever.'

'That's not a hard and fast rule, you know,' Paniatowski cautioned. 'Every investigation is different, and it's always possible to pull back from a slow start if you really...'

'See, if Rodney ... if DCI Mortlake ... wanted to catch mice, he'd just put the traps in the middle of the floor, then expect the mice to set them themselves,' Stevenson interrupted. She giggled. 'No, it's even worse than that. He'd ... he'd expect them to bring their own cheese.'

'So you've got no leads, then?' Paniatowski asked – and her sympathy was only half feigned.

'An' that's how he is with this case, you see,' said Stevenson, who had probably never even heard the question. 'It's almost as if he just expects the kidnapper to walk in and give himself up.' She paused. The aggressive phase of her drunkenness was well passed, and she was now entering the wallowing in self-pity phase. 'Isn't life a load of shit, Monika?' she asked. 'You always think it's going to be better this time – but it never is.'

'There's a coffee bar round the corner that I think will still be open,' Paniatowski said. 'Why don't we go there now? Once you've got a few black coffees down you, the world will start to seem like a much better place.'

'They always let you down in the end, don't

they?' Rosemary Stevenson wailed.

'Who are you talking about?' Paniatowski wondered.

'Men! They promise you the world – they promise to protect you from every little thing that might go wrong – but they never do.'

'Nobody can protect you from everything,' Paniatowski said. 'And if you thought about it, you'd come to accept that you wouldn't want them to.'

'Wouldn't I?' Stevenson asked.

'No, I don't think you would. Because if you don't have to live with your own choices, where's your self-respect going to come from?'

'Don't know what you mean,' Rosemary Stevenson said, and Paniatowski realized that she'd lost her. 'Not making any sense at all.'

'Let's go and get that coffee now,' Paniatowski suggested.

'First it was my father, then it was Martin, and now it's Rodney!' Rosemary Stevenson wailed. 'I've let them have me, but they've never given me what *I* want – what *I* really need.'

Her father, her husband, and Mortlake!

'Have you been sleeping with DCI Mortlake?' Paniatowski asked.

'What if I have?' Stevenson asked, and the aggression was suddenly back in force.

'It's a very bad idea to sleep with your boss,' Paniatowski told her. 'A very bad idea indeed.'

'He *wasn't* my boss when I started sleeping with him.'

Oh God, it was getting worse and worse,

Paniatowski thought.

'How many people have you told about the affair?' she asked.

'Does it matter?'

'Of course it matters, because if it becomes common knowledge, people will start to think that was why you got your promotion.'

'Well, how *else* would I have got it?' Rosemary Stevenson moaned. 'He promised to look after me, but now he can't catch the murderer, and everybody will think it's my fault.'

'I think we should go back to my flat,' Paniatowski said. 'You can stay there overnight, and maybe tomorrow you'll see things differently.'

'Go back to your flat?' Rosemary Stevenson repeated. 'Are you a lesbian or something?'

'No, I...'

'Because it's all right with me if you are. I'll give you what you want – as long as you'll protect me.'

'I'm not a lesbian,' Paniatowski said. 'But I will be your friend – if you'll only give me half a chance.'

'Lady Muck,' Rosemary Stevenson said, afflicted by another mood swing. 'Lady Muck being condescending to poor pissed little Rosemary! Well, it won't work, because I'm better than you any day of the week.'

'Rosemary, please try and get a grip on yourself,' Paniatowski pleaded.

'Bugger off!' Stevenson said. 'Bugger off before I rip my blouse and start screaming that you've assaulted me, you dirty lesbian, you.'

In her present mood, she'd do it, Paniatowski thought. Even if it ruined both their careers. Even if ruined both their lives.

'If you want my help, you know where to find me,' she said.

And then, before Stevenson had time to reply, she turned and walked quickly out of the toilet.

It was the pain that Peter Mainwearing became aware of initially – a dull throbbing ache in his jaw, a series of short stabbing attacks to his ribs.

Then he heard the voices.

'He's coming round,' said the first, a woman's.

'Yes, I believe he is,' replied the second, a man's.

Mainwearing opened his eyes, and discovered that he was staring up at the owners of the voices.

'Where am I?' he groaned.

'In hospital,' the man said. 'Well, you've certainly been in the wars, haven't you, old chap? Though I can assure you that your injuries are not half as bad as they're probably feeling at the moment.'

It was all coming back to him now. Mainwearing told himself – the pub, the big man with the scarred cheek who had lashed out at him...

'Had bad *is* it?' he asked.

'You have a couple of broken ribs, and several others are quite badly bruised. You also have contusions to the jaw and stomach. You're rather black and blue all over, as a matter of fact, but as I said, it feels worse than it actually is.'

263

'And will I ... do I need...?'

'You'll certainly have to take things very easy for quite a while, but there's no reason why, after a good night's rest, we shouldn't be able to let you go home in the morning.'

'The garage!' Mainwearing gasped. 'I have to get back to the garage right away.'

'Whatever do you mean, old chap?' the man asked.

'He's a mechanic, doctor,' the woman – his nurse – explained. 'He's got a small garage about half a mile from Stainsworth. My neighbour says that he does a good job.'

The doctor chuckled. 'So you're a grease-monkey, are you, old man? Well, there's absolutely no point in going to your garage now. As I think I hinted earlier, it'll be quite a while before you're changing tyres, tuning engines, and ... er ... whatever else it is that you chaps do.'

'Have to go there now,' Mainwearing said.

'I've told you that's quite impossible,' the doctor said sternly. 'There's simply no way I'm going to allow you to be discharged before the morning.'

'Then get me a phone,' Mainwearing said. 'I need a phone.'

'If there's anyone you need to call urgently, just give us their name and we'll call them for you,' the doctor said. 'But what you require now – above all else – is a good night's rest.'

'A phone!' Mainwearing said. 'Get me a phone!'

And in the end, because he was growing increasingly agitated, that was what they did.

Woodend's feet and back ached from all the walking he'd done, and for a while he'd seriously considered going home and soaking his body in a hot bath. Then he'd decided that an *internal* soaking would probably do him more good, and he was already on his third pint of medicine when Monika Paniatowski walked into the public bar of the Drum and Monkey, and joined him at their table.

'Did you manage to have a word with DS Stevenson?' Woodend asked his sergeant.

Paniatowski nodded. 'Yes, I did.'

'An' did she happen to tell you anythin' useful?'

'No, but that's because there was nothing useful to tell. The way DCI Mortlake is running his investigation makes a headless chicken look like a potential Nobel Prize winner.'

'You're sure that's true?' Woodend asked suspiciously. 'You're convinced she wasn't just feeding you a line?'

'I'm sure,' Paniatowski confirmed. 'She was not in any state to be playing mind games with anyone.'

'Are you saying she was drunk?'

'Pissed as a rat. Pissed enough to tell me that she's been having an affair with DCI Mortlake – an affair which began even before she was promoted to his team.'

'Good God!' Woodend said. 'That could ruin

them both.'

As it almost once ruined you and Bob, he added silently.

'Anyhow, the point is that they're making no headway at all in their investigation,' Paniatowski said.

Woodend sighed. 'There are some bobbies I've known in my time who've taken great delight in watchin' other bobbies fail – but I've never been one of that breed, Monika,' he said.

'I know you haven't, sir.'

'I really want Mortlake to get a result on this one. I don't even care if he gets promoted over my head because of it, as long as he finds the girl. But he's not *goin' to* find her, is he?'

'Certainly doesn't look that way,' Paniatowski agreed glumly.

'So it's up to us – an' we don't have any more of an idea of how to go about it than he does.' He paused. 'Unless, of course, you've managed to—'

'I haven't,' Paniatowski interrupted, dousing any flicker of hope her boss might have had. 'For one brief moment, this afternoon, I thought I might have found a lead – but it came to nothing.'

'Tell me about it, anyway,' Woodend suggested.

'There was this single-storeyed building, just on the edge of the area that you'd asked me to search. What got me excited about it was that though there had been windows in that back wall, they'd all been bricked in – and, from the

266

state of the brickwork, it was obvious the job had been done quite recently. Anyway, I went round to the front of the place, which was on Gladstone Street...'

'An' that was when you saw that it was Mainwearing's garage,' Woodend supplied.

'Exactly. Mainwearing's bloody garage. And not only does Mainwearing have a solid alibi for the time when Angela Jackson was snatched, but – from what I've heard in the canteen – he also appears to have one for when Mary Thomas went missing.'

'It's a right proper bugger, isn't it?' Woodend said.

'A right proper bugger,' Paniatowski echoed.

They heard the sound of the street door open, and then a familiar – and surprisingly optimistic – voice call out, 'Send us another round of drinks, will you, Jack?'

The explanation for Rutter's high spirits was not long in coming. 'I'm almost certain I know who sold the drug to the killer,' he told Woodend and Paniatowski, the moment he'd reached the table. 'His name's Norman Willis, and he used to work at the Pendleton Clinic.'

'Do we know where can find him?' Woodend asked.

'He lives in a flat on Crimea Road, but he's not there.'

'Then do we have any idea...'

'Every night, he makes a tour of half the pubs in town – and tonight was no exception. I know that because, in a couple of the boozers I visited,

267

I only missed him by a few minutes. The problem is, I don't know what order he makes his calls in.'

'Tours half the pubs in town,' Woodend mused. 'He's a heavy drinker, is he?'

'No! Far from it, in fact. He usually sticks to lemonade.'

'So what's his game?'

'What I suspect has happened is that since he's lost his job at the Pendleton Clinic, drug-pushing has ceased to be a nice little earner on the side, and is now his full-time occupation.'

'That sounds more than likely,' Woodend agreed.

'Anyway, the fact that I haven't found him yet doesn't really matter,' Rutter continued. 'He'll have to go home sometime, and when he does, he'll find Detective Constable Beresford waiting for him.'

'An' you think he'll be willing to tell us the name of the man he sold the drug to?' Woodend asked.

'Yes, after I've told him what that man used the drug for,' Rutter said. 'And if he doesn't want to tell me, I'll arrange for him to fall down the stairs a few times, to see if that makes him more cooperative.'

'That doesn't sound like you at all,' Woodend said.

'It doesn't sound like any of us,' Rutter replied. 'But I've seen what the killer did to Angela Jackson, and I'm willing to use *any* means if it will prevent the same thing happening to Mary Thomas.'

Woodend nodded. 'That goes for me too, an' all,' he said.

'And me,' Paniatowski told him.

Woodend looked at the big clock on the bar wall. It was ticking away the minutes to the closing bell – proving, with every jerk of its big hand, that time was not infinite.

Bob Rutter had said he would do anything to prevent Mary from suffering the same fate as Angela, but though none of them would admit it openly, they all knew, deep inside themselves, that whatever Dr Stevenson had theorized, it might already be too late.

Twenty-Three

Norman Willis arrived back at his flat at just after midnight, but before he'd even had time to open the main door to the block, a dark figure – in the form of DC Colin Beresford – had stepped out of the shadows and informed him that he was being arrested on suspicion of drug-dealing.

Willis had first protested his innocence, then tried to bribe Beresford from the thick roll of cash in his pocket. Finally – when else had failed – he had resorted to taking a swing at the detective constable.

It was at that point he'd learned what a number of other men who'd resorted to violence had found out before him – which was that while Beresford might have a boyish appearance, there was nothing juvenile about the feel of his fist.

Willis had gone down, and – still dazed – had been vaguely aware of Beresford slipping the handcuffs on him.

Now, half an hour later, he was sitting in an interview room in police headquarters, waiting for his interrogation to begin.

He would not have to wait long.

Rutter looked down at the man sitting at the table. Norman Willis, he decided, had just the kind of attractive features which were necessary to get a job at the Pendleton Clinic, but since he'd left the place under a cloud, he seemed to have let himself go a bit. And the black eye certainly didn't help improve his appearance.

'Police brutality,' Willis said, noticing that the inspector was examining his eye.

'Or to put it another way, Constable Beresford beat you to the punch,' Rutter said. 'But let's not waste our time buggering about with small talk – we both know we've got you cold for drug-dealing.'

'Come off it, Inspector,' Willis said. 'I hadn't got a single amphetamine on me when your lad launched his unprovoked attack.'

'But you did have thirty-three pounds in used notes on your person,' Rutter pointed out. 'Anyway, who mentioned anything about ampheta-mines? Maybe I was talking about marijuana.'

'Maybe you were,' Willis agreed.

'But pot isn't really your thing, is it? Everyone should have a speciality – and you've chosen to specialize in *prescription* drugs.'

'Like I said, you didn't find any on me,' Willis said defiantly.

Rutter laughed. 'The boys in our lab can do marvels with the new techniques they've de-veloped recently. They can examine a hundred flies and tell you precisely which one of them it was that shat on your sandwich. So, knowing that, do you really believe that they won't find traces of the drugs you were carrying when they give your clothes the once-over?'

'They were inside plas—' Willis began, then realized he'd been about to say too much, and clamped his mouth firmly shut.

'Plastic envelopes?' Rutter supplied. 'Well, maybe you're right. Maybe we won't find any traces of drugs – unless we decide to plant them ourselves.'

'You can't...'

'According to you, we're already guilty of police brutality, so why wouldn't we go the whole hog – and fit you up for drug-pushing? But to tell you the truth, Norman...' Rutter paused. 'I can call you Norman, can't I?

'I suppose so.'

'To tell you the truth, Norman, I'm not really interested in charging you with drug-dealing.'

'No?' Willis asked, suspiciously.

'No,' Rutter assured him. 'It's not worth my time and effort. Besides, what would be the point of pressing such a pissy little charge as that, when you're already going down for something much bigger?'

'Something much bigger?' Willis asked, with a tremble in his voice.

'Oh, didn't I mention that?' Rutter asked. 'We'll be charging you as an accessory before the fact in the kidnapping and murder of Angela Jackson.'

'Me?' Willis gasped.

'You,' Rutter confirmed.

'But I didn't ... I swear I never...' Willis said hoarsely. 'I promise ... I've ... I've never even met the girl.'

'I believe you,' Rutter told him. 'But you did provide the drug – halothane – that was used to dope her.'

'I didn't know it was going to be used for that,' Willis protested.

'Then what *did* you think it was going to be used for?'

'I don't know.'

'You didn't *think* at all, did you? As long as you were paid, you didn't care *what* it was used for? And that's negligence! That's why you'll end up behind bars until you're a very old man.'

'There was nothing at all in the newspapers about halothane being used,' Willis said.

'Quite right,' Rutter agreed. 'That's one of the details we decided to hold back. But it *is* what he used – and you were the one who made it

272

possible. So why don't you tell me how it happened?'

'I ... I was still working at the clinic at the time.'

'I assumed you were.'

'And ... and I was borrowing a few amphetamines from the dispensary, now and again. It was only for my personal use – you have to understand that – and I'd never have taken them at all if I hadn't been under a lot of pressure...'

'Get on with it!' Rutter growled.

'One night, this man came up to me in a pub. He said he knew I'd been nicking stuff from the clinic, and he had half a mind to report me to the police. But then he went on to say that if I got a bottle of this halothane stuff for him, he'd give me twenty quid for my trouble, and forget all about the other thing.'

Rutter slammed his hand down hard on the table. 'Do I look like a complete bloody idiot?' he demanded angrily.

'No, you—'

'Then don't try to treat me as if I was one. A man comes up to you in a pub, you say. You've never seen him before, but he not only knows who *you* are, he knows you've been stealing drugs from the clinic. And *that's* the story you want to go with, is it?'

'I didn't say I'd never seen him before,' Willis protested.

'*Had* you seen him?'

'Yes. I hadn't actually talked to him, but I'd seen him around – because he was an out-patient at the clinic.'

'What was wrong with him?'

'I don't know. But he was seeing one of the shrinks.'

'And did this man you'd seen around tell you his name?'

'Course he didn't.'

'How very convenient!'

'But I made it my business to find out, because you never know when a piece of information like that might come in useful.'

'So what *was* his name?'

Willis hesitated. 'You'll drop all that "accessory before the fact" stuff, will you?'

'As long as I don't uncover any new information which proves you knew exactly what was going on.'

'You won't – because I didn't.'

'Then you're off the hook for that.'

'An' the drug-dealing charges?'

'You're off the hook for those, too. *Now tell me his bloody name!*'

'Edgar Brunton,' Willis said.

It was two o'clock in the morning, and most of Whitebridge was asleep. The street lights were still on in the centre of the town, but the buildings they stood in front of were in darkness. The only real signs of life in the entire area emanated from police headquarters – an island of light around the duty sergeant's desk in the lobby, another around the custody sergeant's desk in the lock-up, and a third coming from an office on the administrative floor which had been assigned to DCI Woodend.

Woodend sat at his desk, his head in his hands. Facing him were Rutter and Paniatowski. None of them had spoken for some time.

It was Woodend who finally broke the silence.

'Sweet Jesus!' he groaned. 'This is a rapidly turnin' into a complete bloody nightmare. Are you absolutely certain that this Norman Willis feller was telling the truth, Bob?'

'I'm sure,' Rutter confirmed.

'So we had the right man fingered from the very start. I bloody knew we did! It wasn't just the wallet – it was my gut feeling. And then we had to let him go – because the body turned up while he was still in custody.'

'He's got to have had an accomplice,' Paniatowski said. 'That's the only way to explain it.'

'So what do we do now?' Rutter asked.

'Now we'll have to arrest the bastard again.'

'Crawley and Marlowe will never let us get away with that,' Paniatowski cautioned. 'The moment they learn we've taken him in custody, they'll suspend all three of us, and kick him loose.'

'Then we'll have to make sure they *don't* know, won't we?' Woodend said.

'And how can we ever hope to get away with that?'

'By not takin' him to headquarters.'

'Then where can we...?'

'We'll call in a few favours from the troops on the ground, an' lock him up in one of the outlyin' police stations which Marlowe pays so little attention to that he'll have almost forgotten they exist.'

'But the second we've taken him away, his wife will be on the phone to the chief constable,' Paniatowski said.

'Then we'll just have to arrest her, too.'

'On what charge?'

'Murder!'

'Murder?'

'Somebody had to smother that poor bloody girl an' then dump her body on that patch of waste land – an', at the moment, my money's firmly on Mrs Brunton.'

'You do realize that if this goes wrong, we'll all be out on our ears, don't you, sir?' Rutter asked.

'The thought had occurred to me,' Woodend admitted. 'Which is why I'm givin' both of you a chance to pull out while you still can.'

'I'm in,' Paniatowski said decisively.

'What about you, Bob?' Woodend asked.

Rutter hesitated for a second, then he grinned.

'What the hell,' he said. 'If things do go wrong, I'm still good-looking enough to get a job as a porter at the Pendleton Clinic.'

It was three-thirty in the morning when Councillor Polly Johnson – who was by choice a magistrate and by bad luck a widow – heard her front-door bell ringing. At first she tried to ignore it, but when the ringing persisted she forced herself out of bed, threw on a dressing

276

gown, and went downstairs to see who'd had the temerity to disturb her slumbers.

She looked at the big man standing in her doorway with some disdain. 'For God's sake, Charlie, what are you doing here at this time of night?' she asked.

'I need search warrants, Polly,' Woodend said apologetically. 'An' I need them in a hurry.'

'Obviously you need them in a hurry, or you'd have left it till morning,' Councillor Johnson said tartly. 'But let me be clear about this. You are talking about search warrants in the plural?'

'I am.'

Councillor Johnson put her hands on her hips. 'Life's never simple with you, is it, Charlie?' she asked. And then, without waiting for an answer, she added, 'I suppose you'd better come in, then.'

She led him into her kitchen, which was dominated by a large oak table. 'You can sit here while I go and find the warrants,' she said. 'If you want a beer...'

'I wouldn't mind...'

'...then you're out of luck, because there's none in the house. If you want whisky, there's a bottle in that cupboard over there, and you'll find glasses next to the sink.'

When she returned, five minutes later, Polly Johnson had a sheaf of warrants in her hand, and had clearly applied a little light make-up to her face.

Woodend, who had already taken up her offer of a drink, said, 'Shall I pour a whisky for you?'

'Jesus, no!' Councillor Johnson said, sitting down opposite him. 'Not everybody has your cast-iron stomach, you know.'

'When you've heard what I have to say, you might need it,' Woodend advised her. Then he filled a second glass, and placed it in front of her. 'The first warrant is for Edgar Brunton's house,' he continued.

'Is this in reference to the Angela Jackson case?'

'Yes. An' the Mary Thomas case.'

'As far as Edgar Brunton goes, you've already had one bite at that particular cherry,' Councillor Johnson reminded him.

'I've got it right this time,' Woodend promised her.

'I hope you have,' Polly Johnson said. 'Because if you haven't, I'm going to find myself shunned at the few social functions I still attend.' She took a slug of the whisky Woodend had poured her, filled in the warrant, then said, 'What are the others for?'

'I don't know,' Woodend admitted.

'When *will* you know?'

'When I've searched Brunton's house.'

'At which point you can come back here and I'll fill them in for you.'

'There may not be time for that,' Woodend said. 'We've no idea what state the poor kid's *already* in.'

'So you expect me just to give you carte blanche, do you?' Polly Johnson asked.

Woodend grinned. 'Of course not,' he said. 'I

just want you to give me warrants in which the only part that has been filled in is your signature.'

Polly Johnson shook her head. 'I won't do it, Charlie,' she said. 'I *can't* do it, based on what little you've told me.'

'Once before, in the Dugdale's Farm murder, I asked you to take a chance on me,' Woodend reminded her. 'We had even less to go on then than we have now – but we still managed to put a senior policeman, a buildin' tycoon, an' a police surgeon behind bars.'

'Maybe we were just lucky,' Polly Johnson said.

'An' maybe we'll be lucky this time,' Woodend countered.

'I hate it when you put me in this position, Charlie,' Polly Johnson said. 'I really *hate* it!'

Then she drained the rest of her whisky, and signed her name at the bottom of the warrants.

It was five minutes past four when Woodend knocked loudly on the door of the Brunton home, and had his hammering answered by a sleepy live-in maid.

'I have a warrant here to search these premises,' he said, showing the document to her.

'The mister and missis in bed,' the maid replied, speaking with a foreign accent thick enough to wrap butter in.

'Then you'll just have to get them *out of bed*, won't you?' Woodend said.

But that did not prove to be necessary, because

by the time he'd stepped past the maid and entered the hallway, Edgar Brunton had appeared at the head of the stairs.

'Not again!' he groaned angrily. 'I would have thought you'd learned your lesson last time.'

'I shall be takin' you in for questionin', while my colleagues search the house,' Woodend told him.

'You wouldn't dare!' said an outraged female voice, and Mrs Brunton appeared on the staircase next to her husband.

'Let's not make this any more difficult than we have to, madam,' Woodend said evenly. 'I've got my job to do, an' I intend to do it.'

'Your job?' Mrs Brunton repeated scornfully. 'You want even *have* a job by lunchtime!'

Maybe she was right, Woodend thought – but it was too late to turn back now.

Twenty-Four

It was at five-fifteen in the morning that the two officers on motor patrol in the town centre noticed there was a man lying on the pavement outside the Crown and Anchor.

'Dead by reason of heart attack?' PC Roger Crabtree asked his partner, PC Dave Warner.

'More like dead by reason of drunk,' Warner replied.

'Think we should take him in?'

'Don't see why not. He looks very untidy, lyin' where he is, an' it'll at least show the sarge that we've been keepin' busy.'

Crabtree pulled the patrol car into the kerb, and the two officers got out. The stink of stale beer which surrounded the supine man was unmistakable, and if further proof were needed of Warner's assertion that he was drunk, there was a pile of vomit near his head which more than provided it.

Crabtree squatted down, and prodded the man. 'Can you stand up on your own, or are we goin' to have to help you?' he asked loudly.

The drunk groaned. 'All right where I am.'

'I'm afraid that's not the case, sir,' Crabtree said. 'Give it a couple more hours and people will either have to step round you or step over you, so we think it's best if we take you down to the station.'

'Piss off!' the drunk growled.

'I'm sorry, but that sort of attitude will get you nowhere, sir,' Crabtree said, in a mock-prim tone he'd been practising. He turned to his partner. 'Help me get him on his feet.'

They took an arm each, and hauled the drunk up. He was a big man, but so far gone that the only sort of resistance he was capable of was inertia.

It was something of a struggle to bundle him into the patrol car, and it was not until he was lolling on the back seat that they got a proper look at his face.

'Ugly bugger, isn't he?' Crabtree asked.

'Certainly wouldn't win any beauty contests,' Warner agreed. He tilted his head to one side to examine the man from a different angle, then announced grandly, 'We've made an arrest.'

'You don't say?' Crabtree responded. 'Is *that* why he's sittin' in the back of our car?'

'What I mean is, we've made a *real* arrest, rather than just a drunk and disorderly,' Warner explained. 'I recognize this feller. His name's Wally Decker, an' he's wanted for beatin' the shit out of some pervert in a pub yesterday.'

Topton was a moorland village, served by a small stone police station which also had responsibility for the countless isolated farms scattered all over the moors. Woodend had selected it because he knew that the sergeant in charge was close to retirement, regarded Whitebridge as a place which had almost no relevance to him, and didn't give a bugger what the chief constable thought or did. Besides, as small as it was, the police station still had two cells, so that it was possible to keep Brunton and his wife separated.

He arrived there, with his prisoners, at twenty past five. By half-past, he had them both booked in, and was confronting Edgar Brunton across the table in what the local sergeant chose to call the interview room, but was more often used as a kitchen.

'I want to speak to my solicitor,' Brunton said.

'An' you're perfectly within your rights to

make that request, sir,' Woodend said. 'Shall I ring his office now?'

'There'll be nobody there at this time of day,' Brunton said.

'So there won't,' Woodend agreed. 'In that case, we'd better wait until there is, hadn't we?'

'You could ring him at home.'

'I don't like to disturb him, so I think we'll wait for normal business hours. An' if, in the meantime, you don't feel like talkin' without your legal representative bein' present, then you're under absolutely no obligation to do so.'

'Thank you for explaining the law to me, Mr Woodend,' Brunton said, with a sneer.

'My pleasure,' Woodend replied. He leaned back in his chair. 'I used to wonder what made you hate women,' he continued, conversationally, 'but havin' spent half an hour in a car with your missis, I don't wonder any more. What a mouth that woman's got on her.'

Brunton said nothing.

'What's the matter?' Woodend asked. 'Afraid to agree with me, in case I tell her all about it? Worried that if I *do* tell her, she'll tighten the purse strings an' you'll actually have to earn a proper livin', instead of just poncin' about an' *playin'* at bein' a solicitor?'

Brunton looked up at the ceiling.

'Maybe the reason for your sudden feelings of loyalty is that you think the reason she killed Angela Jackson was to save your bacon,' Woodend suggested. 'Well, you're right about that in a way – but *only* in a way. Her real reasons were purely selfish. If she hadn't killed Angela, you'd have gone to jail, an' she'd no longer have had any power over you. Whereas by *killin'* the girl, she's put you more in her debt than ever. If you got away with this – an' you won't – she'd make your life so miserable that the prospect of bein' banged up for thirty years would start to look very appealin'.'

Having completed his examination of the ceiling, Brunton turned his attention to the walls.

'What I'm offerin' you, you see, is a chance of escape,' Woodend pressed on. 'You can argue at your trial that while you admit to torturin' the girl, you never had any intention of killin' her. With a bit of luck, you shouldn't get more than ten years for that. On the other hand, your wife, who *did* kill Angela, will still be inside when she'd drawin' her old-age pension.'

'Have you checked out my wife's alibi for the time the girl was killed?' Brunton asked. A smile came to his face. 'No, I can see you haven't.'

'Are you tellin' me that she's got one?' Woodend asked.

'I don't know for sure, one way or the other. But I would be very surprised if she *hasn't* got one. She needs to have people constantly around her, you see. As far as she's concerned, if there's nobody within easy bullying distance, she doesn't really exist.'

'So if she didn't kill the girl, who did?'

'I wonder how long it will take Henry Marlowe to discover I'm here,' Brunton mused.

'I wouldn't worry about that, if I was you,' Woodend advised. 'You've got bigger concerns to deal with.'

'And I wonder how long *after that* it will be before you find yourself clearing out your desk,' Edgar Brunton said.

Monika Paniatowski glanced up at the clock on the wall of Brunton's study.

Eight thirty-five!

What little advantage their early start had given them was rapidly slipping away, she thought. By now Whitebridge Police Headquarters would be coming to life. Within an hour, someone – perhaps Edgar Brunton's secretary – would begin to wonder what had happened to him, and would only need to ring the maid in order to be told he had been arrested by three police officers who had absolutely nothing to do with the official investigation.

This search had to come up with a lead *soon*, Paniatowski told herself.

The lease to a lock-up garage.

The deeds to a quiet cottage.

Something – anything! – that they could use one of the blank search warrants to investigate.

The phone rang, and Paniatowski picked it up.

'Any luck at your end?' asked the voice on the other end of the line.

'None,' Paniatowski replied. 'How's Brunton holding up?'

'Far too bloody well,' Woodend admitted. 'He's as guilty as sin, but he still seems to believe he has the upper hand.'

That's because he has, Paniatowski thought. The whole investigation's unravelling before our eyes – and there's nothing we can do about it.

'We need to find out how much time we've got left,' Woodend said, with an edge of desperation to his voice.

'How do we do that?' Paniatowski wondered. 'Ring Superintendent Crawley and ask him just how close he is to guessing that we've broken nearly every rule in the book?' She put her hand to her mouth, horrified at what she'd just heard herself say. 'Sorry, sir,' she continued. 'That was uncalled for.'

'It's all right, Monika,' Woodend told her. 'We're *all* a bit edgy.'

'What would you like us to do?' Paniatowski asked contritely.

'I think one of you should put in an appearance at headquarters. Don't speak to anyone you don't have to, but keep your ear to the ground. If it seems to you that the game's nearly up, ring me, an' I'll put more pressure on Brunton.'

'What kind of pressure?'

'Oh, I don't know,' Woodend said – and Paniatowski could tell from the tone of his voice that he'd forced a grin to his face. 'Maybe I'll take a leaf out of Brunton's own book, an' resort to torture.'

'Why not?' Paniatowski said, forcing herself to grin, too. 'Everybody should have a hobby.' She hung up the phone.

'Anything?' asked Rutter from the other side of the room – though there was no evidence of hope in his voice.

'The boss wants one of us to go to headquarters and check things out, while the other carries on the search here. Do you want me to go, or will you?'

Rutter shrugged. 'You go. Since we're all going to hang, it doesn't really matter which of us puts his head in the noose first, does it?'

Twenty-Five

The sun had recently risen, and was casting a warm golden light over the moors. It was going to be a beautiful day, Woodend thought, looking out of the window – at least, it was going to be a beautiful day for *some* people.

He turned around, to face the woman who was sitting at the table in the interview room/kitchen.

When they'd pulled her husband in the first time – in the autumn – Brunton had hinted that the reason she married him was to improve her position in Whitebridge society. Well, maybe there was something in that, Woodend thought, but he didn't think that was the only reason.

She'd been forced to dress hurriedly after her arrest, and looking at her now – without the benefit of her make-up and expensive coiffure – he had to admit that Monika had been spot on when she'd said that Mrs Brunton was plain. And how would such a plain woman have felt when Edgar Brunton – her impoverished but handsome Prince Charming – started paying attention to her? The most likely answer was that she'd been swept off her feet!

So maybe she really *did* love him – and all her bullying was nothing more than a pathetic effort to make sure that she did not lose him.

'If I was in your position, I'd be seriously considerin' what was in my own best interest, Mrs Brunton,' Woodend said. 'Because you know what's goin' to happen if you don't, don't you? Your husband's goin' to stand up in court an' say it was never his intention to kill the girl, an' that it was all your idea.'

'You're mad,' Mrs Brunton said. 'You're completely out of your mind.'

'Your husband's wallet was found at the scene of the first kidnappin' an' we can produce a witness to prove that he bought the drug the girl was doped with. That alone is enough to convict him,' Woodend said wearily. 'It's all over, so why don't you save us all a lot of effort an' just come clean?'

'My husband had nothing to do with the kidnapping and murder of that girl – and neither did I.'

'Why was he seein' a shrink, Mrs Brunton?' Woodend asked. 'An' you must have *known* that he was seein' a shrink – because you're the one who was payin' all the bills.'

From the tortured expression on her face, it was all too clear that Mrs Brunton's mind was in turmoil.

She wants to confess, Woodend thought. She wants to get it off her chest. All it will take is one more push. 'Why don't you come clean?' he suggested softly.

Mrs Brunton sighed. 'You're not going to ease up until I tell you the whole truth, are you?' she asked.

'No,' Woodend agreed. 'I'm not.'

'Don't you even care about how humiliating it will be for me?'

'No, I don't – because I'm tryin' to save a young girl's life.'

'What I have to tell you has nothing to do with her,' Mrs Brunton said.

'Let me be the judge of that,' Woodend countered.

Mrs Brunton sighed again. 'All right,' she said resignedly. 'Edgar puts on a good show of being in charge, but that's all it is – a show. Strip away the smooth veneer, and what you will find underneath is a frightened little boy whose mother used to lock him in the cupboard under the stairs – for hours at a time! – whenever he misbehaved.'

'I don't see what this has to do with the matter in hand,' Woodend said.

'You will, if you'll shut up and listen for a minute,' Mrs Brunton said fiercely. 'Why do you think that the people who matter in this town – most of whom are Edgar's friends – don't take their business to him? It's because they know him well enough to have seen that frightened little boy – and they prefer to have their affairs managed by someone more competent – more *adult*.'

'This is getting' us nowhere,' Woodend said exasperatedly. 'I've asked you why he was seein' a shrink. Why don't you answer that one simple question?'

'He's been seeing Dr Stevenson because he has violent fantasies about women.'

'I think you've just made my case for me,' Woodend said.

Mrs Brunton laughed mockingly. 'I've done no such thing. He has the fantasies – but not the backbone to make them real.'

'You don't really know him,' Woodend said.

'On the contrary, I know him far too *well*.' Mrs Brunton looked down at the table, and Woodend noticed that her hands had started to tremble 'There was a time – when I still hoped our marriage might become more than a sham – when I was more than willing to indulge those fantasies of his,' she continued bitterly. 'I even offered to be involved in them myself. Do you understand what I'm saying? I gave him *permission* to hurt me. And he couldn't do it! He hadn't got the strength to inflict even *minor* pain on me. So don't tell me he tortured that girl. He'd never have had the nerve!'

Woodend turned away, so that Mrs Brunton couldn't see the troubled look on his face.

The problem was that he believed her when she said *she* didn't believe her husband could have tortured the girl.

And even if she was wrong about that – and she had almost convinced him that she wasn't – he was now certain that she herself had had absolutely nothing to do with Angela's death!

Before she'd even entered police headquarters, Monika Paniatowski had already made a conscious decision to stay there for half an hour, and no more.

Thirty minutes! Just long enough to establish whether or not Marlowe and Crawley had any idea that there was a mutiny going on below decks, and not quite long enough for anyone to begin wondering what she was doing, and if *she* knew where Woodend was.

Once inside, she glided around the building almost like a ghost – hearing what was being said, seeing what was happening, but touching nothing and leaving no impression of herself anywhere. Yet she was far from unaffected by the experience. Just observing the normal life of the station taught her something she should already have known for some time – that the three of them, herself, Rutter, and Woodend, were further out on a limb than they'd ever been before; that they'd reached the point of no return.

The thirty minutes she'd allowed herself soon passed, and though she'd heard nothing to suggest that the powers that be were aware of what was going on in Brunton's house and Topton police station, she felt no sense of relief – because she knew it could only be a matter of time before they did.

As she walked down the corridor which led to the car park, she turned her mind to the search that Rutter was still conducting at Brunton's home, and in which she would soon be joining him.

They would find nothing, she told herself. They'd been fools to ever imagine that they would.

'Sergeant Paniatowski!' boomed a voice in the corridor behind her.

Superintendent Crawley! she thought. Bloody Superintendent Bloody Crawley!

She froze, rearranged her face into a look of complete innocence, then turned around. 'Yes, sir?'

'Are you busy at the moment, Sergeant?'

'Yes, sir, as a matter of fact, I am.'

'Only, as it happens, I've got a little job I would like you to do for me.'

'As I've just said, sir, I'm always willing to help out in any way I can, but I really am rather—'

'Don't give me a hard time, Sergeant,' Crawley growled. 'You're one of the few officers in this building not involved in the search for young Mary Thomas. And we all know why that is, don't we?'

Yes! Because you and your arse-licking cronies pulled me off the case, Paniatowski thought viciously. Because you decided you knew better than Cloggin'-it Charlie, whereas, the truth is, you haven't got a bloody clue what's going on.

'I said we all know why that is, don't we?' Crawley repeated.

'Yes, sir, I expect we all *do* know,' Paniatowski replied, through gritted teeth.

'So, bearing that in mind, I don't think it's unreasonable of me to expect you to take on a minor job which will relieve the pressure on those of us who are doing the real work,' Crawley said.

Paniatowski sighed. 'What is it you want me to do, sir?'

'An old friend of yours got beaten up in the Dog and Duck yesterday.'

'An old friend?'

'Peter Mainwearing.'

'I'd scarcely call him an old—'

'Anyway, the uniformed branch have only just got round to collaring the man who committed the assault. Now, if it was left up to me, we'd give the feller a medal, but we still have to do things by the book, apparently, so somebody needs to take his statement and charge him. And that someone, Sergeant Paniatowski, is going to be you.'

'I'll get right onto it, sir,' Paniatowski said.

It had been easy enough to make the joke about getting a job as a porter at the Pendleton Clinic, but the joke was wearing a bit thin now, Bob

293

Rutter thought, as he surveyed the pile of documents on Edgar Brunton's desk.

The team had been hopelessly optimistic to ever imagine, even for a moment, that if there *were* any incriminating documents which might lead them to where the girl was being held, Brunton would have been stupid enough to leave them in his own home.

Such documents – if they even existed – would be safely tucked away in a safe-deposit box, in a bank somewhere. And though someone with determination could probably track them down eventually, the only people who *had* that determination would already be out on the street.

The phone rang.

Was it Woodend, desperate to hear that he'd found something useful? Rutter wondered. Or was it Paniatowski, calling to tell him that Marlowe and Crawley were already onto them?

Rutter picked up the phone.

'Edgar?' asked a hoarse, worried voice at the other end of the line.

'Yes,' Rutter replied, in a tone a little deeper than his normal one.

'Your voice sounds strange. What's the matter?'

'I have a cold.'

'But that didn't stop you from going out last night, did it?'

Whoever the caller was, he seemed to be having difficulty with his breathing, Rutter thought.

'Please tell me it didn't stop you seeing her?'

the man on the other end of the line begged.

'No. It didn't stop me seeing her,' Rutter agreed.

'And how is she?'

The unknown caller was talking about Mary Thomas, Rutter thought. He *had* to be talking about Mary Thomas!

'She was scared out of her wits,' Rutter said.

There was a pause long, then the caller said, 'Who are you?'

'I'm Edgar.'

'No, you're not,' the caller said with a horrified gasp. 'Edgar would have described it better. Edgar would have told me *just* how she was feeling.'

Rutter could no longer hear the other man's heavy breathing, but now there was a new sound – a slow, rhythmic banging.

The bastard's dropped the phone, he thought. He's dropped it so suddenly that it's swinging from side to side, and banging against the walls of the booth.

And then Rutter heard something else – a metallic voice which said, 'Would Dr Traynor please report to Casualty.'

Appearances could sometimes be deceptive, Paniatowski thought on first seeing Walter Decker from the door of the interview room – but that didn't seem to be a very likely possibility in this case.

Decker not only looked like a thug, but his record confirmed that was exactly what he was

– and, it also suggested, not a very bright one.

Paniatowski crossed the room, and sat down opposite him. 'You've been advised of your rights, have you?' she asked.

Decker sniffed. 'I suppose so.'

'So you know that anything you say can be taken down and used in evidence against you?'

'Yeah, yeah, I know the drill,' Decker said. 'Let's get it over with, shall we?'

'All right,' Paniatowski agreed. 'Your name is Walter Archibald Decker, you're thirty-eight years old, a jobbing builder, and you reside at 38 Wesley Terrace. Is that correct?'

'Reside?' Decker repeated, questioningly.

'Is that where you *live*?'

'Oh, yeah.'

'This is not the first time you've been arrested for violent assault, is it, Mr Decker?' Paniatowski asked.

Decker's lip curled. 'He had it comin',' he said.

Paniatowski looked down at the record sheet in front of her. 'Who had it coming?' she asked. 'Are you talking about Peter Mainwearing, who you kicked the shit out of in the Dog and Duck? Or do you mean Simon Burgess, whose arm you broke a couple of years ago? Perhaps it was neither of those men. Perhaps Harold Decker – who I assume is your brother – had it coming. Then again, it could just as easily have been...'

'All right, so I've got a bit of a temper,' Decker admitted.

'Let's talk about the attack on Mr Mainwearing,' Paniatowski suggested. 'Did he provoke you in any way?'

'You could say that.'

'*How* did he provoke you?'

'He provoked me by bein' what he was. He provoked me, 'cos after I worked for him, all my mates said I must be a pervert, just like him. But I didn't know! When I built that room for him, I had no idea he was a perv.'

Paniatowski felt a sudden, unexpected tingling in her nerve endings. 'Room? What room?' she asked.

'At the back of the garage.'

'What was it? A toilet? A kitchen?'

'No, it was just a plain room,' Decker said, obviously mystified by this new line of questioning. 'Must have been for storin' things in, or somethin'.'

'What makes you say that?'

'Well, he told me to brick up all the windows, didn't he? An' he got me to put in this heavy steel door.'

'Did you see anything of particular value in the garage?' Paniatowski asked. 'Something he would have needed to keep secure? Something he would have wanted to protect behind a steel door?'

'No, there was just the usual sort of clobber you'd expect to find in a workin' garage.'

'So why did Mainwearing need a room which was so secure at all?' Paniatowski wondered.

Decker shrugged. 'Never really thought about it,' he said.

No, I bet you didn't, Paniatowski thought. I bet you don't think about much at all – other than boozing and beating people up.

The ambulance and the police cars arrived at Mainwearing's Garage almost simultaneously, the fire engine a little later.

It took the firemen fifteen minutes to burn their way through the steel door with their oxy-acetylene cutting tools, and when they had it finally opened it, the stench which wafted out of the room – a mixture of sweat and fear and faeces – was almost overpowering.

The girl was naked, and huddled in the corner of the room. She seemed to have no idea who these people were, or that they had come to rescue her, but she did not resist when she was wrapped in a blanket and carried out to the waiting ambulance.

The doctor who examined her said later that she had suffered very little bodily abuse and that – physically, at least – she should make a full recovery.

Twenty-Six

There had never been an armchair in Interview Room Two before, and the only reason there was one there now was because it had been deemed unreasonable to ask the suspect to sit on one of the straight-backed chairs.

Woodend looked down at the man in the armchair, and said, 'You'll never guess what they're doin' downstairs.'

'You should never have had me brought here,' Peter Mainwearing complained. 'I'm a sick man. It isn't right.'

'Bollocks!' Woodend said lightly. 'If you were well enough to be discharged from hospital, you're well enough to be questioned by me.' He paused. 'Don't you *want* to know what they're doin' downstairs?'

Mainwearing sighed. 'What are they doing downstairs?' he asked.

'They're havin' a whip-round for Wally Decker's defence fund. Funny that, isn't it? A couple of hours ago, he was nothin' but a common thug, an' they wouldn't have pissed in his mouth if his throat was on fire. But now he's a hero – the feller who kicked the shit out of Peter Mainwearin' – an' the boys in blue want to get him the best lawyer that money can buy.'

'I'm tired of this conversation,' Mainwearing said.

'Fair enough,' Woodend said easily. 'I'll do all the talkin', then, shall I? An' don't you go worryin' about that bein' any hardship on me – because I love the sound of my own voice.'

'You're a buffoon,' Mainwearing said.

'The last time I interviewed you, you warned me that sex offenders are very good actors – an' you were quite right about that,' Woodend said. 'When I realized that Edgar Brunton had to have had an accomplice, the first person who came into my head was his wife. I never thought of you. Partly, of course, that was because you had an alibi. But partly it was because you were so convincin' during that interview that I really thought you were what you were pretendin' to be – a reformed sex offender, weighed down by guilt for his past mistakes.'

Mainwearing smirked. 'Yes, I could see that I had you completely fooled,' he said.

'But now you've given up playin' games with me, have you?'

'What would be the point in continuing them? You have enough evidence to convict me a dozen times over, so why pretend any longer? Now, finally, I am free to act like the man I really am – the man I am proud to be!'

'The man who tortures little girls?'

'The man who knows what he wants out of life, and – unlike most of the miserable creatures who attempt to pass themselves off as men – has

300

the courage to take it!'

'Well, you certainly *did* have me fooled,' Woodend admitted. 'Your partner, on the other hand, put up a very poor showin'. I knew he was guilty right from the offset.'

'Don't call Brunton my partner!' Mainwearing snarled.

'Then what *should* I call him? Your assistant?'

'My disciple would be more accurate,' Mainwearing said. 'My *slave* would be even closer. He would have been nothing without me. He would never have achieved anything at all on his own.'

'You almost sound as if you despise him,' Woodend said.

'I do despise him.'

'Oh, I don't think that can be quite true,' Woodend said airily. 'After all, you sacrificed a great deal of the pleasure you'd been anticipating by killin' Angela Jackson earlier than you'd intended to. Because it's not the same, inflictin' the wounds after she's dead, now is it?'

'Not the same at all,' Mainwearing agreed.

'An' why would you have made the sacrifice, if it wasn't to save a dear friend?'

'You really are a fool,' Mainwearing said. 'I didn't do it to protect Edgar Brunton.'

'No?'

'No! I did it to protect myself. If he'd been in police custody for much longer, I simply couldn't have trusted him not to betray me.'

'You mustn't have thought he was much of a disciple, then, must you?' Woodend asked. He frowned. 'Are you sure you were the one in charge? The only reason I ask is that he seems to have made most of the runnin'.'

'What are you talking about?'

'Well, you did the first kidnapping together – or, at least, you each played a part in it. Brunton snatched the girl in the park, put her in the boot of your car and drove to a point close to the bus station, which is where you took over. You did it that way so you'd both have partial alibis, didn't you?'

'Of course!'

'But Brunton snatched Mary Thomas all by himself. Now why was that? Because you'd bungled your part of the first kidnappin' – an' he wasn't goin' to trust you again?'

'I *ordered* Brunton to grab Mary Thomas,' Mainwearing said angrily. 'I decided he should do it because I thought that, as a result of the way *you* bungled the first kidnapping investigation, you had placed him above any suspicion of taking part in the second.'

And you were right about that, Woodend thought. Nobody even considered asking Brunton for an alibi covering the time when Mary Thomas was snatched.

'Did you also order him to get the drug that was used to dope Angela Jackson?' he asked Mainwearing.

'Of course.'

'An' did you tell him where to get it from?'

'Yes.'

'Specifically?'

'Yes, *specifically*. I told him to get it from the Pendleton Clinic.'

'Where he was a patient, and you weren't.'

'So what?'

'So why did you choose the Pendleton Clinic? Why not Whitebridge General, instead?'

'I had my reasons.'

'An' what were they?'

'I forget.'

'There's another thing that's been puzzlin' me,' Woodend said. 'How did the two of you ever happen to link up in the first place?'

Mainwearing looked at him blankly. 'I don't understand,' he said.

'I should have thought it was a simple enough question,' Woodend said. 'Did you meet at school?'

'No.'

'In the army?'

'No.'

'Through some interest that you shared? I mean *another* interest. One that didn't involve torturin' little girls.'

'No.'

'So it must have been through a classified advert in the *Perverts' Weekly*.'

'There's no such magazine – and I'd never have risked using it if there had been.'

Woodend shrugged his shoulders. 'Then I give up,' he said. 'How *did* you first get together?'

Mainwearing was beginning to look distinctly uncomfortable – perhaps even frightened. 'I don't want to talk about it,' he said.

'Let's move onto somethin' else, then,' Woodend suggested. 'I assume that since you were the
master, and Brunton was the slave, it was your
idea to put in the spyhole.'

'What spyhole?' Mainwearing asked.

'The one set into the wall, between your
garage an' the derelict buildin' next door.'

'There *is* no such spyhole.'

'I can assure you there is,' Woodend told him.
'It's quite cleverly hidden, but even so, it didn't
take our technical boys more than a few minutes
to find.'

'You're making this up!' Mainwearing said,
getting angry again. 'I don't know why you're
doing it, but you have to be making it up.'

'That's certainly one possibility,' Woodend
admitted. 'But there's another one, isn't there?
Maybe it was Edgar Brunton who installed the
spyhole. Maybe he wasn't quite as submissive
to your wishes as you like to believe. Maybe
instead of you playin' him, he was really playin'
you.'

'Impossible!' Mainwearing said. 'He wouldn't
have dared do something like that without my
permission. And anyway, why should he want
to?'

The door opened, and Superintendent Crawley
walked into the room. He looked first at Woodend, then at Mainwearing, then back at Woodend again, and said, 'Thank you, Mr Woodend,
you may leave now.'

'What!' Woodend exploded.

'You're dismissed,' Crawley said. 'I'll take

over from here.'

'But it's my collar,' Woodend growled.

'How could it *possibly* be your collar, when you weren't even assigned to the case?'

'It's my collar because I'm the one who arrested the bugger.'

'And if a uniformed constable, pulled off the street, had made the arrest, would that have made it *his* collar?'

'You'd never have caught this swine if it hadn't been for me.'

'I think you over-estimate both your own importance and your contribution to the investigation, Chief Inspector,' the superintendent said coldly. 'We were closing in on Mainwearing and Brunton. We'd have had them in custody by lunchtime, even without your help.'

'That's bullshit, an' you know it,' Woodend said.

'You have two choices, Chief Inspector,' Crawley told him. 'You can leave without another word, and I will include some mention of your contribution to the case in my report. Or you can continue to defy me, and I will bring you up on charges of insubordination. Which is it to be?'

What was the point in arguing, Woodend thought. He'd always told Rutter and Paniatowski that his main interest in the case was not self-advancement, but to save the girl. Well, the girl *had been* saved, hadn't she? So why not live up to his word? Why not go quietly?

'I asked you which it is to be?' Crawley

repeated.

'I'll leave now,' Woodend said.

The superintendent nodded gravely. 'A very wise decision, and one I'm sure you'll not regret.'

Woodend walked over to the door, opened it, and stepped out into the corridor. Then he froze for a second, as if some nagging doubt at the back of his mind had suddenly been resolved. And when he moved again, it was not to go down the corridor, but to step back into the interview room.

'There was a note pinned to Angela Jackson's body,' he told Mainwearing. 'It said somethin' like, "This is a gift from the Invisible Man to all my fellow sufferers everywhere." Did you write that? Or was it yet again a case of Brunton – your *supposed* underling – takin' the initiative?'

'I wrote it.'

'On what?'

'On a piece of cardboard I'd torn off a baked-beans box.'

'Chief Inspector...' Crawley said.

'So you're the Invisible Man, are you, Mr Mainwearing?' Woodend asked, totally ignoring the superintendent.

'Of course I am,' Mainwearing replied. 'You didn't think it was that pathetic wretch Edgar Brunton, did you?'

'I did for a while, but now I see I was quite wrong.'

'Mr Woodend, I really must insist that you leave now,' Crawley said forcefully.

Woodend turned towards him. 'I've got one more question for Mr Mainwearin', an' then I'll go,' he promised.

Crawley strode angrily across the room, and pushed Woodend into the doorway.

'You'll leave *now*!' he shouted.

The expression on Woodend's face was probably enough to tell Crawley that he'd just made a big mistake, but if it wasn't, then Woodend's grabbing him by the lapels, swinging him round, and slamming him against the wall certainly succeeded in getting the message across.

'How dare you?' Crawley gasped.

'Listen to me, you stupid bastard!' Woodend said, with considerable menace. 'I'm goin' to ask Mainwearin' one more question, an' if you interrupt, I'll drop you where you stand. Understood?'

'This is ... this is totally outrageous,' Crawley spluttered.

'Understood?' Woodend repeated.

'Since I have no intention of indulging in further fisticuffs with a man from a lower rank, I have no choice but to agree. But I warn you—'

'Good,' Woodend interrupted. 'Now here's the question, Mr Mainwearin' – why *do* you call yourself the Invisible Man?'

Mainwearing gave him another totally blank look. 'I don't understand what you mean,' he said.

Twenty-Seven

It was early afternoon, and the two men were walking along that section of the canal bank which ran close by the University of Central Lancashire. They were dressed similarly – Woodend in his customary hairy sports jacket, Martin Stevenson in the same tweed jacket and brown trousers he had been wearing when the chief inspector had first met him. They were moving at a leisurely pace, which suggested that even if they had a particular destination in mind, they were in no hurry to get there – and that what really mattered was the conversation they were having en route.

'I have to confess to you, Chief Inspector, that I'm feeling rather guilty,' Stevenson said.

Woodend chuckled. 'I thought you trick cyclists always preached that guilt was nothin' but a weight around your neck, an' that it should be thrown off at the earliest opportunity,' he said.

'It's not quite as simple as that,' Stevenson replied seriously. 'What I actually tell my patients is that if the guilt is there – and if it has good reason to be there – they must find a way to assuage it.'

'So what are *you* feelin' guilty about?'

'That I never raised the possibility that there might be two men involved in the kidnapping and murder, rather than just one. But, you see, it was really a very remote possibility. The only recent case I can think of is that of the Moors Murders, and the two people involved in that – Myra Hindley and Ian Brady – were very much *disorganized* killers, who murdered largely on impulse. And that sets them a world apart from people like Mainwearing and Brunton.'

'Is your guilt assuaged now you've explained to me why you couldn't really have known?' Woodend asked.

Stevenson smiled wanly. 'Not really,' he admitted. 'Because there's a part of me which will keep insisting that I *should* have seen the possibility.'

'Perhaps it might make you feel a little better if you could help sort a couple of other things that are still puzzlin' me,' Woodend suggested.

'Perhaps it might,' Stevenson agreed.

'I've interrogated any number of murderers in my time,' Woodend said, 'an' one thing they've all had in common, once they've admitted to the crime, is a willingness to fill me in on all the details. They seem to want me on their side, you see – as if *that's* goin' to make any difference to the eventual outcome – an' they see cooperatin' fully as being a part of that. Now, it wasn't like that with Brunton an' Mainwearin'. They were very open about some things, but very cagey about others. An' I was wonderin' why that should be.'

'Would you care to give me a specific example?' Stevenson asked.

'Certainly. They both denied any knowledge of the spyhole.'

'The spyhole? What spyhole?'

'Sorry, I didn't explain that, did I?' Woodend said. 'There was a spyhole in the wall between the house next door an' the room where the girl was bein' held. Now what kind of man is it who'll confess to torturin' a girl, but refuse to admit he's been watchin' her through the wall?'

'A very strange kind of man,' Stevenson said pensively. 'And certainly not a kind that I've ever come across myself. I suppose there's no chance that this spyhole was there previously – that it had nothing to do with Brunton and Mainwearing's activities?'

'You're suggestin' that a previous tenant of the house next door might have installed it to spy on a previous tenant of the garage?'

'Yes, essentially.'

'It's a temptin' theory. But, you see, Mainwearin' had that room completely rebuilt by a jobbin' builder called Decker, an' during that rebuild, the spyhole was bound to have been discovered.'

'Then I can't explain it,' Stevenson said.

'No matter, let's move on to somethin' else,' Woodend said easily. 'There are other questions I put to Mainwearin' that he seemed unable to answer.'

'You mean *wouldn't* answer?'

'No, I meant exactly what I said. He should have known the answers – but he plainly didn't.'

'For instance?'

'He signed himself the "Invisible Man". I think I must have told you that before...'

'Yes, you did.'

'...and there's no doubt that he was the one who left the note which was nailed to Angela Jackson, because he described the piece of cardboard on which it was written perfectly. But, you see, he can't tell me *why* he chose that name for himself. So I'm thinkin' that maybe it's buried deep in his subconscious...'

'That's a possibility.'

'...an' that we just might be able to unlock that subconscious mind by the use of hypnotism.' Woodend paused. 'Do you use hypnotism yourself, Doc?'

'I have done,' Stevenson said. 'On occasion.'

'An' does it work?'

'It depends on exactly how you define the term "work". In helping a patient to remember his childhood, for example, it can be a useful tool. But that's all it is – a tool – and one of many available. It's certainly not the miracle cure that some people believe it is.'

'So you couldn't, for example, change somebody's personality with it?'

'Most definitely not. All you can use it for is to build on what's already there. You're not going to change an introvert into an extrovert by a couple of sessions of hypnosis. You have to turn him around by other means – or rather, he has to turn *himself* around by other means – and, once that process is under way, you can *then* use hypnosis as a reinforcement.'

'Fascinatin',' Woodend said. 'But to get back to the point. Do you think there's a chance I can use hypnosis to make Mainwearin' tell me why he calls himself the Invisible Man?'

'As I've said, it's a possibility. But why should you even want to? You know he's guilty. Isn't that enough? Do you really need to probe every little corner of his psyche?'

'Not really,' Woodend admitted. 'It's just that I like to know these things. I suppose it's because when I was a kid—'

Stevenson laughed. 'If you want to tell me about your childhood memories, you need to be lying on a couch first,' he said. 'And you're going to have to pay me for the privilege.'

'On *my* salary?' Woodend asked wryly. He stopped walking for a moment, to light up a cigarette. 'The drug Mainwearin' used to dope the girls isn't well known to your average layman – an' that bothered me at first,' he continued. 'Then Dr Shastri explained to me that anybody with a reasonable head on their shoulders could find out all there is to know about it by spendin' half an hour in the library.'

'I expect they could.'

'But what's still got me confused is why Brunton decided that the best place to get it was the Pendleton Clinic.'

'*Is* that where he got it from?'

'Yes.'

'Well, I suppose it was because he was a patient there. In fact, he was *my* patient there.'

'True enough,' Woodend agreed. 'But he'd only be at the clinic for ... what? An hour a week?'

'Two hours a week. Tuesdays and Thursdays.'

'An' I wouldn't have said that was long enough for him to have learned how the hospital ticked. Certainly not long enough for him to have found out that one of the fellers workin' in the dispensary was bent.'

'Perhaps someone else told him about the pharmacist.'

'A doctor, you mean?'

'I consider that particular possibility highly unlikely,' Stevenson said severely. 'We do have certain standards in the profession, you know, and I can't see any doctor risking his reputation in that way. It's much more likely that Brunton got the information from one of the ancillary staff, who would probably be only too glad to earn some extra money by providing it.'

'So doctors are true paragons of virtue, but wave a few quid in front of one of the members of the lower orders, an' you'll have him rollin' over like a puppy?' Woodend asked.

'I didn't say that,' Stevenson protested.

'No, not *quite* you didn't,' Woodend agreed.

'I suppose it did sound rather snobbish of me to insist it couldn't have been one of the doctors,' Stevenson said, in a placatory manner. 'After all, there are a few bad apples in every barrel.'

Woodend slapped his forehead with the palm of his hand. 'Idiot!' he said loudly.

'I beg your pardon?'

'I'm losin' my grip on my argument completely, which is hardly surprisin', considerin' I've had no sleep for last thirty-six hours an' I'm so tired that I'm almost on the point of droppin' where I stand.'

'You *should* get some sleep, you know,' Stevenson said solicitously.

'As soon as I've tied up a few loose ends, I will,' Woodend promised. 'Anyway, here we are debatin' about whether it was a cleaner or a doctor that told Brunton who he should approach, when, in fact, it was *Mainwearin'* who decided to obtain the drugs from the Pendleton Clinic.'

'And he wasn't a patient there.'

'Well, exactly! An' not only that, but he couldn't explain to me *why* he chose the clinic – just like he couldn't explain why he decided to call himself the Invisible Man.'

'Perhaps he was lying about choosing the clinic himself,' Stevenson suggested. 'Perhaps it was Brunton's choice after all.'

Woodend shook his head. 'Mainwearin' didn't lie to me durin' that interview. He might not have always known the truth – but he certainly didn't *lie*.'

'I couldn't comment on that,' Stevenson said. 'I wasn't there.'

'No, you weren't,' Woodend agreed. 'An' it wouldn't have been proper to have you there.

Because not only was *Brunton* one of your patients, but *Mainwearin'* was an' all.'

'I wouldn't exactly call him a patient of mine – not in the same way as Brunton was – though I did see him a few times, at the request of his probation officer. I believe that was one of the conditions of his parole.'

'It's funny that neither of them tried to get close to the investigation, isn't it?' Woodend asked.

'What do you mean?'

'Well, if I'm recallin' what you told me correctly, you said that the *organized* killer takes a great interest in the investigation. He'll keep a scrapbook of the newspaper reports, an' may even try to insinuate himself onto the periphery of the investigation itself. But Brunton an' Mainwearin' *never* tried to do that. An' when we searched their properties, we found no evidence of scrapbooks.'

'If you remember, I also used the word "likely" quite a lot,' Stevenson said. 'The organized killer is *likely* to keep a scrapbook, and *likely* to want to get close to the investigation. But dealing with the human mind is a tricky business, and there are no hard and fast rules.'

'On the other hand, *you* did sort of become part of the investigation,' Woodend said.

'Only because my wife asked me to,' Stevenson pointed out. He laughed. 'Only because she *insisted* on it.'

'Aye, she's a very formidable woman, is Sergeant Stevenson,' Woodend agreed. 'But even formidable women can be manipulated, if you go about it in the right way.'

'What do you mean?' Stevenson asked.

'I remember the first time you turned up at my office as if it was only yesterday,' Woodend mused, ignoring the question. 'You were wearin' the same brown tweed jacket and brown trousers that you're wearin' today, an' I thought at the time that they looked rather new. Were they?'

'I can't honestly remember.'

'You were wearin' the same outfit when we met in the Drum, just after I'd been kicked off the case. But the *next* time I saw you – when I popped into your office unexpectedly – you were wearing a smart suit. Now you're back to the jacket an' trousers again. But then, that's understandable – because I did tell you in advance that I was comin' this time, didn't I?'

'Are you trying to make some kind of point?'

'I once had a mate who was a salesman, an' he said the key to successful sellin' is to do all you can to convince the customer that you're very much like him. If you go out for a meal together, eat what he eats an' drink what he drinks. If he's a follower of rugby league, find out all about it, an' pretend it's the drivin' passion of your life. An' if you seem to have the same taste in clothes, well, that can't do any harm either.'

'But I'm not a salesman.'

'Of course you are.'

'And what am I supposed to be selling?'

'Your ideas. An' even more importantly, your-

316

self – which is what all salesmen are really sellin' anyway.'

Stevenson glanced down at his watch. 'I have to get back to the university,' he said. 'I'm due to give a lecture in an hour, and there's still some preparation I need to complete.'

'See that bridge up ahead of us?' Woodend asked, pointing.

'Yes?'

'Just walk that far with me. It won't take more than a couple of minutes, an' if you put a spurt on when you turn round again, you'll easily make up the time. All right?'

'All right,' Stevenson agreed, though he didn't seem entirely happy about the prospect.

'I got on really well with my old mam,' Woodend said. 'She was that proud of me when I became a sergeant in the army, an' she was that proud of me when I became a police inspector. But, do you know, she'd have been just as proud of me if I'd stayed in the mill all my workin' life, like my dad did.'

Stevenson sighed. 'Look, I should never have agreed to go any further with you,' he said. 'I really *do* have to get back.'

'Did you disappoint your mam as much as you've obviously disappointed your wife?' Woodend wondered.

'What!'

'I expect you did. That's probably why you married Rosemary in the first place – because she was so much like your mam that you thought you could relive your childhood, an' get it right

317

this time. But that kind of thing never works out, Doc. You of all people should know that.'

'How dare you try to analyse me like that?' Stevenson demanded. 'You've no idea what you're talking about. You haven't had the training.'

'No, I haven't,' Woodend admitted. 'But I've seen a great deal of life – an' that's been an education in itself. So tell me, when did you come up with the idea of turnin' Mainwearin' and Brunton into your puppets? When exactly did you decide to use them as the instruments for fulfillin' your fantasies?'

'This is ludicrous!' Stevenson said.

'My guess would be it was at some point in their treatments – when you realized they were both a lot like you.'

'They're nothing like me!' Stevenson said, in a voice so loud it was almost a scream.

'You're not bein' quite honest with yourself there, Doc,' Woodend said. 'If they weren't like you, you'd never have been able to get them to do what you wanted them to do. If they weren't like you, you'd never have been able to hypnotize them so successfully.'

'I never hypnotized either of them.'

'Of course you did. That's why Mainwearin' could sign himself the Invisible Man, even though he had no idea where the name came from. That's how he could know that the pharmacist at Pendleton Clinic was bent, without ever havin' been to the place – because *you* worked there, *you*'d heard the rumours, and *you* put the idea into his head. But most important of all, there's the fact that Brunton an' Mainwearin' have no idea that the reason they got together in the first place is because you *put* them together.'

'This is all pure speculation,' Stevenson said. 'I was teaching a class of thirty students when the first girl was kidnapped, and I wasn't even in the country when the second one was snatched.'

'You didn't need to be there for the thing to happen,' Woodend said. 'All you had to do was programme Brunton an' Mainwearin' beforehand. They did the dirty work for you, didn't they?'

'Of course not.'

'So tell me, Doc, do you think you'd have eventually plucked up the nerve to hurt the girls yourself – or would you never have got beyond keepin' a death watch from the house next door?'

'I had nothing to do with any of this – and you'll never be able to prove I did,' Stevenson told him, with a show of contempt.

'Don't talk so bloody stupid!' Woodend said dismissively. 'This is what I do for a livin'. Crime's my business, just like shrinkin' heads is yours. So of course I can bloody prove it.'

'How?' Stevenson challenged.

'Well, for starters, you had quite a cosy little set-up in that house next to the garage. You needed to be sure that you wouldn't be disturbed, which in turn means you either had to own the place yourself or have a hold over whoever else owns it. It shouldn't be too hard to uncover that link.'

'I do own the place, as a matter of fact,' Stevenson admitted. 'I bought it as an investment, some time ago. But I haven't been near it since the day I purchased it.'

'Bought it as an investment,' Woodend scoffed. 'An almost derelict house like that! Some investment!' He paused for a moment. 'An' then there's the spyin' equipment which you installed in the wall, so you could get your nasty little thrills from watchin'a poor innocent girl suffer. Very specialized, is stuff like that. There won't be more than a few places in the country that sell it – an' it should be a doddle to trace it back to you. An' when we search your house, we'll be sure to find your scrapbooks, won't we?'

'My ... scrapbooks?'

'Aye, I thought we would. Brunton an' Mainwearin' didn't keep them, but then they were not so much *organized* offenders as *bein' organized* offenders.'

'Everything you have is purely circumstantial,' Stevenson said. 'You'll never make it stick.'

'If it'll help, you just go on tellin' yourself that,' Woodend said encouragingly. 'Keep on sayin' it right up to the point that you hear the steel door slam behind you for the last time. Because it *will* be the last time, you know? They're never goin' to let you out.'

They had almost reached the bridge, and two uniformed constables emerged from the shadows.

'I've finished with him. He's all yours now,' Woodend said.

The constables advanced, placed Stevenson's hands behind his back, and cuffed him.

'Any last words you'd like to say to me?' Woodend asked Stevenson, as he was about to be led away.

'What are you *expecting* me to say?' Stevenson asked. 'That I realize now that I've done wrong. That I'm sorry about what happened to the girl. Because if that's what you were waiting for, you're going to be sorely disappointed.'

'No, I wasn't expectin' anythin' like that,' Woodend said. 'But I might have done, if I hadn't had the advantage of spendin' so much time with you.'

'What are you talking about?' Stevenson asked.

'You're a very good teacher, Dr Stevenson,' Woodend said. 'Possibly even a remarkable one. An' one of the things you've taught me is just how sick bastards like you actually think.'

Twenty-Eight

It was over three hours after Martin Stevenson's arrest that Woodend found himself standing in front of the chief constable's desk and looking down at the seated Henry Marlowe, while Marlowe, in turn, glared back up at him.

'Why *exactly* do you think I've sent for you, Chief Inspector?' the chief constable asked.

Woodend shrugged. 'I suppose it could be to congratulate me on solvin' yet another crime that has had fellers with more pips on their shoulders completely baffled,' he suggested.

'Your position is already precarious enough as it is,' the chief constable said. 'Insolence will certainly not improve matters for you.'

'Insolence, sir?' Woodend repeated. 'I thought I was statin' no more than the simple truth.'

'Superintendent Crawley tells me you physically manhandled him in front of a suspect who he was about to begin questioning,' Marlowe said. 'You may deny it if you choose to, but I'm confident the suspect will confirm Mr Crawley's version of the events.'

'Aye, an' if you can't take the word of a sexual deviant who tortures little girls, whose word can you take?' Woodend mused.

'So are you denying it or not?'

'Depends which part of your statement we're talking about. I deny the part about Crawley questionin' the suspect. *I* was the one who was questionin' Mainwearin' – *he* was the one who was buttin' in.'

'Do you deny that you *manhandled* Superintendent Crawley?'

'I slammed him up against the wall an' told him that he'd only got to interrupt one more time an' I'd deck him – if that's what you mean, sir. An' the *reason* that I did that was because I needed to have one more piece of information before I could go after Dr Stevenson – an' Mr Crawley was doin' his level best to prevent me from gettin' it.'

'But you had no right to "go after" Dr Stevenson in the first place. If you knew he was guilty, you should have informed Superintendent Crawley and DCI Mortlake immediately.'

'Ah, but that's the point,' Woodend said. 'I didn't know – I only strongly suspected. It wasn't until well into our walk along the canal bank together that I became absolutely convinced Stevenson was my man.'

'Very well, then, if you weren't sure you should still have informed Superintendent Crawley of your *strong suspicions*, and then stepped aside while he continued the investigation.'

'What? An' have him bugger the whole thing up?'

'It was his investigation to bu— to conduct,

and the one thing I will insist on in this force is the proper respect for the chain of command.'

'I'll bear that in mind in future,' Woodend promised.

'If I have my way – and I sincerely believe that this time I finally will – there won't *be* any future for you,' Marlowe promised him.

'You're sackin' me?'

'After the abominable way you behaved with Superintendent Crawley, that is certainly my intention.'

'I did crack this case, you know,' Woodend reminded him. 'It was me who actually put the villains behind bars.'

'There is more to policing than simply catching criminals,' Marlowe said.

'Is there? Like what?'

'There is orderliness. There is image. These are essential elements of modern police work, but you have never made any attempt to come to terms with them. And that, Mr Woodend, is why you will simply have to go. Have I made myself clear to you?'

'Clear enough,' Woodend said.

The phone rang, and Marlowe picked it up.

'I said I didn't want to be interrupted, except in an emergency,' he barked into the receiver.

In spite of the situation he found himself in, Woodend couldn't help grinning at the turn events were taking. Marlowe had been waiting for this confrontation for a long time – he probably even dreamed of it – and now his big dramatic moment had finally come, it had been interrupted by a phone call. It seemed a real shame!

The colour had drained from the chief constable's face, and his hand was gripping the receiver so tightly that his knuckles had turned white.

'What?' he said into the receiver. 'You're absolutely sure of that? ... But it's a nightmare. It's a bloody disaster!'

He slammed the phone down on its cradle.

'Bad news, sir?' Woodend asked, the grin still on his face.

'Shut up, Chief Inspector, and listen very carefully to what I have to tell you!' Marlowe said angrily. 'When you leave this office, I want you to go straight to your own. And once you're there, you're to stay there – and talk to no one – until I summon you again. Is that perfectly clear?'

'Perfectly,' Woodend said, mystified.

It was over two hours before the promised summons from the chief constable came, and, when Woodend returned Marlowe's office, the first thing he noticed was that his boss had changed into his best dress uniform.

Marlowe ran his eyes briefly – and distastefully – up and down Woodend's frame, then said, 'I don't suppose you keep a decent lounge suit in your office, do you, Chief Inspector?'

'Afraid not,' Woodend told him.

Marlowe sighed heavily. 'I suspected as much. Well, you'll just have to do as you are.'

'Do as I am for *what*?'

'We're going to attend a press briefing, you and I,' the chief constable said grimly.

'A press briefin'?' Woodend repeated. 'Look, you can try an' get me sacked if you like, but if you think that while you're crucifyin' me for the benefit of the media I'm goin' to just stand there an' take it—'

'For God's sake, man, shut up!' Marlowe screamed. 'Shut up! Shut up! *Shut up!* I am not about to crucify you, however much I might wish to. All I'm asking you to do is to attend a press briefing, and listen to what I have to say. You'll get your chance to put your own point of view when I've finished speaking, and I promise you that there'll be no comeback from me, whatever you choose to say. That's fair, isn't it?'

'Very fair,' Woodend agreed. 'In fact, considerin' you're the one that's makin' the offer, sir, I'd have to say it's *remarkably* fair.'

Woodend had expected to see both Superintendent Crawley and DCI Mortlake at the briefing, but there was no sign of either of them. In fact, the only two people on the platform were the chief constable and himself.

Marlowe stood up and outlined the details of the case with a briefness and lack of self-aggrandizement that left Woodend almost breathless with amazement. But the cabaret had only just begun.

'There have been some wild rumours flying about, to the effect that the hero of the hour –

Detective Chief Inspector Charles Woodend – is to be brought before a disciplinary board,' Marlowe said.

Woodend looked around him, wondering if there was another DCI with the same name in the room.

'Nothing could be further from the truth,' Marlowe continued. 'As some of you – especially the members of the local press – may know, Mr Woodend has spent the last six months serving this police force in a purely administrative capacity. This, I need not add, was entirely at his own request. He felt, and I agreed with him, that after so many years at the sharp end of policing, he needed a period to recuperate and reflect in more tranquil surroundings.'

Does he seriously think I'm goin' to let him get away with this crap? Woodend wondered.

'Mr Woodend's work while in administration has been truly excellent,' the chief constable lied, 'but when this current serious case broke, I felt the need to call on his investigative expertise again, and he agreed to provide it. He did not "front" the investigation, as I believe the current popular term would have it, but any of you who have covered his previous cases will have felt his driving force and guiding hand behind the more visible presence. With the successful conclusion of the case, DCI Woodend has now agreed that the time is right to return to his old job in the CID. Needless to say, I am delighted by his decision.' Marlowe paused, and gulped in a little much-needed air. 'And now, I expect Mr

Woodend would like to say a few words himself,' he concluded.

What the bloody hell is goin' on here? Woodend asked himself. Have I finally lost my bloody mind?

The chief constable bent down, so that his mouth was almost touching Woodend's ear. 'Happy now, you bastard?' he hissed.

Woodend and Rutter were sitting at their usual table in the public bar of the Drum and Monkey. Paniatowski, though absent, had promised to put in an appearance before closing time.

'I don't understand it,' Woodend said, for perhaps the tenth time. 'An' if I live to be a hundred, I'll *still* never understand it. Marlowe was so intent on bustin' me. An' given the number of regulations I've broken this time – plus the fact that I assaulted a superior officer – he could probably have got away with it. Then, all of a sudden, I'm not just reprieved, but I'm a bloody hero. It doesn't make any sense.'

'There's a lot of things that don't make any sense,' Rutter replied. 'Like the fact that neither Crawley nor Mortlake have been seen since this afternoon. There's a rumour going the rounds that they're both being transferred, though no one seems to know why.'

'Well, it can't be for incompetence,' Woodend said. 'If they were bein' moved for that, they'd have gone long ago.'

Rutter glanced down at his watch. 'Better go and give the nanny a ring, just to let her know

I'm going to be a bit late,' he said.

Woodend grinned. 'Well, she's certainly got you well house-trained,' he said.

Paniatowski appeared in the main doorway, just as Rutter disappeared into the corridor. She was holding a newspaper in her hand.

'This is the first edition of tomorrow morning's *Daily Gazette*,' she said, slapping the paper down on the table. 'It came in the nine o'clock train from London, so you won't have seen it yet.'

'Quite right, and I can think of no reason why I should want to look at that particular rag now,' Woodend said.

'You will when you've read the article on the front page,' Paniatowski said confidently.

Woodend had finished reading the article by the time Rutter returned from using the phone, and had folded the newspaper up in front of him.

'Something the matter?' Rutter asked, sensing a change in the atmosphere at the table.

'Have you, by any chance, spoken to your friend Elizabeth Driver today?' Woodend asked.

'That's not really any of your business, sir,' Rutter said, slipping into the defensive position he always adopted when Driver's name came up.

'I'll take that as a yes, then,' Woodend said. 'An' when you were talkin' to her, did you happen to discuss the Mary Thomas case?'

'It's about time you started to understand that Liz is perfectly capable of wearing different hats at different times,' Rutter said, 'and that before I tell her anything about my work, I make sure she's wearing her "friend" hat, rather than her "reporter" hat.'

'Her "friend" hat!' Paniatowski repeated, with some disgust.

'You don't know her as she is now,' Rutter said. 'She's changed a great deal since you last met.'

'So you *did* discuss the case with her?' Woodend persisted.

'Yes, I did,' Rutter said defiantly.

'An' when would that have been, exactly?'

'An hour or so before your first interview with Mr Marlowe. I was very disturbed about what was probably going to happen to you. I needed to talk to someone about it, and I knew Liz wouldn't abuse my confidence.'

'Wrong!' Woodend said.

'Wrong?' Rutter repeated.

Woodend unfolded the newspaper. 'Take a look at this!'

Rutter quickly scanned it. 'Bloody hell fire!' he said.

'That's exactly what I thought when I read it,' Woodend told him.

BLIND JUSTICE!
by Elizabeth Driver

The statue of Justice which sits proudly on top of the Central Criminal Court wears a blindfold to demonstrate her impartiality.

330

The law treats everyone equally, which is only how things should be.

But there are other ways in which justice – or perhaps I should say the police – can be blind, as is shown in the case of Chief Inspector Charlie Woodend of the Whitebridge Police.

I have been a big fan of 'Cloggin'-it Charlie', as he is affectionately known to his colleagues, for a number of years. The brilliance of his detection work is universally admitted, though his unorthodox approach can sometimes make other, less imaginative officers, feel uncomfortable.

Yesterday, Cloggin'-it Charlie brilliantly cracked another difficult case, the brutal murder of one little girl, and the kidnapping and physical abuse of another. And what is to be his reward for this new triumph, you ask your-selves. A medal, perhaps? Promotion to the rank of superintendent?

Not according to my sources close to the Central Lancs Police. They claim that Charlie is be hauled up before a disciplinary board, and may even lose his job.

There was more in the same vein, but Rutter had read enough to get the general idea.

'Good old Liz!' he said. 'Well, that explains Marlowe's sudden turn-around, doesn't it?'

Yes, it certainly did, Woodend agreed. The phone call that had come through while he was getting slated in the chief constable's office must have outlined exactly what this article was going to say, and Marlowe – like the coward he was – had been thrown into a complete panic.

'You must thank Miss Driver for the article the next time you talk to her,' he told Rutter.

'I rather think you should thank her yourself,' Rutter said, with a hint of a rebuke in his tone.

'Aye, you're right,' Woodend agreed.

And Bob *was* right. He should do it personally.

But he didn't like being indebted to a woman with the moral standards of a slug. And what was really concerning him was that he couldn't work out *why* she'd gone in to bat for him.

There was one thing he *was* certain of – that he wasn't buying into Bob's vision of her as the new improved Elizabeth Driver, with her halo sparkling brightly in the golden sunlight. No, she was playing some devious game of her own, and though he had no idea what it was yet, he was sure he would find out soon enough – and that when he did, he wouldn't like it at all.